W9-BKR-259

the Goodbye Bride

Center Point
Large Print

Also by Denise Hunter and available from Center Point Large Print:

Barefoot Summer
The Wishing Season
Married 'til Monday
Falling Like Snowflakes

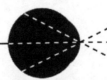

the Goodbye Bride

—A Summer Harbor Novel—

DENISE HUNTER

CENTER POINT LARGE PRINT
THORNDIKE, MAINE

This novel is a work of fiction. Names, characters,
places, and incidents are either products of the
author's imagination or used fictitiously. All characters
are fictional, and any similarity to people living
or dead is purely coincidental.

The text of this Large Print edition is unabridged.
In other aspects, this book may vary from the original edition.
Printed in the United States of America on permanent paper.
Set in 16-point Times New Roman type.

ISBN: 978-1-62899-931-0

Library of Congress Cataloging-in-Publication Data

Names: Hunter, Denise, 1968– author.
Title: The goodbye bride : a Summer Harbor novel / Denise Hunter.
Description: Center Point Large Print edition. | Thorndike, Maine :
Center Point Large Print, 2016. | ©2016
Identifiers: LCCN 2015050952 | ISBN 9781628999310
      (hardcover : alk. paper)
Subjects: LCSH: Amnesia—Fiction. | GSAFD: Love stories. | Christian
fiction.
Classification: LCC PS3608.U5925 G66 2016b | DDC 813/.6—dc23
LC record available at http://lccn.loc.gov/2015050952

the Goodbye Bride

Chapter 1

Lucy Lovett had barely opened her eyes when she took notice of the pain hammering at the back of her head. She groaned, her fingers finding the tender spot, a lump that pushed up through her thick brown hair.

She closed her eyes again as other details registered. Her cheek, pressed to a cold, hard surface. A girdle-like squeeze in her middle. Pinched toes.

The squeak of shoes sounded somewhere in the distance, then a thud. Cool air whooshed over her. Someone gasped. "Oh no! Miss? Miss, you okay? Oh mercy."

Lucy opened her eyes, rolling over, the lump connecting with the hard surface. "Ow."

Her gaze drifted over the water-stained ceiling tiles, then fell to the chubby cherub-like face of a middle-aged brunette.

"How many fingers?" the woman said.

Three thick fingers blocked Lucy's vision.

"Whatever happened?" she asked.

"Oh dear, you don't remember?"

Lucy's gaze bounced around the room. Gray stalls, a speckled floor, two porcelain sinks, their rusty guts exposed from her vantage point. Her eyes lit on a yellow folded sign on the floor nearby. *Caution! Slippery When Wet*, it warned above a stick figure doing the slippety-do.

"I fell."

Didn't she? She must've. Why else would she be lying prone on the floor—wet, she realized now, as the dampness registered—with a lump on her head? She winced as her hand found the bump again.

"Can you get up? Oh, have you hit your head? Maybe we should call 911."

"No!" Just the thought of the hospital had her sitting up. "See, I'm just . . ." Her eyes dropped to her lap and took in the frothy white skirt. She followed the delicate beading up the bodice to her bare shoulders. Her thoughts raced, searching for answers, but all she found were scrambled puzzle pieces.

"Well, who are you here with? I'll let them know what happened."

"I—I'm alone." Wasn't she? Why couldn't she remember?

"Let's call somebody then. Your groom perhaps? I'll get some ice for that head, then we'll call. He must be worried silly."

The woman bustled out the door while Lucy tried to assimilate the facts floating through her ringing head. It couldn't be her wedding day. That just made no sense whatsoever. It was over a month away. Maybe this was just her fitting. But why didn't she remember a single thing? Why didn't she remember getting into the gown or coming here or falling?

Think, Lucy. Think.

Her last memory was of cleaning up the restaurant with Zac the night before. He'd walked her to her apartment afterward, the cool fall wind ruffling his longish black hair. He'd slipped his coat over her shoulders, and they'd talked all the way to her door. There, under a puddle of light, she'd looked up into his handsome face, into his stormy gray eyes, and felt a pinch of fear. That niggling worry that something would go horribly wrong and she'd lose the one person she needed more than air.

A shuffling of feet sounded outside the door, pulling her back to the present. She was fine. She just needed to get up and find Zac. He'd help her make sense of all this.

Lucy pulled her knees in and braced herself against the subway-tiled wall. As she got to her feet, her eyes fell on the white satin heels pinching her toes. Heels she'd admired a few weeks ago on Nordstrom.com. Kate Spade slingback peep-toes with tiny demure bows. Shoes that were far out of her budget. She hadn't ordered them. She'd settled on a cute (if not darling) pair of pumps from a Summer Harbor boutique.

She looked down at the shoes. And yet, there they were.

The door burst open, and Cherub reappeared

9

with a baggie of ice. She helped Lucy to her feet, and Lucy set the ice against the lump. A jack-hammer was going in her head, and she blinked against the pain.

"Let's get you to a chair, honey. I think you should get an X-ray or something. You seem a little muddled."

"I'm fine. But I need to call my fiancé."

"Of course you do. My cell's about dead, but the manager will let you use her phone. I think she's worried about a lawsuit."

The bathroom door opened to a bustling diner that looked straight out of the 1950s with red stools and a black-and-white tiled floor. Lucy didn't recognize the place. A savory smell hung in the air, making her stomach churn.

She looked out the big picture window. The sun sparkled off the ocean in the distance, but the shops across the way were unfamiliar. Some corner of Summer Harbor she hadn't set eyes on? Though the little town only had so many corners, and she thought she'd seen them all.

Cherub retrieved a phone from the frowning lady behind the counter and handed it to her.

"You call that fiancé of yours. I'll be right back." She disappeared into the ladies' room.

"There was a sign," the woman said, glaring. "Soon as you walked in the door. You couldn't miss it."

Lucy nodded, making her head pound harder.

Her breaths were quick and shallow. She was sitting in a room full of people, but she couldn't remember ever feeling so alone. Well, except the one time. But that was so very long ago. Way before Zac.

He's only a phone call away.

Lucy punched his cell number into the handset, trying to ignore the frowning manager and the prying eyes. She supposed it wasn't every day a person saw a bride in a diner.

Zac must be fretting about her, she thought as the phone rang. She did hope he wasn't waiting at the chapel. She glanced at the clock on the diner wall. No, it was too early for that. The wedding didn't start until five thirty.

My wedding day. What happened to the past month?

She pushed the questions away. Needing Zac more than ever, she dialed the Roadhouse.

Zac Callahan lined up the shot, drew back the stick, and struck the cue ball. It rolled forward, spinning across the green felt, and kissed the solid blue ball, which shot off at an angle and sank into the corner pocket.

The bystanders erupted in cheers. Wagers always had a way of upping involvement.

"Of all the luck," Beau said.

Zac straightened to his full six-four height. "Luck's got nothing to do with it, big brother."

"Yeah, whatever." Beau surveyed the table, his near-black eyes narrowing in a frown.

Zac had left him nothing. With the rest of his evening on the line, he wasn't leaving it up to chance. Marci, one of his servers, had called in sick, and the crowd was picking up. He was going to need the extra hands.

"I can't wait to see you in that apron," Zac said.

"Not happening." Beau's dark hair hung forward as he took a shot and missed.

His new fiancée, Eden, consoled him with a pat on the arm and mouthed to Zac, *I'm so there.*

"Zac, you're wanted on the phone!" his hostess called on her way past the poolroom.

He set down the cue stick and pointed at Beau. "No cheating."

Beau gave a *Who, me?* face as Zac headed toward the counter. The restaurant was already half full because of the Red Sox game on TV. The crowd gave a hearty shout as the tying run crossed home plate.

Zac paused a moment to watch, then continued on his way. He patted Sheriff Colton's shoulder as he passed and avoided the booth where Morgan LeBlanc sat with a friend. He'd had a couple dates with Morgan, and they were going out again soon. He tried to work up some excitement about that and failed.

He slipped behind the counter and snapped up the handset. "Zac speaking."

"Zac! Oh, thank heavens."

Adrenaline flushed through his body, tingles zinging across his skin. His shoulders went rigid. He hadn't heard her voice in seven months. That sweet Southern drawl that used to give him palpitations. Now it made his heart stop in its tracks.

"Something awful's just happened. I—I fell, and I don't rightly know where I am. Can you come for me?"

He rubbed his forehead, his thoughts spinning. *"What?"*

"I don't want to be late, and I'm already just sopping wet, and my hair—"

"Late for what?"

"That is not funny, Zac Callahan." She sounded near tears. "My head's cranking, and I—I need you to come fetch me."

"Lucy, you're not making any sense. Why are you even calling me?"

There was a long pause. "Are you kidding me?"

He remembered that day seven months ago, returning from his weekend trip. The unanswered calls, the unanswered knock at her door. Being worried, calling her landlord only to find her apartment empty and Lucy gone.

His fingers tightened on the handset. "Call somebody else. You're not my problem anymore."

She gave a little gasp. "Why are you being so hateful?" The last words wobbled.

13

Why was he—? He pulled the phone from his ear, scowled at it, and put it back in place. "You're the one who left, Lucy. If you need a ride, call a cab." He started to hang up.

"Wait, Zac! Please. Oh my gosh, you can't do this to me. I hit my head and there's a great big lump and my head is pounding and I need help. I need *you*."

His gut clenched hard. How many times in the recent months had he longed to hear those words from her lips? She sounded so . . . confused. So lost. And it wasn't like she had any family left.

And you're a great big sucker, Callahan.

"Please. I don't know where I am or what's going on. You have to help me."

He leaned back against the bar. "Lucy. You need to go to the hospital. You must have a con—"

"I can't go to the hospital!"

Zac dragged his palm over his scruffy jaw, remembering Lucy's phobia. He'd never be able to talk her into an ER visit over the phone. Even when she'd torn a tendon in her ankle, she'd refused to go. An EMT friend of his had treated her in his apartment upstairs.

If she really had a head injury, it could be bad. She could even have bleeding on the brain or something.

He sighed hard, knowing he sounded put out and not caring. He really was a sucker. "Where are you?"

"I—I don't know. Hold on. Don't hang up."

A shuffling noise sounded in the phone. He strained to hear over the clamor of voices and clanging of silverware.

On Lucy's end a woman rattled out a street address.

"Wait," Lucy said, her voice muffled. "Summer Harbor?"

"No, honey. Portland."

"Portland . . . ?" Lucy asked. "Portland, *Oregon?*"

"What? No. *Maine.* Portland, Maine."

Ah, for the love of— Zac poked his fingers into his eye sockets. "Lucy." More shuffling. *"Lucy."*

"I'm right here. Zac, I'm in—"

"I heard." He gave a quiet growl. He shouldn't even be thinking about doing this. She was gone from his life. He was finally over her.

Sure you are. That's why you're going to rush to her rescue.

He'd always been so weak where Lucy was concerned. She'd had him in the palm of her hand since the day she'd walked into the Roadhouse. Right up until she stomped all over his heart with her fancy pointy-toed heels.

"This better not be some trick, Lucy."

"Why would I even do that?" Her voice was a mixture of outrage and hurt.

He huffed. Like he'd ever been able to figure her out.

"Please, Zac. I'm truly desperate."

His resolve crumbled at the sound of tears in her voice. *Aw, dang it.* He'd never be able to live with himself if something happened to her. He ran his palm over his face as resolve settled over him.

"Sit tight. I'll be there in a few hours."

Chapter 2

Lucy stared out at the bustling harbor. Her backside was numb from the wooden bench she'd been sitting on since her call to Zac. After she'd hung up she'd been eager to escape the glowering manager, curious patrons, and nauseating smells coming from the kitchen. She'd hiked up her skirts and crossed the street, relieved to find an out-of-the-way bench where she could ruminate in private.

She'd had hours to think, or so it seemed, and she'd reached a disturbing conclusion. She'd definitely lost a month of her life. There was no getting around it. She wasn't sure why she was in Portland or why Zac was in Summer Harbor, but she had to face it—her brain wasn't operating at optimum capacity.

She felt mildly dizzy, and her vision was slightly blurred no matter how hard she tried to blink it away. The sunlight glinting off the water felt like knife blades jabbing her in the eyes. She closed them against the pain and focused on breathing.

While the headache and dizziness were disorienting, the anxiety roiling in her gut was even worse. What was wrong with her? Were the memories of the past month gone forever? Did she have a serious injury? How long would this befuddled state last? What if it never went away?

She watched a lobster boat coming in off the water, the men quitting for the day. What time was it? What was taking Zac so long?

What if he didn't come?

Ridiculous. Of course he'd come. He loved her.

She thought back to their phone call. The sound of his voice, his Mainer accent, had been so reassuring, the dropped *r*'s as familiar as the sound of waves rolling ashore. *Lobstah. Satahday. Chowdah.*

She frowned, the memory of the call digging in deeper. The conversation was fuzzy. He'd seemed out of sorts, but she couldn't remember exactly what he'd said.

What if she had a brain injury? She was going to have to go to the hospital, she just knew it. Anxiety swelled inside. She was suddenly eight years old and sitting alone by her mother's hospital bed. A machine beeped quietly, keeping track of her heartbeats.

Until it stopped altogether.

Lucy's heart pounded at the memory, making her headache worse. The hospital felt like death. Smelled like death. But she would have to go.

You won't die, Lucy. What is the matter with you?

She didn't have the time or mental capacity to answer that question. And why could she remember something that happened sixteen years ago when she couldn't remember putting on her wedding gown only hours ago?

"Lucy?"

She turned at the deep timbre of Zac's voice. Her heart soared at the sight of his familiar face. His strong, masculine features, the sharp turn of his jaw. She knew every curve and angle by heart. She frowned at the sight of his short beard. His black hair was longer than she remembered too, a thick curl falling over his forehead.

Shaking the confusion, she jumped up and took a step toward him, eager for the safety of his arms. But the world tilted, and she stumbled sideways on the walkway.

Zac sped to her side, catching her by the elbows. "What are you doing?"

She winced at the gruffness in his voice. Her grip tightened on his forearms. She blinked away the dizziness and stared into his gray eyes, wishing she could see more clearly. He felt stiff and sounded cold. Not at all like her Zac.

"Zac . . . I'm so glad to see you. Will you take me home? Please?"

"Just sit down for now." He eased her back until she hit the bench, letting go as soon as she was seated.

She looked down at the dress, clutching the frothy material. Their wedding day was ruined. Completely ruined. After all that work.

Sudden tears clogged her throat, filled her eyes. "You weren't supposed to see me yet."

Not until she came down the aisle. There was supposed to be awestruck wonder on his face. It was a bride's right, for gosh sakes. She'd wanted the altar lights on just to be sure she caught a glimpse of his expression.

She frowned at the thought. The chapel was in Summer Harbor, and she was in Portland. It was all so confusing. She rubbed her temple. "I'm afraid I'm a bit befuddled."

"Where'd you hit your head?"

"In the ladies' room." She gestured over her shoulder. "At the diner. The floor was wet, and I guess I just . . . slipped."

"I mean where on your head?"

"Oh. Here." She took his hand and placed it gently on the lump.

He pressed his lips together. "You've got a good-sized lump going. Were you knocked unconscious?"

"I—I don't know. I think so. Maybe?" She couldn't even remember that!

He withdrew his hand, and she immediately missed the comfort of his fingers. Why wasn't he touching her? Holding her? She needed comfort, daggonit!

"Lucy . . . you were unconscious, you're dizzy, and you've got some time gaps. You need to get looked at."

She looked at him pleadingly, tears welling up in her eyes. "No . . ."

"I'll go with you. There's no choice. We need to see what's going on."

Where was his warm voice? His tender touch?

"What about the wedding? We need to call people. I can't believe this is happening." Her breaths were coming hard and shallow, like her lungs couldn't keep up.

"Slow down, you're going to hyperventilate. Think you can make it to my truck?"

She didn't want to go to the hospital! *God, please. Don't do this to me.* She just wanted to go home and curl up in her bed. She wanted Zac to tuck her in like he did some nights when she was really bushed. And she was really bushed just now.

"Lucy, can you walk?" The impatience in his voice was like a dagger in her chest.

"I don't want to go to the hospital." She couldn't control the tremble of her voice.

"Well, that's where I'm taking you."

She rocked back and forth, soothing herself. Only it wasn't working. It wasn't working at all. She knew he was right. Something was terribly wrong. She could get by if Zac stayed with her. Couldn't she?

"Will you take me home afterward?"

"Yes."

She tried to block the thoughts, but the memories surfaced anyway. The antiseptic smell, the beeping of machines, the cold, sterile floor. And her mama, what was left of her, still and pale in the bed.

"Maybe you can get someone to come look me over," she said. "That nice EMT from before." She looked at him hopefully.

"We're in Portland, Lucy. I don't know anyone here."

He-uh.

"Oh . . . right."

"That's exactly why you need to get checked out. You don't even know where you are, for heaven's sake."

She winced at his harsh tone, her eyes burning. He sounded put out. Like he didn't give a flying fig about what was happening to her. That she might have bleeding on the brain or drop dead in two minutes!

He stood. "Come on now. There's no choice. Let's go." He scooped her up into his arms, frothy skirt and all. His grip was gentle enough, but he held her stiffly, carried her mechanically. She laid her head on his shoulder and closed her eyes. Maybe when she woke up, this nightmare would be over.

Chapter 3

Zac settled his elbows on his knees, watching as the nurse finished with Lucy's IV. They'd given her something to settle her stomach, something for her headache, and a little something to take the edge off. Her eyes were closed, her brows losing that pinched look as the medication took effect.

The nurse left, and Zac let his gaze wander over Lucy's face. Her delicately arching brows, her creamy skin, her pink kiss-me lips. She hadn't changed at all. She still had those vulnerable blue eyes that tugged at him. Reeled him right in. She'd taken the pins out of her long dark hair, and now it cascaded over her shoulders in waves, covering a portion of the ugly hospital gown. He'd been so glad to see her lose that wedding dress.

Wedding dress. He'd about turned around and left when he saw her at the harbor. It had only been seven months since she'd left. How had she managed to fall in love and get engaged so quickly? Or maybe she'd been in love for longer than that. Maybe that's why she'd left him in the first place. The thought was a punch in the gut.

He leaned back in the chair and crossed his arms, frowning. What the heck was he doing here? She had a groom somewhere, a groom she loved, and a church full of people wondering what had happened to her.

It didn't add up though. What had she been doing alone in a diner bathroom right before her wedding?

Lucy wasn't the only one with questions.

But he'd have to put his aside for now. The doctor would be in soon with another set of questions. Lucy had filled out her own forms in the busy waiting room, and her pen hadn't even paused over the address line. She'd jotted down the address of her Summer Harbor apartment, only pausing when she'd reached the insurance information.

Lucy had no idea of the extent of her memory loss, and regardless of how she'd left things with him, he still felt protective. He'd have to break it to her easy.

Lucy's eyes fluttered open. She felt ever so much better. Thank God for medication. She was floating a little, but that was just fine. Better that than the horrible anxiety that had sent panic racing through her veins.

Her eyes drifted to Zac, hunched over in the bedside chair. Thank God he was still there. But even with her blurry vision she could see the scowl on his face. It hurt. He'd always been so tender toward her. So protective and sweet.

"Why are you mad at me?" she whispered.

His eyes darted to hers, his face softening. "Feeling better?"

"Much."

"Good." He stood and paced the length of the room.

He was so tall. So broad shouldered. He towered over her five-foot-four-inch frame, and when he took her in his arms, she felt safe and loved in a way she hadn't since she was a young girl. His confident presence just took over a room, and right now his long-legged stride was making quick work of the space.

He turned and faced her. "Lucy . . . there are some things you need to be aware of."

She pulled the sheet up against her chest. "What is it?"

"This . . . wedding." He gestured toward her gown hanging in the small wardrobe with the door ajar. "It wasn't ours."

She blinked, trying to see him. Trying to make sense of what he was saying. "Whatever are you talking about?"

He drew a breath and blew it out. "We're not together anymore, Lucy."

Why was he saying this? A burn started behind her eyes. She shook her head as a knot hardened in her throat.

"We were over months ago. I'm sorry to break it to you like this, but the doctor is going to have questions, and you need to know—you're missing a lot of time."

Her heart was an aching hole in the center of her chest. It couldn't be true. They couldn't have parted ways. Zac loved her, and she loved him. So much.

She shook her head. "No."

He neared the bed, stopping just shy of the rail, his hands stuffed into his jeans pockets. "It's true. You've lost a good seven months at least." He kept on in that matter-of-fact voice she was growing to hate.

"Why are you doing this?" Her voice cracked.

"I'm telling you the truth. You need to know, and the doctor needs to know so they can figure out what's—" His eyes stopped on something. He reached over and grabbed the newspaper he'd brought from the lobby. "What day is it, Lucy?"

"It—it's . . . I don't know. Our wedding day. November seventeenth." She stared into his eyes at the long pause, feeling more vulnerable than she remembered feeling in a long time.

"We were sitting outside on the harbor," he said. "Did it feel like November to you?"

She blinked away, thinking. She couldn't remember what it felt like. Had she been chilled?

"It's not November, Lucy. It's June."

She shook her head. No, it couldn't be summer. She'd just finished decorating her apartment for

Thanksgiving. She'd put out the festive table-cloth and the brown pillar candles and the big stuffed turkey Zac had given her, the one that gobbled when you squeezed its belly. Just a couple nights ago she'd laughed herself silly at the ridiculous sound.

He held the paper in front of her, and her eyes worked hard to focus where he pointed. Today's date. June 15. And a year she didn't even remember ringing in.

Her head spun, and her skin felt hot. A fine sheen of sweat broke out on the back of her neck. She wished that nurse would come back and double her anxiety med because it wasn't working anymore. Not even close.

"Calm down now . . ."

"I've lost seven months? *Seven months?*" It all spun in her head. What had happened in those months?

Her chest tightened, and she palmed the spot. "We broke up?"

"Yes."

He was the one thing she had going right in her life. The one thing she couldn't live without. Her gaze touched on the wedding dress.

"If we're not together anymore, why was I wearing a wedding gown, huh? Answer me that."

His lips formed a tight line. "I don't know."

"You're wrong. You're making this up!"

"Why would I do that?"

"We're engaged!"

"Are we, Lucy? Where's the ring I gave you?"

"Right here." She held up her hand, noticing the ring for the first time. A diamond twinkled back. An awfully large one.

Not the one Zac had given her.

A whimper escaped her throat as panic crept in. "What's going on?"

An orderly slipped into the room. "Okay, time for pictures." Working quickly, he verified Lucy's identity, took care of the IV, and set the bed in motion.

Lucy turned toward Zac as she was wheeled from the room, her gaze aligning with his guarded eyes. He stood immobile, his hands in his pockets, his jaw hard, his lips pressed into a tight line. He disappeared as quickly as her memory had.

Chapter 4

"What's the last thing you remember, Miss Lovett?"

It was midnight, and the doctor had been quizzing her for ten minutes. Her thoughts were so fuzzy. The CT was normal. Everything looked fine, he'd said. How could everything look fine when it clearly wasn't?

The doctor looked to be in his thirties with messy brown hair, blue eyes, and round glasses.

He looked like Harry Potter. How could she remember Harry Potter when she couldn't remember losing the only man she'd ever loved? How could seven months of her life simply slip her mind? She had a man—a fiancé!—she didn't even remember. What had she been doing the last seven months? Where had she been living?

"Lucy . . . ?" Zac said. "Your last memory."

She cleared her throat and thought hard. "Um, we were walking home from the Roadhouse—Zac's restaurant. It was cold. We said goodbye at the door."

She had a sudden flash of memory, and her eyes cut to Zac. "You picked up the pumpkin on my porch and pretended it was talking."

She'd laughed at his antics, and she'd been relieved to see a glimpse of his old self. He'd been so blue since his daddy had passed. After he'd set the pumpkin down, he'd pulled her into his arms and told her he couldn't wait to spend the rest of his life with her.

She searched his eyes now and saw the glimmer of memory before he looked away.

"How long ago was that?" the doctor asked Zac, oblivious to the tension hovering in the room.

"The end of October," Zac said.

The doctor closed his chart. "Well . . . you've obviously got a concussion and some retrograde amnesia. That means your injury caused a loss of memory."

"Will she get it back?"

The doctor shrugged. "She may or may not. It varies by person. Sometimes being around familiar things and people helps. Sometimes it doesn't. I'm inclined to check her in for the night to keep an—"

"No, sir," Lucy said. She couldn't get out of this place quick enough. "I don't want to stay. I need to get home. You said my CT was just fine."

"Perfectly normal. And I'm open to the option of sending you home, but only if someone stays with you for at least twenty-four hours."

Her eyes darted to Zac, pleading. They couldn't give her enough drugs to keep her here.

His eyes tightened, and a shadow twitched in his jaw. "Fine."

"You'll need to wake her every few hours tonight. She needs to take it easy until her symptoms are gone. I've prescribed a pain med for her headache and something for the nausea. The nurse will get you some information on post-concussion care. She should schedule a checkup with her regular doctor."

"What about my memory?" Lucy asked. "Will I get it back?"

The doctor's eyes shot to Zac's, then back to her. "We'll have to wait and see. Try not to worry too much about that. Just rest up and take care of yourself."

After he left, Lucy pressed her fingertips to her

forehead. "Try not to worry that I can't remember the last seven months of my life?"

"Being upset isn't going to help anything."

"Easy for you to say! You're not the one with the huge, gaping hole in his life." Or in love with someone who apparently hated her now.

Zac sank into a chair. "At least you don't have to stay. We'll get your prescriptions filled and find a nearby hotel. In the morning I'll start doing some research and see if I can't figure out where you live and get you connected with your—friends."

Lucy came upright. "You said you'd take me home. You promised."

Zac gave her a patient look. "I meant to your home *now*."

"Well, I don't even remember that home! Or those people. I want to go back to Summer Harbor with you."

"Lucy, that's not—"

"This isn't my home. I don't remember any of it."

"Well, that could change. You could wake up tomorrow and everything could be different."

"Or I could never remember any of it!"

Something flickered in Zac's eyes. Something she needed. He still had to care for her deep down, didn't he? After all they'd shared?

"Please, Zac. Take me home. It's where I belong." Her eyes burned, and when she fought to hold back the tears, her feelings spilled out her lips instead. "You have to take me home. I love you."

His eyes hardened. "Don't say that."

"It's true."

"You only think it's true. You've got a life here, Lucy. You've got a job, and a home, and a freaking fiancé."

"Well, I don't remember any of it! I only remember Summer Harbor and my little apartment and you." Her last words broke off.

Zac bolted to his feet and paced away, his hands laced behind his head. He wouldn't turn her down. Not the Zac she knew. Would he? He faced a blank wall, his shoulders rigid, his body stiff.

It seemed forever before he finally turned around. "Fine."

She was glad she couldn't see the look in his eyes from across the room. Her imagination was filling in the blanks only too well.

"I'll take you back. But we're going to figure this out whether your memory comes back or not. Your life is here now, not in Summer Harbor."

Not with me.

The unsaid words hung in the air between them, cutting off her breath. She couldn't imagine ever wanting to come back here or ever wanting to leave Zac.

But she knew enough to quit while she was ahead. "All right. Fair enough."

She'd get back to Summer Harbor and figure out what went wrong. Then she'd fix it. Because she knew she'd never love anyone else the way she loved Zac Callahan.

Chapter 5

Zac turned onto Harbor Drive and followed the two-lane highway up the coastline. The headlights of his Silverado cut through the darkness, lighting the way, but he'd barely seen the road the entire drive back to Summer Harbor.

It was three thirty in the morning, and Lucy had succumbed to sleep long ago. She wore some ill-fitting clothes from the hospital's lost and found. He'd shoved her wedding dress into the backseat.

Her slight weight had fallen against him as they'd passed through Ellsworth, and now her head rested on his arm. The familiar apple scent of her shampoo or perfume or whatever made her smell so fresh wove around him. The fragrance drew him right back to when they'd been together.

She turned her face into his arm, cuddling closer, and gave a deep sigh.

Come on, God. I'm only a man. What are You doing? Why's she back in my life?

Twelve hours ago he'd been minding his own business, getting ready for a busy night at the

Roadhouse. Now here he was, bringing his ex-fiancée home.

He rounded the last curve and applied the brakes as the Roadhouse came into view, his eyes swinging to his darkened second-floor apartment. He pulled into the parking lot and killed the engine.

Lucy didn't budge. In the sudden quiet he could hear her gentle breaths. Feel the expansion of her lungs against his elbow. He looked down at her. The golden glow of lights washed over her face. Her long lashes swept the tops of her cheeks, and her long hair cascaded over her shoulders.

Lucy used to say she'd never rise above "cute" because of her dimples and compact size. But she was wrong. She was beautiful. His fingers itched to brush her hair back, to linger on the softness of her cheek. To glide across her generous lips. To pretend, just for a few minutes, that everything was the way it had been.

He ground his teeth together. *Enough, Callahan.*

He nudged her with his shoulder and she awoke, lifting her head. She looked around, seemingly lost for a moment. And he wondered if she'd miraculously regained her memory.

Then her eyes met his, and her face fell. "What time is it?"

"After three."

"I thought—what about my apartment?"

She was still loopy from the drugs or concussion, and she looked so vulnerable. He steeled himself against the need to comfort her. Reminded himself of the way she'd left. Of her groom back in Portland.

"Your apartment's long gone. You can use Riley's old room for tonight."

He got out of the truck and came around to help her in case she was still dizzy. His baby brother had rented out the room for a while. When Zac took over the Roadhouse, the room was full of storage. Riley fixed it up in exchange for cheap rent.

"He's not here anymore?" she asked when he opened her door.

"He joined the marines. Easy does it," he said when she wobbled on her feet. "You should take your meds before you turn in."

He unlocked the door and led her through the darkened restaurant and down the short hall past his office and private bathroom. Beyond that was a small room with the bare necessities. He couldn't remember the last time the sheets had been washed. The air was stale, so he cracked open the window.

He got her a glass of water and helped with her pills. Her eyes had that sleepy look, and her makeup was smudged underneath, making her look younger and helpless somehow. He'd fetched her a T-shirt from upstairs that would probably hang to her knees.

34

When she was settled, he turned at the door. "I'll wake you in a few hours."

She was sitting on the edge of the bed, the T-shirt clutched to her chest. She stared at him with those wide blue eyes he'd once been a fool for. "Thank you, Zac."

He gave her a tight smile before pulling the door. He walked around for a while, busying himself with a few things in the restaurant. His thoughts were spinning, his nerves jacked up like he'd had a full carafe of coffee.

Around four thirty he forced himself to lie down on his office couch. His legs hung off the end of the lumpy sofa. He set his phone alarm for six to check on Lucy, but he was still wide awake when it went off. It was fair to say he wasn't going to make it to church this morning.

He slipped into her room. Morning sounds filtered through the cracked window. Dawn glimmered through the sheer curtain, washing over the form of her quilt-covered body. She slept on her side, facing the door, her knees drawn up in fetal position.

For a moment he imagined that the past seven months hadn't happened. That she'd never left Summer Harbor. That they'd married on November 17. She was lying in their bed, and she was *his*. His heart thrashed against his ribs.

Stop it. Just stop it. Jeez.

Zac crept over to the bed and touched her

shoulder. "Lucy." She didn't stir, so he nudged her again. "Lucy, wake up."

He felt her go still.

"Zac?" Her voice was rough with sleep.

"You okay?"

"Mmmm."

"All right. Just checking." He turned to go.

She grabbed his hand. "Stay."

She was killing him. He pulled his hand from hers. "I'm right next door in the office. Go back to sleep."

Back in his office he set his alarm for nine, then lay awake, staring at the darkened ceiling, planning what he'd do. He'd start with a search for weddings in Portland. There'd be a church listed, and he'd call the pastor for contact numbers. Once he got in touch with her fiancé, he was home free. The thought made his chest feel hollow inside. But the sooner he got her back to Portland the better.

He must've drifted off because light was peeking through the window when his eyes opened next. The alarm was going off. He checked on Lucy, then stumbled back to the sofa and fell promptly asleep.

A pounding noise woke him. He bolted upright, his thoughts spinning. Last night came bounding back. Lucy's call. The ER. Lucy in his guest room.

He ran a palm over his face.

The pounding started again, and Zac unfolded

himself from the dinky couch and went to the back door.

Beau stood on the porch in his church clothes, giving him a black look. "Where you been? You didn't show up at church."

Zac turned back inside. It was too early for this. "I got in late. Didn't get much sleep." He headed upstairs to his apartment, dreaming of coffee, Beau on his heels.

"I've been texting all morning."

"What's the big emergency?"

"You kidding me? You take off last night with no explanation, leave the restaurant in my hands, and don't show up for church?"

Zac entered his living room, leaving the door open, and headed straight toward his kitchenette, his coffeemaker, like a zombie. "Were there any problems?"

"Naw, there were no—Zac, what's going on? You look like crap."

"Can you at least let me get some coffee in me? Jeez." He filled the machine with water and grounds and hit the Power button. He heard his brother pacing in the living room. Beau was in his oldest-brother glory.

Zac pulled out a mug, then looked over his shoulder. Beau was staring out the window that faced the harbor. "Want some?"

"No thanks."

The thought of the research he had to do today,

of Lucy sleeping downstairs, made his head throb. A quick check of his watch showed it was going on twelve thirty. After he got rid of Beau he'd check on her, then start Googling. Surely it wouldn't take long to find her wedding information, her fiancé.

He glared at the slow trickle of coffee. *Come on.* With any luck he'd figure this out and get her back to Portland before the sun set. Maybe she'd even get her memory back. Then they could all have their happy endings.

He gave a quiet *humph.* His mind wandered to the man Lucy had been about to pledge her life to. Poor schmuck. He had no idea what he'd gotten himself into.

Even as the thought formed, he had a gut check. He remembered the sweet Lucy, the sassy one. The one who'd turned him upside down and inside out in all the best ways. She'd been everything he'd dreamed of.

And then she left you high and dry.

The coffee machine began the blessed gurgling sound that indicated his drug of choice was ready for consumption. He filled his mug, took a sip, and started toward the living room. Maybe he could just give Beau some vague excuse and get him out of his apartment.

Zac froze on the living-room threshold as Lucy appeared in the apartment doorway. Her dark hair was all tousled and sexy, the loose T-shirt falling to mid-thigh. She offered Zac a tremulous smile just before her eyes swung to Beau's back.

Her lips pulled higher. "Beau . . . hey there."

Beau turned, his lips parted, his eyes widening. "Aw, no . . . No way." His gaze flitted off Lucy, then his lips tightened and he nailed Zac with a look.

Well, shoot. Couldn't a man have a cup of coffee in peace?

"You shouldn't be up here," Zac said, his voice sounding harsher than he intended.

Lucy seemed to sink in on herself as she crossed her arms. "I can't find—"

"I'll be down in a minute." He should probably offer her a cup of coffee, but he couldn't get her out of there quick enough.

Her eyes toggled between Beau and Zac. "O-okay."

Zac shut the door behind her and took a long sip of his coffee, barely noticing the burn at the back of his throat. He felt Beau's dark eyes on him as he settled in the recliner and tried to forget that his ex-fiancée was downstairs in his T-shirt, still in love with him.

"What. Have. You done?"

Zac looked up, his gaze glancing off his brother's face. Not quick enough to miss the way his neck bent forward in disbelief or the shock that registered in his eyes.

"It's not the way it looks."

"Then what way is it?"

"She's hurt. I'm helping her, that's all. I'll have her home by—"

"Helping her?"

"—tonight, if all goes as planned."

"She left you!"

"She has a concussion! And memory loss. What do you expect me—?"

"That's what that phone call was about? She just calls you out of the blue, after all she did, and you go running—"

"Oh, here we go."

"—to her rescue?"

"She has memory loss—or did you miss that little piece of the puzzle?"

Beau plunged his hands deep into his khaki pockets. "I don't care if she has malaria. What problem is that of yours? She lost the right to call on you for help when she deserted you with an entire wedding to cancel. With a broken heart, in case you forgot."

"I haven't forgotten anything! She's the one who's forgotten. She doesn't even remember leaving Summer Harbor. She woke up on some bathroom floor with a knot on her head and the past seven months gone."

Beau studied him intently, as if he were trying to piece it all together.

Good luck with that. He hadn't even gotten to the wedding dress.

Beau walked to the sofa and sank down across from Zac, his elbows planted on his knees as his eyes narrowed knowingly. "She's playing some kind of game, Zac."

"Believe me, my mind went there too. But I took her to the hospital. She has a concussion. It's true."

"How do you know she's not faking the memory loss?"

"I just do."

"Come on, Zac, don't be so gullible."

Okay, now that smarted. He glared at Beau. "I'm not freaking gullible. What do you want, a medical report? I sat right there and listened to the doctor say she has amnesia."

"Because she *said* she didn't remember? Come on, man. You know she's your weak spot. After what she pulled, I wouldn't put it past her."

"You didn't see her last night. Didn't see how upset she was. She went to the *hospital*. You know how hard that is for her. Besides, why would she lie? She's the one who left *me*."

"Well, maybe she's changed her mind. Maybe this is some devious play on your sympathies so you'll—"

"She was in a wedding dress, all right?"

"What?"

"She was wearing a wedding dress. And some other dude's engagement ring. It was her flipping wedding day, and she can't even remember who she was marrying."

Beau's brows pulled together in confusion. "That doesn't make any sense."

"Well, I'm going to figure it out. I'm going to find her—people—and get her home ASAP. She'll be gone before you know it."

"Where was she at?"

"Portland."

Beau shook his head. "It just doesn't make sense. It's only been, what, six months since she left?"

"Seven." And eighteen days. But who was counting?

"And she's not only moved on, but she's ready to walk down the aisle with some other dude?"

Zac shrugged. It stung, he wasn't going to lie. Here he was, forcing himself to date other people, and she was about to take the plunge.

"You think she was cheating on you before?"

"I don't know." He thought back to last fall. They'd been so happy. Or so he'd thought. "It didn't seem like it. Everything seemed fine." As Beau's eyes met his, the silent words filled the gap between them. *Obviously it wasn't.*

"I don't even want to think about it. I just want to find her fiancé, hand her over to him, and forget she was ever here."

"I'm not sure it's going to be that simple."

"I'll make sure it is. In the meantime maybe you can keep this to yourself. I really don't feel like having a bunch of people slapping my shoulder again and asking me how I'm doing. Or worse, gossiping about what a gullible fool I am."

"People are going to see her, Zac."

"I'm closing the restaurant today. And I'll have her back in Portland by tonight if it's the last thing I do."

Chapter 6

Lucy loosened the edges of the eggs with the spatula and with a quick jab of her wrist flipped the omelet. She liked to cook at the Roadhouse. The walk-in was always well stocked, and the pans were top of the line.

Had it really been seven and a half months since she was here? It didn't seem possible. It went against everything her mind was saying.

She couldn't forget the way Beau had looked at her upstairs. Like she was the last person he'd expected—or wanted—to see. She couldn't help but feel she was missing some part of the equation, some critical piece of the past.

After being chased from Zac's apartment, she took a quick shower and slipped back into the loose jeans and T-shirt she'd been given from the hospital lost and found. Her stomach growling, she'd scrounged up some fresh ingredients. They'd both perk up after a nice breakfast.

She'd heard Beau leave fifteen minutes ago,

and her nerves were wired waiting for Zac to come down. As she slid the omelets onto plates, she heard his footfalls on the steps. A moment later he entered the kitchen, stopping short when he caught sight of her at the stove.

He wore a black T-shirt that hugged his muscular torso and a pair of fitted jeans. His hair was still damp from his shower, his goatee trimmed tighter than it had been last night.

"How are you feeling?" His remote gray eyes erased any warmth his words may have engendered.

"Better now that the meds have kicked in. Thanks for checking in on me last night."

"How's your vision?"

"Still a little blurry. It comes and goes." She held up the plates. "Hope you're hungry."

"You should be resting." If his tone weren't so gruff, she might think he still cared. But no. He only wanted her out of his life as quickly as possible.

The backs of her eyes stung. She swallowed hard as she set the plates on the prep table where they usually ate.

Used to eat.

After he retrieved some juice they dug in quietly, tension weaving around them like a sticky spiderweb. His stool couldn't be farther away. He hadn't even looked at her after that first glimpse of her at the stove.

How could he not love her anymore? After all

they'd meant to each other? It seemed impossible. Her feelings were real. How could she have been in love with another man, ready to pledge her life to him, just yesterday?

A part of her was curious about this man she'd been engaged to. But another part just wanted to erase the past seven months so she could be back where she belonged—with Zac.

"Has anything come back to you?" he asked.

The hope in his voice deflated her. As much as she wanted him to remember his love for her—that's how much he wanted her to remember that they'd parted ways.

He'd moved on without her. He really didn't love her. Maybe he—oh dear—maybe he was dating someone else. Maybe he was in love with someone else.

Her appetite was suddenly gone. She pushed her egg around the plate with her fork.

"Lucy?"

"Um, no. I don't remember anything else." She cleared the emotion from her throat. "Beau seemed a bit cross this morning."

"He's—distracted. He just got engaged."

"To Paige?"

"What? No. Her name's Eden. She's from away. Came to Summer Harbor last Thanksgiving."

"Oh." A lot had changed since she'd left. Riley was gone, Beau was with someone else, and Zac was completely over her.

He didn't say anything for a minute. "Listen, I'm going to shut down the restaurant today. Get online and figure this out. Sooner we can get you back to your old life the better."

She pinned him with a look, but he kept eating, eyes on his plate.

"Better for whom?" she said. "I don't even remember that life."

"Being back in your normal surroundings, your regular routine, will help."

"I don't even know where I lived."

"We're going to figure all that out." He shoved a bite into his mouth.

Lucy studied him. His evasive eyes, his stiff shoulders, his detached demeanor. She thought of Beau's reaction to her. Not at all consistent with his usual warm, friendly nature.

Maybe her brain wasn't operating at full speed, but something was wrong. "What's going on, Zac?"

His eyes came up, meeting hers for a long-drawn-out moment.

"Why are you being like this? So . . . distant and angry. And Beau . . . he didn't even say hello to me."

Zac dropped his fork onto his plate and got up, his stool scraping across the ceramic tile. He scraped his plate off and set it in the sink. "Things didn't end well between us, that's all."

"What happened?"

Zac grabbed a rag and began wiping down the counter. "You left, that's what happened."

"What do you mean I left?"

"Out of the blue. Just like that. No explanation."

Her mind rejected his words. The air left her lungs. "No."

"Ayuh. I went away for a weekend. When I came back, you were gone. Your apartment was empty, your things were gone." His voice was tight. "You didn't even leave a note, changed your number. I had no idea where you went. You left the ring, though, thanks for that."

She shook her head. "No. I wouldn't do such a thing." She loved Zac. It was the kind of love you lived for. The kind you died for. Surely he knew that.

"Something happened. Something more than that. What aren't you telling me?"

He fixed her with a look. "I'm telling you everything I know. It's precious little—believe me, I'm aware."

The food congealed in her stomach. She pushed her plate back.

His hand moved across the stove top, working fast. His words were measured, careful. "When I couldn't get hold of you, I figured you were done. We were done. I called the florist and the photographer and the bakery and every guest on our wedding list and told them the wedding was off."

47

A yawning ache opened in her middle. Her eyes stung hard. This was horrible. She couldn't have ditched him like that. She wouldn't have done that to him. Not to Zac.

"But you did."

She hadn't realized she'd spoken aloud. Her face was warm, like she'd sat out in the sun too long.

"Something must've . . . I don't know how . . . It doesn't make any sense to me at all."

"Well, that makes two of us." Zac pitched the rag into the sink and turned to her, drawing a deep breath. Two. His chest rose and fell, and she got a little inkling of the pain she'd caused.

No wonder he was treating her so differently. No wonder his brother was so mad. He was protective of Zac. She wanted to continue to deny what he was saying. As much as she loved Zac, she couldn't even imagine bailing on him like that.

But then she remembered other instances. Times before she'd even known Zac, when leaving was exactly what she'd done. Who she'd been. Other times when her feelings for Zac had scared her down to the marrow of her bones.

She watched him gather himself, and she wanted to walk over to the sink and comfort him. She wanted him to lift her onto the counter, like she was a little bit of nothing. She wanted to kiss him until she made all his pain disappear.

Until they both forgot everything that had happened.

But he wouldn't welcome her comfort or her kisses.

"I—I can hardly believe I did that. But if I did—"

"You did."

"I'm awful sorry. It doesn't seem real. I can't even imagine why I'd—" She shook her head. "I love you, Zac."

A shadow flickered as his jaw twitched. "Stop saying that. It isn't doing anybody any good."

She blinked the tears away. "But it's true. I still feel like our wedding is days away. I still want to spend the rest of my life with you."

Emotion tightened the corners of his mouth. "Well, you won't when you get your memory back. You were headed down the aisle toward someone else, remember?"

The cords of his neck stood out, and his jaw was knotted, his eyes tight. "Listen. Let's just focus on gathering information today. Let's figure this out. Get you back to your life and your job and your—"

Fiancé.

His lips flattened. He grabbed her plate and glass and set them in the kitchen sink. "I'll be in my office. Maybe you should get some rest."

Chapter 7

Zac dropped his head back against his office chair and stifled the urge to throw his laptop across the room.

How could it be so hard? It was a wedding, for crying out loud. Weddings were announced. They were publicized. And yet he couldn't find one mention of Lucy's wedding anywhere on any Portland site. He'd looked up her name in the *Portland Press Herald* and in the *Daily Sun.* He'd Googled her name with "wedding" and "engagement." He'd checked the social media sites to see if she'd joined the rest of the world sometime over the past seven months. She hadn't.

Of course not. She didn't want you to find her.

He drew in a deep breath and blew it out, his eyes drifting over to the sofa where Lucy had lost her battle with fatigue. She'd followed him into the office hours earlier, much to his dismay. He needed to keep as much distance between them as possible, and she wasn't making it easy. Looking at him with those soft blue eyes. Saying things he'd only dreamed of hearing since she'd left.

She was easy to read, an open book. He could see the guilt in her eyes and the remorse in the slope of her shoulders. In the kitchen she'd reached out a hand as if she'd wanted to comfort him. But just as quickly, it had fallen to her side. Just as well.

How many times had he gone over those days before she left, trying to figure out why she'd done it? It was true he'd been distracted. Moody. Had he chased her away? Or had she never even loved him as she should have? There'd be no answers for him now. Not unless her memory returned.

She helped him with ideas as he researched, offering quiet suggestions. But he sensed her conflicting emotions. She wanted to help, but she wasn't eager to return to Portland. She made no bones about that.

Well, that was too bad. She'd wanted it seven months ago. He'd darn well figure this out and get her back home.

Resolved, he went back to work, trying to ignore the little sounds she made in her sleep. She'd dozed off right where she sat, her head drooping against the wingback part of the sofa. The quilt he'd used last night was spread across her. Okay, so he'd put it there awhile ago when he'd needed to stretch his legs. She'd been curled up in a ball like she was cold. What was he supposed to do?

Frowning, he forced his mind back to his search. What else? What wasn't he thinking of? The wedding license. Were those a matter of public record? He did a search, his spirits buoying when he discovered they were. There were even online records!

He scrolled quickly to the bottom of the page where the county links were. His eyes scanned the counties once. Twice. Cumberland wasn't on the list. They didn't offer the online feature. His spirits sank again. So many roadblocks.

He'd have to wait until they opened tomorrow. He'd get the name of her fiancé from the license, then he'd track the guy down. He hated the delay, but maybe he'd find something else yet today.

His eyes swung to the sofa again, to Lucy with her hair sticking up at all angles. With her small hand curled under her delicate chin, her long lashes kissing the tops of her cheeks. She looked so vulnerable. She hadn't been herself sincehe'd pulled up to the curb in Portland. She was lost and confused, and it pulled at every protective instinct he had. But she wasn't his to protect anymore.

She made a little *hmm* sound as she resituated, curling into the sofa arm and letting out a soft sigh. Where had the bold, quirky Lucy gone? The one who'd snagged his attention the moment she'd walked into his restaurant? Maybe time hadn't stopped when she'd entered his world, but it had seemed to.

His brothers were hanging around that evening, the first day of the year that was warm enough to make people believe spring really was on its way. There was a jubilant feeling in the air. The Red Sox home opener had ended in a triumphant win over the Phillies, and the town was in the mood to celebrate.

The jukebox cranked out country tunes, and a few brave souls danced on the wide-open space in front of it. A rowdy game of pool ensued in the back room, and his well-staffed kitchen was hopping. His servers scurried around with fragrant trays of buffalo wings, seafood platters, and bowls of chowder.

With all the commotion, people coming and going, he didn't even know what it was that pulled his eyes to the door the minute she walked in. Dark hair framed a pixie face that seemed lit from within. She wore a pair of fitted jeans, a glittery black top, and a pair of high-heeled boots that made her legs go on forever. A blingy leather bag was slung over her shoulder.

He was no fashion expert, but she looked a little upscale for Summer Harbor. She was alone, but she had a confident air about her that said she didn't mind her own company.

She paused in the entry, probably wondering if she should seat herself. He had just begun to move from behind the counter when Beau intercepted her on his way to the poolroom. After a quick exchange she headed toward a small empty table across the room.

A server called for help, and Zac got lost in his work for a while. Correcting a customer's order, refilling drinks, cleaning up a spill in the pool-room.

The next time he had a chance to look up, her table was empty, and disappointment settled like a weight in his gut. But a few seconds later he found her on the dance floor, moving fluidly to "Country Girl." Nice moves. She was short with subtle curves. Compact. Tousled brown hair moving around her shoulders.

He liked women of all sizes and shapes, but because of his height he tended toward tall women, usually willowy ones with short hair. But he suddenly felt like he'd been missing out.

Several local women were dancing near her, and she was chatting them up like they were old friends. She smiled at something one of them said, and two adorable dimples came out to play.

He fought the urge to make the sign of the cross—and he wasn't even Catholic.

"Something catch your eye?" Riley sank onto an empty stool in front of him.

His younger brother was built like a tank, barrel-chested, his arms thick and strong from his days on the lobster boat. At just under six feet he was the shortest of the three Callahan brothers.

"She's cute, huh?" Riley was watching the new girl dance.

"Cute" didn't do her justice. The upbeat song

faded away, replaced by the poignant strains of "I Don't Dance." Jared Watkins, one of his old schoolmates, swept her up in his arms, and Zac felt a prickle of annoyance.

"She's from the South," Riley said.

Zac pulled his eyes from the dance floor. "How do you know?"

"She asked me where the restroom was. Nice, slow Southern drawl. Tennessee, maybe."

"Naw." Beau appeared on the stool next to Riley. "You see those boots? I'm guessing Texas."

Riley gave a laugh. "Not even close."

"Can I get a refill, bro?" Beau asked Zac. "Ten says I'm right." He fished a ten-spot from his wallet and slapped it on the counter.

"You're on." Another ten landed on the bar. "You in, Zac?"

"Sure." He refilled Beau's glass, then fished a bill from his pocket. "It'll give me a reason to talk to her."

"Like you needed one." Riley smirked. "You've been eyeing her since she walked through the door."

Beau quirked a brow. "Aw, that's so cute. You smitten, little bro?"

Zac shot him a look as he moved to take a drink order from a fellow down the counter.

"Better hurry up before Jared stakes his claim."

"She kind of looks like the chick in that movie," Beau said. "Mandy something. What was it . . . ?"

He snapped his fingers. *"A Walk to Remember."*

Zac lifted a brow.

"Don't judge. It was a date."

Zac's eyes swung to the dance floor on his way to the kitchen. He fetched a seafood sampler and delivered it to the end of the bar. When he returned, he took a phone call from a customer's wife, asking Zac to tell her husband to stop on the way home for a gallon of milk. By the time he passed on the message, the slow dance was over and the dance floor was hopping again. The object of his attention was right in the middle of it all.

He caught up with his brothers between customers, and a few songs later a flash of glitter caught his eye. He turned to see the pretty girl approaching the counter. Her eyes sparkled as they settled on him.

His mouth dried up, and his entire body started buzzing like a neon sign.

She walked with an easy grace, her hips swaying just a little in those trendy jeans, her chin tilted at a jaunty angle.

He felt his lips turn up of their own accord. He was vaguely aware of his brothers talking but couldn't be bothered to listen.

She didn't take her eyes from him as she neared the bar. She smoothly pulled out an empty stool, hitched her hip, and . . .

Missed.

She wobbled for a moment, then caught her balance before he could lean across the bar. "Whoopsie," she said.

Twin flags of pink brightened her cheeks, and he fell just a little in love with her right then. She righted herself on the stool, cleared her throat, then turned her eyes up to his. Blue, with flecks of silver. Mesmerizing.

"Guess I danced my legs right off." She bit her lip. "That's a lie. Actually I'm just a little clumsy sometimes. A lot of times. Okay, most of the time."

He gave her a crooked grin, her slow drawl weaving around him like a spell. "I find that hard to believe. What can I get you, Georgia?"

Surprise flared in her eyes before they narrowed on him. "How'd you know where I'm from?"

He barely heard Beau's and Riley's groans over the music.

Not taking his eyes off her, Zac scooped up the bills and shoved them into his pocket. "I have an ear for accents. Lots of people pass through."

"Can I get a sweet tea?" she asked.

"Coming right up." Zac filled a glass with ice and tea.

A mutual friend of his brothers' showed up, and Zac was glad when they drifted away from the bar, leaving him alone with Georgia.

He set the tea in front of her and braced his elbows on the counter, praying everyone would leave him alone for two seconds. "What brings you to Summer Harbor?"

She shrugged a slender shoulder. "Just doing a little traveling up this way."

"Passing through?"

She tilted her head. "I don't know. I like the feel of this town. Nice vibe." Her ice tinkled against the glass as she played with her straw. "I might stick around awhile."

That was the best news he'd heard all week. "What's your name? Or should I just keep calling you Georgia?"

She sighed, her piercing eyes never leaving his. "Yes, please," she whispered.

He quirked a brow.

Her eyes took on a deer-in-headlights look as the pink on her cheeks deepened. "I said that out loud, didn't I?"

"You kinda did."

"I do that sometimes. Add it to the long list of ways in which I embarrass myself."

He chuckled. Everything about her was so . . . delightfully unexpected. And he could listen to that drawl of hers all night.

He held out his hand. "Zac Callahan."

She gave a chagrined look. "Lucy Lovett."

Her hand was small and warm, and he found himself reluctant to let it go. "Lovett—as in Audrey Lovett, the actress?"

"She's my great-aunt, actually."

"No way. My mom used to watch her movies all the time." He tilted his head, scanning her heart-shaped face, her big blue eyes. "You have the look of her."

"Thank you. She was quite the star back in her day."

His eyes dropped to the necklace she was toying with—a dainty silver heart with a cross inside. Was it too much to hope they shared the same faith?

"Like your necklace."

She glanced down. "Thank you. My mama gave it to me the day I was baptized."

"We have something in common then."

"Your mama gave you a heart-shaped necklace?"

Her saucy smile made his heart race, and he smiled in return. "I was referring to faith."

"Well . . . I am from the Bible Belt, you know. Can't throw a rock and not hit a church."

"Not such a bad thing."

"No, it's surely not." Her gaze rose to the top of his head. "Are you really that tall, or do you have a platform back there?"

"I'm really that tall. Can I get you anything else? An appetizer?"

"I already ate. The chowder was really good. Have you worked here long?"

"Since high school. It's mine now. The owner retired, and I'm buying him out."

"Isn't that something." She looked around the

restaurant, her eyes taking in the high rustic ceilings, the eclectic wall of license plates, the worn plank floors.

She seemed a little high society for his place.

"It's the gathering place, right?" she said. "Where everybody knows your name?"

He smiled. "Something like that."

Her eyes smiled first, followed by her lips. "It's awful nice. Has a lot of energy, but it's warm too. Invitin'."

Invitin'. He was pretty sure men weren't supposed to swoon, but dang it all if he didn't feel like doing it anyway. "Glad you like it."

"So, being the town's social hub, you must be connected. Know where a girl might find employment around here—if she *were* to stick around?"

"Whatcha looking for?"

She shrugged. "I'm flexible. I like people, so anything in retail would suffice. I have a sociology degree, but honestly I haven't had much use for it."

"Sociology, huh? Where'd you go to school?"

Her eyes fluttered down, then back up. "Um, Harvard."

He lifted his brows. "I think you might be over-qualified for anything around here."

She waved him off. "I'm not particular. And like I said, I probably won't hang around that long."

"Well, I know they're looking for someone to

run the visitor center. It was previously just the Natural History Center, but the town recently voted to make it a visitor center also. Lots of small-town controversy there, but I'll spare you the details. My aunt manages it, and she's looking for someone to welcome tourists, hand out maps, point them in the right direction. Like I said, you're way overqualified . . ."

"No, it sounds fun. I'd learn about the area too, so that's a bonus. And at some point I'd love to hear the story of the controversy. I find such things fascinatin'."

Fascinatin'. That's exactly what he found her to be. He pulled a pen from his pocket and jotted down Aunt Trudy's number on a napkin. The restaurant phone was ringing, but for once someone else could get it.

He slid the napkin across the counter. "Give her a call if you want. Tell her I sent you. She's a little gruff, but don't let that put you off."

She snapped up the napkin, her eyes sparkling. "Thanks. I'll do that."

"Phone, Zac!" one of his servers called.

Lucy slid off the stool, hitching her purse onto her shoulder. "Well, I should get on and let you get back to work. Maybe I'll see you around."

He gave her a smile. "Maybe you will."

A humming sound pulled him from the past, and he leaned back against the desk chair. Across the office Lucy shifted on the sofa, the quilt puddling in her lap. She stilled, her eyes remaining closed.

He blinked away the remnants of the memory. It was a rude transition from that heady first meeting to today. Falling in love with Lucy had been as easy as drawing a breath. Falling out of love, not so much.

Chapter 8

Lucy paced the office, her gaze swinging to Zac as she walked. He was on the phone with the people from county records. He'd made the call at the stroke of nine.

She hitched up her lost-and-found jeans. While they accommodated her generous backside, they failed to follow the curve of her waist. She needed a belt. Or a heavy-duty pair of suspenders.

"Yes," Zac was saying. "Okay . . . I'm not sure . . . Thank you." A long pause ensued. His expression gave away no more than his words. He ran a hand over his jaw. She could hear the rough scrape of his tightly trimmed beard in the quiet.

As curious as she was about her old life—and as much as she longed for some decent-fitting clothes and maybe a thriving bank account—she dreaded the answers he was about to find.

"Yes, I'm still here," Zac said.

He wouldn't even look at her. Couldn't wait to get rid of her, obviously. And no wonder, after what she'd pulled. Her pulse pounded in her temples.

She let her eyes rove over his handsome face, the chiseled features that had melted her on the spot the second she'd seen him. He had masculine brows that shadowed his deep-set eyes. Those gray eyes, so serious now, could light up so quickly. He had a goofy side. Could make her laugh until her jaw ached.

But he hadn't so much as smiled since her return. He was so distant. As if he were determined to keep her far away from his heart.

This whole situation boggled her mind. How could all her feelings for Zac be intact when she had a fiancé waiting in Portland? How could she possibly have fallen in love with someone else?

She couldn't. She refused to believe it. Whoever he was, he couldn't have captured her heart the way Zac had. She didn't want him. Didn't want to love him, didn't want a life with him.

And yet any moment the person on the phone was going to tell Zac his name, and Zac was going to escort her out to his truck, tuck her inside, drive her back to Portland, and hand her over to some stranger.

"Ayuh," Zac said.

She stopped in front of his desk. Her heart rate accelerated, the headache thumping in her temples until she felt dizzy with it. Her fingers itched to hit the End button on the phone's base. She didn't want to know his name. She didn't want to go anywhere.

"I see," he said. "When?" His lips pressed together as he listened to the county clerk. "Fine. Okay. Thank you for your help." He turned off the handset and set it on the desk with a loud *thunk*. His eyes were glued to the desk. A shadow flickered over his jaw as it clenched, and his nose flared.

What? she wanted to ask. But nothing came out. She watched him collect himself while her own heart threatened to explode from her chest.

"Their computers are down," he said finally.

Her breath released in a quick puff. Thank God. A reprieve. Maybe a short one, but she'd take what she could get.

"They're hoping they'll be back up later today."

"Hoping?"

He nailed her with a look. "They *will* be," he said as if he could will it to happen.

"What—what do we do till then?"

"I have a restaurant to open. You should go . . . get a nap or something."

"It's a little hard to sleep when my entire future's up in the air." Edginess crept into her tone.

"You heard what the doctor said. You should take it easy. Maybe your memory will come back if you—"

"I don't want it back!"

He blinked at her, those inscrutable gray eyes giving away a flash of surprise.

"I don't! I don't want to go back to Portland, I don't want to know whose name was on that stupid marriage license, and I don't want—"

"We've been through—"

"—my memory back!"

They stared at each other, silence pushing in around them, thick and heavy like a fog rolling into the harbor. The same fog closed over her mind. She fought to hang on to her thoughts, but the wispy edges of them slipped away.

Her pounding head took front and center, stealing any rational thought she might have left.

Zac's chair squeaked as he got up. He skirted the desk, heading toward her.

Finally. Suddenly all she could think about was his arms around her. She ached for his embrace. She wanted to sink her weight into him and pretend none of this was happening. Her heart sped as he neared, and she stepped toward him.

But he passed by her and went out the door.

Her breath escaped in a little whimper. Her eyes stung and her vision went blurry. Not from the concussion this time, but from the tears. She wouldn't cry, daggonit. She would. Not. Cry.

She counted the number of books on his shelves to distract herself. There weren't many, so she mentally alphabetized them. Why should she be so upset when he was apparently just going along like she wasn't in the middle of a crisis?

She might as well take control of her situation. Make a plan. Maybe she had a memory lapse, but she wasn't helpless. She'd walk right to the store and find some suitable clothes. Buy a curling iron and some decent conditioner. And lipstick. She'd feel so much better once she—

What was she thinking? She didn't have a cent to her name. She *was* helpless. Leastwise until she returned to Portland.

Zac walked back in and stopped, extending his hand. There were two pills in the bowl of his palm. A glass of water in his other hand.

Her eyes stung again at his kindness. What was wrong with her? Why was she so blubbery?

She took the pills and sank against the desk, weariness draping over her like a heavy mantle. She suddenly wanted to fall asleep for a very long time. Who knew forgetting could be so exhausting?

He stuffed his hands into his pockets. She could feel his eyes on her but didn't look at him. Didn't want him to see her vulnerability, not when he had that thick wall up between them.

"Lucy," he said, his tone full of reason. "I know this is hard, but the last seven months happened whether you want to remember them or not. You've moved on. I've moved on. Whether you remember it or not, that doesn't change that it happened. The sooner we figure this out, the sooner we can both get on with our lives."

"What if I never get my memory back?"

"That doesn't change the fact that it happened. You have a job you can go back to. People who care about you."

She sniffed. "I don't care about them."

But a small part of her rejected the claim. She was the same person she'd been yesterday before the fall. Somewhere inside, she must care about this other man. Somewhere out there, he must be fretting over her. Whether she remembered him or not, she owed it to him to set his mind at ease.

"I've been thinking about yesterday," Zac said. "Maybe it wasn't your actual wedding day. Other-wise, why would you have been alone in a diner? Maybe you were having your fitting or something. Did you notice if there was a wedding shop nearby?"

"I can't say as I did." She pushed against the anxiety threading through her. Bridal shops had restrooms. Maybe she hadn't been thinking straight since she'd konked her head, but there was only one logical explanation why she was in that diner.

"I guess it's possible you hadn't even gotten a license yet. There's no waiting period, remember?"

He was wrong about all of this. She knew it deep inside, but she grabbed onto the thought like a lifeline. "That's true."

"I guess we'll find out this afternoon."

・・・

Zac hung the order and went to refill drinks at table eleven. Marci had missed her last two shifts.

Lunch rush was just about over, but a Red Sox game was coming on shortly and that meant extra customers. The retired population often stopped by to enjoy the afternoon games. They didn't order much, but Zac enjoyed their company.

By the time the restaurant cleared out, the supper crew was arriving. A quick check of his watch told him he needed to make that call to the county. He'd been too busy. At least that's what he told himself. Maybe somewhere deep inside, he didn't want to let go of Lucy just yet.

You're a regular masochist, Callahan.

He tossed down the rag he'd been using to clean the bar and strode to his office. He was going to get this over with, and he was going to do it now.

Seconds later he was dialing the number he'd jotted on a scrap of paper. It took forever to reach the right person, but when he did, he found that their computers were back up.

Hallelujah.

He paced the floor as he waited for the clerk to pull up the license. She'd put on some kind of easy listening music that was probably supposed to keep him calm. Instead, his nerves jangled like loose change in a server's apron.

The music cut off. "Mr. Callahan, are you there?"

"Yes."

"I found the record. Would you like me to fax you a copy?"

"That'd be great." He gave her his fax number. "How long do you think it'll take?"

"I'll send it as soon as I hang up."

"Thank you so much."

Zac signed off and pocketed his phone. He walked over to the machine and waited, hands on hips. Soon as he had a name, he'd do a little Googling and find Mr. Right's phone number. Or maybe the license had that information. Could it really be so easy?

Maybe the guy would even come pick her up. He felt a pinch in his gut at the thought. Could he put her in a car with someone who was a stranger to her? Maybe he should—

No, he chided himself. *She's not yours anymore.*

The machine whirred to life, and a paper fed through. As soon as it was done, he picked it up and scanned it.

Brad Martin. Portland, Maine. Age 29. Caucasian.

Bingo.

He headed down the hall and knocked on Lucy's door.

"Brad Martin," Zac said the instant she opened

the door. His eyes studied her intensely, the silver flecks sparking.

Lucy stood in the doorway, conscious of her sleep-tousled hair and makeup-free face. The pills made her so drowsy. Maybe that's why she couldn't think straight.

"What?"

"Brad Martin. Mean anything to you?"

"Um . . . no."

"Are you sure?"

"I've never heard—is that his name? My . . . fiancé?"

He held up a paper. "They faxed your wedding license."

"Let me see." She took the paper and scanned the information. *Brad Martin.* She frowned. *Brad Martin.* The name meant nothing to her.

"Maybe he goes by Bradley." His tone was urging, hopeful.

She shook her head, staring at the paper a moment before she handed it back. "Nothing. Sorry."

He turned around and walked away. She followed him to his office where he sat behind his desk and went to work on the computer.

She stepped behind him and watched as he typed the name into the search engine, confining the search to the Portland area. A moment later twenty-seven results appeared.

He sighed. "Great."

"Look. It lists their ages." *Why are you helping?* Leaning forward, he scrolled through the list. "There's no twenty-nine-year-old Brad Martin," he said a couple minutes later. "But this one's twenty-eight. Got to be him, right?"

"Maybe."

He picked up the handset and began dialing.

Her heart pounded. "Wait. You're calling now? What are you going to say?"

He spared her a look. "Me? Oh no. It's your fiancé." He finished dialing and handed her the phone.

Panic tumbled through her. "What do I say?"

"Ask if he knows who it is. If it's him, he'll know your voice."

Her face must've shown the panic she was feeling because his eyes warmed. "He'll be relieved to hear from you."

"Hello?" a male voice said on the other end of the phone.

Her throat closed up, her eyes locked on Zac. Was this him? The man she was engaged to? The man she was supposed to love? Wouldn't some part of her know his voice?

"Hello?" His tone was impatient. Or maybe expectant. Hopeful?

"H-hello. Is this Brad?"

"*Lucy?* Lucy, is that you?"

"Y-yes."

He swore. "Do you have any idea—" A hard

71

sigh cut through the words. "Where are you?"

She was suddenly reluctant to give her exact location. "I—I'm up north. I had an accident. I hit my head. I don't remember anything."

"I know. I've been in touch with the hospital. They're looking for you, Lucy."

"Who?"

"Who? The police. Everyone. I filed a missing person report."

"The police?" Her eyes shot to Zac's.

His brows pulled together.

"I'll let them know I found you. Why didn't you call me? I've been worried."

"I told you, I don't remember anything."

Silence spread across the line until she was almost ready to call his name and make sure he was still there.

"What do you mean by 'anything'?" he asked finally.

"I—I don't remember the last seven and a half months."

More silence. *"Nothing?"*

"No, I—I'm afraid not. I don't even remember moving to Portland. I don't remember meeting you at all. I don't remember dating or anything. We—I had to research on the computer to even find your name."

"No kidding."

His reflective tone struck her as odd. But she wasn't processing things correctly. He was

72

probably in shock. He'd been going through a crisis of his own.

"You don't remember our wedding day?"

"No. Only waking up on the floor of a diner."

"Will it come back—your memory?"

"I don't know. The doctor said it might or might not. I was afraid. I—I came up north."

"I'll come get you. Where are you?"

She recoiled at his offer. She knew she was being silly, but there was something about him she didn't like. He seemed . . . calculating somehow. *It's all in your head, Lucy. He was your fiancé, for heaven's sake.*

"Thank you, but no. I'm—I'm going to stay put awhile. I need to rest and recover."

Zac shook his head adamantly, mouthing, *No,* while Brad tried to talk her into coming back. Her head was pounding again. Brad continued to reason with her, but his strident tone grated on her. She wanted to hang up the phone.

"I have to go, Brad," she said, interrupting his speech.

"You can't just walk away, Lucy. You have a job here, friends . . . me. Just let me—"

"I'll call you later." She hung up the phone before he could argue. Her heart was pounding, and her breath felt squeezed into her lungs.

"Lucy, you have to go back," Zac said. "You have an apartment or a house, a job, and all your money is—"

"I know! I will." But she wouldn't be going with Brad. She was so tired of people telling her what she had to do. She knew she had to go back. She surely couldn't stay here and mooch off Zac. But she had to sort out her life somehow before she made any kind of decision.

"Why didn't you tell him where you are?"

"I don't know." She rubbed her temples. "I didn't want him to know. I don't like him."

Zac smirked, his eyes mocking her. "Well, you must've liked something about him."

Lucy pulled her shoulders back. "This isn't funny, Zac. You got your way. You're getting rid of me like you want, so just . . . just put a sock in it!"

She stormed out of the office and returned to her room. She shook out two more pills and washed them down with the lukewarm water on the nightstand, then sank onto the edge of the bed and closed her eyes. She'd probably be passed out again in twenty minutes, but that was just fine. She was starting to prefer unconsciousness.

Chapter 9

It was late by the time they entered Portland. Lucy had dozed part of the way, gladly giving in to oblivion. She didn't want to think about the moment when Zac would leave her. Just the thought that she'd never see him again made her chest so tight she could hardly breathe.

She watched him from the corner of her eye. The streetlights washed over his face, highlighting the masculine angles. Shadows crouched below his brows and in the hollows of his cheeks. Her eyes fell to his lips, drawn out in a tight line. She would never kiss those lips again. Never feel the gentle sweep of his fingers across her skin. Never enjoy the safety of his strong embrace.

She'd thought she'd bought some extra time when Zac was unable to find her address, and she'd pleaded with him not to call Brad again.

But he had an ace up his sleeve—his cousin Abby, a private detective who lived in Indiana. She'd found the address in under an hour. Lucy lived in a downtown apartment on Park Street, unit 6.

Zac took an exit, and they coasted through a residential neighborhood. His hands gripped the steering wheel as he wordlessly navigated the darkened streets. Eventually the neighborhood gave way to a commercial area with higher buildings and stoplights at every corner—none of it familiar. She tried to picture her apartment and failed. But a different problem came to mind.

"Wait a minute. How are we going to get in?"

He cleared his throat, speaking for the first time in miles. "We'll find the super."

"What if he's not home?"

"Then we'll check next door. Maybe you left a key with a neighbor like you did in Summer Harbor." His low voice rumbled through the cab.

"And if I didn't?" He wouldn't just leave her there on the stoop, would he?

"Abby's taught me a few tricks over the years. I can pick a lock when I need to."

He turned onto Park Street and slowed, coasting as he read the street numbers. They were in the three hundred block, so he accelerated. Soon they entered a residential neighborhood that had a Boston feel, with tall, narrow buildings crammed together, stoops leading up to sets of double doors.

His foot eased off the pedal and the car slowed. His brows pinched together as he stared out the front windshield, and his lips went tighter still.

She followed his gaze to a handful of people gathered on the stoop of a brownstone.

"Oh boy," he said.

"What's wrong?"

"Is there a back—? Never mind."

He passed the building, and the people watched them go by. A couple of them stood. A man swung a camera to his shoulder. She noticed a white van that said KPTV on its side. And another white van with an unreadable logo.

Zac turned into a parallel slot just down the street and cut the ignition.

"What's going on? Was that my building?"

He looked at her across the darkened space. "Here's what we're going to do. We're going to walk fast, pass by them. Stay close to me, and don't say anything. Nothing at all. Got it?"

"This is about *me?*"

His sigh was long and steady. "Your fiancé must've contacted the police and let them know you're all right. It must be public record. You're a missing person, suffering from amnesia, and you're Audrey Lovett's great-niece to boot. I guess that's news. You ready? We need to make this quick."

No. Heck, no, she wasn't ready. But Zac was already out of the truck and heading round toget her.

He opened her door and took her arm. Her legs wobbled as they marched toward the small crowd. Her heart raced, her lungs struggling to keep up. She clutched Zac's arm, needing support.

As they neared, the people turned and headed toward them, microphones in hand, two video cameras. A light flashed, making her blink. Then another. She ducked into Zac, and he put his arm around her, drawing her into his side.

And then the mob was upon them.

"Lucy, is it true you have amnesia?"

"Where have you been, Lucy?"

"What can you tell us about your accident?"

"Who's the guy, Lucy?"

"No comment," Zac growled, turning a shoulder in and plowing through the group.

Lucy almost had to jog to keep up. They reached the stoop, and she scampered up the steps beside him.

"Lucy, how much do you remember?"

"What's your prognosis?"

"Why'd you leave your wedding?"

"They're calling you the Runaway Bride. Any thoughts on that?"

They slipped through the door and darted for the stairs. Behind them the door fell closed, shutting out the questions. Zac stayed close as they climbed a flight of steps, then another.

Her breaths were heavy by the time they reached the top. "What about the super?"

He pulled two little tools from his pocket. "We're going straight to plan C."

Lucy looked down the stairwell while he worked, afraid the reporters were going to come crashing in the door. Their questions haunted her. How long would they stay out there? Was she going to be trapped here?

Runaway Bride?

"Maybe we should just find the super. It'll say on the mailbox."

His hands went still, and he angled a look up at her, his eyes intense. "You remember the mailboxes?"

"No . . . I just assumed."

He visibly deflated, then went back to his tools. "I almost have it."

A few minutes later he turned the knob and the door opened. He held it for her and she crossed the threshold, finding a light switch on the wall beside her. The apartment smelled like new carpet and lemons. Zac shut the door behind her, fiddling with the doorknob.

"You're going to need a better lock. A dead bolt."

She entered the living room, looking around at the unfamiliar sleek furniture. The walls were dove gray, the carpet white. The charcoal leather sofa looked like it was built to admire, not sit on. The end tables were glass and metal. On the wall was a Georgia O'Keefe floral print, nicely framed, and a skyline of a city—Portland, she presumed. It was a nicely appointed apartment, but it was not to her taste.

She felt Zac's presence as he entered the room. "Nice place. Anything seem familiar?"

She shook her head. "Zac, this isn't even my style. Or in my budget. Are you sure this is my place?" What if they'd picked someone else's lock?

"The camera crew wouldn't be here if it weren't."

"Oh. Right." She hoped she would get her brain back soon.

His eyes drifted around the room. "Maybe it was furnished." He walked toward a table while she wandered down a short hall.

A nice bedroom. A fancy bathroom with a big garden tub. She stopped in the bathroom doorway as her eyes caught on her red can of Big Sexy Hair. She picked up the mousse and the familiar hairbrush and pulled them close. Her eyes fell on her facial cleanser, and she grabbed that too.

Zac appeared in the doorway, his eyes dropping to the products she cradled like a baby in her arms. Heat rushed to her cheeks as she set them down on the marble counter, one by one, her hands shaking.

You're really losing it, Lucy.

"I found some stuff." He held up some envelopes. "Mail. Looks like a bank statement and a few bills. A paycheck."

"A paycheck? From where?"

"Someplace called Vacasa."

She took the check, frowning at the place of employment she'd never even heard of. At the amount of the paycheck. Even if it was only a weekly paycheck, it wasn't enough to justify a place like this.

She shook her head. "It doesn't make any sense."

"You probably had a second job. Let's see if we can find some car keys."

She followed him into the living room, through a tiny dining room, and into a kitchen. Maybe Brad had forked out the money for the apartment. She couldn't imagine living off a man like that, but nothing else made sense.

"Bingo," he said, scooping an unfamiliar leather purse off the counter. He handed it to her.

"Why would my purse be here? Wouldn't I have taken it with me?"

He shrugged.

But no, she would've carried a dainty little white one to go with her dress. And likely a small suitcase or overnight bag. She'd had to change and get ready, after all.

Runaway Bride.

She pushed the thought away as she rifled through her bag. "I doubt if my car's even here." Her fingers connected with the metal edges of keys. She pulled out the ring containing three keys and a Buick remote fob.

But she drove a 2010 Mini Cooper, and she'd never had the luxury of remote start. She frowned. "These aren't mine."

"I'm betting they are."

He walked to the window and peered through the sheers before pulling them back an inch. "They're still there."

She came up behind him, close enough to smell his spicy, woodsy scent. She drew in a deep breath, committing the smell to memory.

Zac aimed the fob toward the street, pushing a button.

Lights flashed on a Buick sedan parked just down the street.

"Bingo." He handed the keys back to her.

Their eyes met and clung, the lamplight washing over his handsome features. Was he really going to leave her here? Had she really lost him forever?

How can this have happened, God? I love him so much.

He cleared his throat and palmed the back of his neck. "Um, you should check your purse for your phone. It'll have your contacts and texts. Maybe it'll help you remember something."

"It wasn't in there."

"Right. I guess you would've had it on you when you fell. You should call the diner in the morning and see if they found it."

She nodded absently. She didn't even remember the name of the diner or have a clue where it was. She was going to have to call Brad back whether she wanted to or not. Maybe he could point her toward a friend she'd trusted. Maybe then she wouldn't feel so alone. So sad.

"What do you think they meant, Lucy?" His deep voice cut straight through her. She met his silvery eyes and gloried in the tenderness she saw there. "About the Runaway Bride thing?"

She wrenched her eyes away, shifting under his steady gaze. He had a way of making her feel like he could see right through her. Right down to the center of her heart. Somehow he'd loved her anyway.

"How would I know?"

"Right." He shifted away, driving his hands into his pockets. His eyes flittered around the sterile apartment, then came back to rest on her. "You're all settled then. I should get going."

Her heart drummed against her ribs as he headed toward the door. Adrenaline emptied into her system, making her pulse race and her limbs tremble.

"Can't I get you something to drink?"

"It's late. I have a long drive."

"Something for the road then? Some iced tea?" Surely she had iced tea.

"No thanks."

She followed him, fighting the insane urge to grab his shirt and drag him back. Or race ahead and throw herself in front of the door.

But he didn't want her. Didn't love her anymore. He was eager to get back to his Lucyless Summer Harbor life. And what did she have? An unfamiliar apartment in a foreign city, a fiancé she didn't remember, and oh yes, a gaggle of reporters on her front stoop. Panic rose in her throat, adding to the lump of emotion already knotting there.

Zac opened the door and turned, looking down at her with his cool, steely eyes.

Her feelings must've been written all over her face, because his eyes softened the smallest bit. "You'll be fine. You know where you work, and you have your car and your money, and your . . . fiancé."

I don't love him. I love you.

"I left his number on the table. You should call him. He'll help you get all this straightened out."

His words didn't even register. She stared at him, mentally begging him to stay. Why was everyone always leaving her? What was wrong with her?

Panic bubbled up, swelling inside. Her heart thrashed in her ears. *Do not beg, Lucy Lovett. Do not.*

The softness was gone from his eyes. Now they were just cold, hard pewter. His jaw was set in a stubborn line, his lips pressed together. As much as she might want to curl up in his arms one last time, it would be like hugging a cold marble statue. And she didn't think she could take one more rejection.

"Be sure and lock up behind me," he said in a tight voice. "Take care, Lucy."

Her lip trembled, and she caught it between her teeth and gave a little nod. It was all she could do.

And then he was gone, the door falling shut in front of her as so many others had before.

Chapter 10

Zac pushed open the main door of Lucy's apartment and plowed through the paparazzi.

"Where's Lucy?"

"Can we get your name?"

"Where's she been since Saturday?"

"Are you the reason she left Brad at the altar?"

Zac clamped his lips under the barrage of questions, his eyes straight ahead. He made quick work of the ground between the building and his truck and was glad for the silence once he was inside.

They were still on the stoop. He wasn't important enough to follow. But Lucy was another matter.

Not your problem.

But the image of Lucy's face as he'd left surfaced in his mind. Her skin pale and ghostly, her eyes flashing with panic.

He pushed the image firmly away as he pulled from the curb. His heart fought a battle with his rib cage, and an achy feeling was swelling in his gut.

She's a grown woman. She'll be fine.

He turned on the radio as he accelerated onto the highway a few minutes later. A mournful country song bled into the cab, and he switched the station to something more upbeat.

Lucy was where she belonged, and he was on his way back to normalcy. If normal wasn't all that great, well, he could work with that. He'd been doing it since she'd left. Picking up the pieces was never fun. And if she'd put another dent in his heart, well . . . it would heal. Eventually. He'd forgotten the pull of her sweet

Southern drawl, of her liquid blue eyes. The heady draw of her small hand in his.

But she'd seemed so forlorn tonight. So lost as she looked around her unfamiliar apartment, her arms wrapped protectively around her waist.

She has her fiancé. He'll help her through this.

He had to stop this. He turned up the radio and tried to lose himself in the country tune.

It was late. Almost eleven. Time for the TV news, he realized. Would they cover Lucy's story? Would everyone in the city soon be in Lucy's business?

"Why'd you leave your wedding, Lucy? They're calling you the Runaway Bride."

He frowned at the street in front of him, the words marching like soldiers through his mind. Was that really what had happened? Was that why she'd been alone in the diner when she'd fallen? Had she left yet another groom at the altar? He almost felt sorry for the guy.

A part of him felt vindicated. If he wasn't the only one she'd left, the problem wasn't him. Wasn't *them*. It was her. He chided himself for the thought. This wasn't about him or them. This was about Lucy.

Lucy, who no longer had a fiancé.

And why hadn't the guy mentioned the small matter of getting ditched at the altar on the phone? What did Zac even know about this guy? Just because he'd been engaged to Lucy didn't mean he was on the up-and-up. She hadn't known him long. He could be a real schmuck. Maybe that's why she'd dumped his sorry rear end.

If he'd kept the one secret from her, who knew what other lies he'd tell? And how would she know any better if she couldn't remember anything for herself? She was in a vulnerable position.

And you're just leaving her at his mercy?

His heart rate kicked up, and his breaths came short and quick.

Don't do it, man. Don't go back.

He gripped the steering wheel, wishing he could pick up the phone and call his dad. He'd had a way of cutting through all the details and getting down to the nitty-gritty. He'd know what Zac should do. But he was gone, and Zac was on his own.

He'd have to sort through the details himself.

Lucy didn't belong in Summer Harbor. She'd already broken his heart once. Beau had been texting him regular reminders since he'd stopped over yesterday. He'd been pushing Zac to get her back to Portland as soon as possible. Beau knew she was Zac's kryptonite.

But then he pictured her face as he'd turned to leave. He saw her lips wobbling. Watched the tears trembling on her lashes. Heard the thready whisper of her last words.

And he knew he couldn't do it. He couldn't

leave her there. He pounded his palm on the steering wheel, then did it again for good measure. *Dumb, stupid . . .*

He drifted into the right lane and took the next exit, hoping he wasn't making the biggest mistake of his life.

The pounding on the door made Lucy jump. Her heart skittered across her chest. Had the reporters slipped inside? They'd still been out there a few minutes ago when she'd watched Zac leave.

Or maybe it was her fiancé. Maybe Brad had gotten wind of her return.

Please no. She just couldn't deal with him right now.

She crossed the room and moved down the short hall. Just a little peek out the peephole. She didn't have to answer. She pressed her finger-tips against the door and leaned in. Her eyes widened on Zac's figure. His eyes were cast on the floor, his lips tight.

Zac! She didn't even care why he was back; she was just so happy to see his face again. Her heart found a new speed, and her fingers shook as they twisted the lock and opened the door.

His eyes pierced her. Something glimmered there. Anger? Frustration?

She studied his face for a hint of the reason for his return, but it was an inscrutable mask.

Her mouth went dry. Words stuck in her throat.

Hope clawed at her chest, her limbs tingling with it.

"Pack a bag." His voice was gruff. "And make it quick."

Air whooshed from her lungs. "You're taking me home?"

"You're going to follow me." His lips tightened. "And this is just until your memory's back."

Tension she didn't even know she held drained away, replaced by a light, giddy feeling. The backs of her eyes stung. She pressed a palm to her pounding heart.

"Come on, get moving," he said tersely. "The vultures are still out there, and I'd like to get at least a little sleep tonight."

Chapter 11

Lucy approached the wide front-porch steps of the Primrose Inn in Summer Harbor. The sun was high overhead, chasing away the morning chill. The lush landscaping dazzled with colorful blooms, and raw green stems peeked through the mulch as if wanting to join the summertime fun. Her mama would've loved it.

She looked up at the beautiful old mansion. An enormous veranda, complete with swings, warmed the stately brownstone exterior. The inn had advertised its need of a desk clerk in the help-wanted section of the *Harbor Tides*, and Lucy figured she had a good chance at the job. The owner, Margaret LeFebvre, a bird-watching enthusiast, had often visited the Natural History Center when Lucy worked there, and they'd hit it off.

Lucy had woken this morning feeling decisive and optimistic for the first time since she konked her head. She called the company she'd worked for in Portland and quit, explaining her situation. It seemed like a large company, as the person in human resources didn't even seem to recognize her name. She canceled her lease and made plans to store her belongings—the apartment had come furnished, so she didn't have much. She'd collect them later. Lastly, she had her mail forwarded.

She was staying in Summer Harbor, with or without her memory. She had yet to mention that fact to Zac. She'd left while he was busy, saying she was stepping out for a bit. But the sooner she got a job the better. If the Primrose Inn didn't work out, there was also a position open at the Unique Boutique.

She could do this. She felt more like her old self in her favorite gray slacks and a lightweight sweater that matched her blue eyes. She'd found a pair of gray Michael Kors wedges that added four inches to her height.

A bell jingled as she pushed open the heavy wooden door. The house carried the fragrant scent of bacon backed with a sweet cinnamon smell. The aroma made her stomach growl.

There were voices in the back room, and she was about to follow them when Margaret came through the doorway, a warm smile on her face. The woman had always reminded her of Diane Keaton, with her smart fashion sense and elegant figure.

"Mrs. LeFebvre, how are you?"

The woman's smile diminished by a few watts. "Lucy. You're back in town."

Lucy smiled wider, trying not to be discouraged by Mrs. LeFebvre's lack of enthusiasm. "I am. I arrived Saturday. Your primroses are so lovely! You have a very inviting home. I can see why your inn is so popular."

Mrs. LeFebvre removed her readers, letting them dangle from the chain around her neck. "Thank you."

"Have you done much bird-watching lately?"

"Not much. We've been quite busy with tourists since the weather turned warm. Are you looking for a place to stay?"

"Oh! No, I'm not. Actually I came across your ad in the paper for a desk clerk. I was hoping the spot might still be available."

The woman gave a thin smile. "I see. So you're here to stay."

Her flat tone made Lucy's heart feel as if it were shrinking. "Yes, ma'am."

"I didn't realize you and the Callahan boy were back together."

Lucy's smile wobbled. "We're—well, we're not, exactly. But I'm moving back to town. I missed Summer Harbor." Not that she remembered missing it, but she must have. "I have a lot of experience working with the public, as you know, and I worked as a—"

"I'm sorry, dear," Mrs. LeFebvre said, her gaze direct. "I'm afraid you're not quite right for the position."

Lucy squirmed as a heavy feeling settled in her stomach. "Oh. Well, I see. I—I do hope you'll keep me in mind if something else opens up." She lifted the edges of her mouth in the semblance of a smile.

"Thank you for stopping by."

Lucy turned and left, navigating the porch steps on wobbly legs. The woman was a lifelong friend of the Callahans, and obviously she was bitter about Lucy leaving Zac.

She thought of all those calls he'd had to make, canceling their wedding, of the humiliation he'd suffered. Shame stole over her, making her cheeks fill with heat. What had made her do such an awful thing?

She turned onto the sidewalk, making a valiant effort to shrug off the depressing thoughts. There was nothing she could do about the past. At the corner she turned, heading toward the Unique

Boutique. She'd splurged on a baby-blue sundress there last summer. She'd been wearing it the night Zac proposed.

Two hours later Lucy sat on the beach, heedless of her nice pants. She removed her wedges and dug her toes into the coarse sand. The coolness felt good against her aching arches.

Out in the harbor, lobster boats bobbed in the water. The wind tugged at her hair, and she drew in a deep breath, letting the salty tang of the air fill her lungs. The water kissed the shore in quiet ripples, a sound that failed to soothe her troubled spirit. Overhead a seagull gave a lonesome cry.

She'd put in an appearance at the boutique and had spoken with the owner. The thirtysomething woman had taken one look at Lucy, put her twitchy nose up in the air, and said in a clipped tone that the position had already been filled.

So had the opening at the bookstore, though the help-wanted sign still hung in the window. She'd stopped in other shops, but no one else was hiring.

She'd finally gotten desperate enough to check Frumpy Joe's diner. She'd spent many hours at the café with Zac, and the owner was one of the friendliest women she'd ever met. Lucy had worked as a server during college. Maybe she'd dropped a few trays, but she was efficient, and she had a great memory. Well. Normally.

Turned out she needn't have fretted about

dropping trays at Frumpy Joe's. Charlotte Dupree took her number, but her tone gave Lucy little hope of hearing from her.

Lucy's brain may not have been operating at full capacity, but she'd have to be dead to miss the cold shoulders turning her way. The enormity of what she'd done seven months ago was sinking in, and it wasn't feeling too good.

She couldn't bring herself to go back to the Roadhouse. Zac was as eager to get rid of her as everyone else in town. Probably more so. The thought was a kick in the gut.

Hearing footfalls behind her, she turned and spotted a young woman jogging on the board-walk. She felt a moment's envy at the peaceful expression on her face. That was what she needed right now. There was nothing like a nice, long run to wash away a person's troubles.

Wanting to think about something else—any-thing else—she rooted through her purse and pulled out a bundle of envelopes. Between her and Zac they'd managed to find some mail and papers lying around her apartment. Maybe they'd give her a clue about what she'd been doing in Portland and provide the information she needed to resettle.

She pulled an envelope from the stack and saw it was from a bank. After her disastrous afternoon, she hoped she'd spent the last several months putting away some serious money. She pushed a finger under the flap and tore it open. She'd need to contact the bank and get another ATM card. She only had twenty-seven dollars in her wallet.

As she unfolded the paper, a gust of wind took the envelope, and she reached out for it. But as she did so, the wind swiped the papers from her hand, and they went scuttling across the beach.

Lucy jumped up and followed their harried path up the beach and across the boardwalk, grabbing at empty air. When she reached the boardwalk, she snatched one of the pages from the air while someone's tennis shoe stomped on the other.

"Oh! Thank you!" She looked up to see the woman jogger. Her chestnut hair was clasped in a perky ponytail.

The woman chuckled through her ragged breath as she handed Lucy the paper. "I'm not sure who's getting the best workout this afternoon."

Lucy couldn't help but smile at the woman's friendly expression. "I was just thinking I needed to go for a jog." She looked down at her outfit. "This wasn't how I planned it."

"Are you visiting? Your accent places you well south of here."

"Georgia, actually. But I'm moving here—if I can find a job, that is. I didn't have much luck this afternoon."

"I don't know of anything, but I'll keep my ears open."

"I'd be much appreciative. I should let you get on with your jog."

"I was just cooling down. I'm new at this. A mile feels like a cross-country trek."

"Sounds about like me. I do like the way it makes me feel though."

"Afterward." They spoke at the same time, then laughed.

"You should meet me out here sometime," the woman said. "I could use an accountability partner. I usually jog in the morning, but I got a late start today."

"I'd like that. Maybe it'll go faster with company."

"We can only hope." The woman put her hand on her waist, still breathing hard. "The wind's ferocious on the harbor today. Did it blow your shoes away too?"

Lucy laughed as she wiggled her bare toes. "No, but I'd better get back to them before it does."

The other woman held out a hand. "My name's Eden, by the way."

"Lucy," she said as they shook hands.

The woman's smile froze. Recognition dawned in her eyes, stealing the sparkle. She shuffled back a step.

Lucy bristled. Really? Someone she'd never even met? "I guess my reputation precedes me."

Eden's mouth worked, and her hands fluttered around her body. "I—I'm Beau's fiancée."

Lucy gave a tight smile. "Of course you are. Well, no worries, Eden. I won't hold you to your

96

offer. Go ahead and walk away. Everyone else has." She turned toward the beach, her back as stiff as a flagpole.

"Wait," Eden called after her.

Lucy turned, her lips pressed together.

"Is it true—you have amnesia?"

The wind whipped her hair around her face. "I don't remember the last seven months."

Eden's brown eyes squeezed. "Not at all? That's . . . that must be hard."

Still being in love with the man whose heart you didn't remember breaking? Not exactly a walk in the park. But she didn't know this woman. Didn't owe her an explanation.

"Look." Eden stepped off the boardwalk and onto the sand. "I don't see any reason why we can't be friends. Or jogging buddies. I mean, you and Zac are history, right?"

Lucy's chest tightened. She offered a weak smile. "It appears that way."

Eden's lips parted as realization flared in her eyes. "Oh, you—you don't remember leaving, so . . ."

"Yeah, I'm pretty much operating on the emotions I had when we were still engaged."

Eden winced. "Ouch. Do they expect your memory to come back?"

Lucy lifted a shoulder. "God only knows."

Eden studied her for a full ten seconds while the wind fluttered her jogging pants. She seemed to be weighing something out.

A seagull cried out, its lonely call echoing across the harbor.

Lucy dug her toes in the sand, fixing to turn. "Well, I should let you—"

"How about tomorrow?" Eden said. "Eight o'clock?"

Was this woman really giving her a chance? Beau's fiancée? "I'm not really supposed to jog until my symptoms are gone."

"Oh, that's right. Your head injury. We could walk . . . ?"

She was pretty sure a walk wouldn't be much of a challenge for Eden. But she needed a friend too badly to turn her down. "All right. If you're sure."

Eden smiled brightly. "My legs thank you." She backed up a few steps. "So right here at eight a.m.?"

"See you then." Lucy watched her hop onto the boardwalk and head toward the cars parallel parked along the curb. She turned and headed back to her bag and shoes. Maybe things were finally looking up.

Chapter 12

Zac locked the door and shut off the restaurant lights. It had been a long day. He'd filled in for Marci since she'd called in sick again. He was glad to stay busy, but he was getting behind on paperwork. Three advertising proofs sat neglected on his desk, and he still had payroll to do.

He headed down the hall toward his office. Lucy was sitting behind the computer when he entered. He'd told her to help herself, and apparently she had. She was in a pink tank top, and beneath the desk he could see a pair of pajama pants that were scattered with tiny cows. Her hair was in a floppy ponytail, and her face looked fresh-scrubbed. He admitted, if only to himself, that she was the most adorable thing he'd ever seen.

"How you feeling?" he asked.

"About the same. Have you seen the articles?"

"What articles?"

She flipped the laptop around, and he saw an article from a Portland newspaper. He stared at the photo, which had been taken in front of her apartment, of Lucy ducking into his shoulder.

"The article refers to my aunt as 'the late Audrey Lovett.' "

His eyes found hers.

"She died . . . and I don't even remember."

His heart softened as her eyes glossed over with sadness and something else. Guilt? "I'm sorry. I should've thought to tell you." He'd heard it on the news a couple months after Lucy had left. He couldn't even pass on his condolences at the time, since he had no idea where she was.

"I wasn't awful close to her, as you know, but

she was my guardian for years. My only relative. How can I not even remember her dying?"

"It's not your fault. You have a brain injury."

"I know you're right, but—" She seemed to shake the thought away. "Anyway, the article spells out what's happened to me. Now all of Portland knows."

He propped his palms on the desk and scanned the article.

Missing Woman with Amnesia Turns Up

A missing young woman who was diagnosed with amnesia turned up last night at her Portland apartment.

Lucy Lovett, great-niece of the late-sixties starlet Audrey Lovett, failed to show up at a private wedding ceremony where she was to wed local businessman Brad Martin. After being unable to reach his fiancée, Martin filed a missing person report the next day.

Police discovered Lovett had been treated at the hospital Saturday evening. They have since learned that Lovett fell and struck her head at Dee Dee's Diner after her disappearance Saturday. Martin received a phone call from Lovett, during which she said she had been diagnosed with amnesia and had subsequently left town.

Lovett showed up yesterday at her Park Street home in the company of an unidentified man. "I never saw him before," neighbor Dorinda Evans said. "Lucy's always coming and going, but her fiancé was the only man she ever brought around."

Shortly after Lovett's return she left again to an undisclosed location.

"That fellow left for a while, and then he came back," Evans said. "A few minutes later he and Lucy both left with luggage. I don't know where they came from or where they went off to. I don't think she's thinking straight."

Lovett served as a project coordinator at Vacasa, where she's worked for the past six months. Her employer failed to comment on the circumstances, and Martin was also unavailable for further comment.

Zac's eyes flitted off Lucy. "Well, maybe they'll drop it now."

"That's not the only article. There's a clip from the TV news with footage at the apartment. They know more about me than I do." She sank back against the chair.

She was at least three feet away, but that familiar, fresh apple smell wafted by. He drew in a breath, letting it fill his lungs. Man, he'd missed that. He'd missed so much about her. He'd forgotten the delicate curve of her eyebrows, the gentle dip of her top lip.

He gave his head a shake. He needed to get her out of here. She was already messing with his head.

"Anything at all coming back to you?" he asked.

"Afraid not."

"Did you look through all those papers from your apartment?"

"Sure did."

"You were gone a long time today."

He'd been worried that something had happened to her. What if she'd fallen again, or what if they'd missed some swelling and she'd dropped dead on the beach somewhere? Relief had poured through him when she walked through the door.

"I was out looking for a job."

He gave her a long look. "A temporary one?"

Her eyes searched his as she rubbed her hands down her pant legs. "Zac . . . I've decided to stay in Summer Harbor for good."

"Stay in . . ." No. Just no. That was the last thing he needed. He hadn't been able to get over her when she was gone, much less if he was tripping over her every day. It was torture having her here. She still looked at him with love shining in those beautiful blue eyes. Still begged without words for him to take her into his arms.

As much as he longed to accommodate, it would all be gone the split second her memory returned.

His teeth locked together even as his breath caught in his lungs. "No, Lucy."

She notched her little chin upward, resolve etched in the firmness of her features. "That's not for you to say."

"The heck it isn't. You're staying at my place, eating my—"

"I'll get my own place."

"You bet your sweet rear end you will."

Hurt flickered in her eyes. Her full lips pressed into a straight line. Then her eyes began to fill, and once again he felt like a dog. She looked away, down to her lap where her fingers twisted in the fabric of her pajama pants.

A moment later she looked back up, nailing him with those liquid-blue eyes. "You want me gone. Message received. But where I live is not your decision, Zac. I'm a grown adult, and I can live wherever I want, and I want to live here, so you'll just have to get over it."

The phone rang, shattering the tension. Why had he brought her back? He should've just left her in Portland to fend for herself. She would've been fine. She always landed on her feet.

Zac wrenched his eyes away from Lucy's and answered the phone. "Hello," he said gruffly. A slight pause ensued. He should just hang up. He didn't want to talk to anyone anyway.

"Who is this?" a male voice finally demanded.

Zac frowned at the caller's rudeness. "Who's calling?"

"This is Lucy's fiancé. Is this the same guy who—"

"*Ex*-fiancé."

"—showed up with her in Portland? Put her on the phone."

"Listen, pal—"

"No, you listen. I don't know who you think you are, but you can't just run off with Lucy. She has a brain injury, and this is tantamount to kidnapping. I'll see to it that . . ."

He kept talking, but Zac stopped listening when Lucy came over and stood in front of him. Resolve in her eyes, she extended her hand.

Fine. He was her problem. Let her deal with it.

Lucy took the phone and met Zac's eyes as she put it to her ear. The voice on the other end was rambling on about legal charges. She cut him off. "Brad—Brad, it's me."

"Lucy! Why didn't you tell me you were coming home? I would've met you there, picked you up. What's going on? You're all over the news. They're calling me, asking me where you are, and I don't know. I don't know where my own *fiancée* is, Lucy. Who's that man, and why are you with him?"

Her head spun until she was dizzy with all his questions. She steadied herself with a hand on Zac's desk. "I just need some time to think."

"Where are you? Who's the guy?"

She had no idea how much she'd told him while they were together. "I'm—I'm up north a ways.

104

He's an old friend." Her eyes connected with Zac's, and she watched his jaw tick. He was staring intently at her, and she couldn't pull her eyes away from the hurt that lingered there.

"You're not thinking straight, Lucy," Brad said. "I don't know what happened before the wedding, but I still love you, and you must love me too, deep down, whether you remember it or not. Let me come and pick you up. I'll take care of you."

Her voice softened, not from his words, but from the sadness she saw in Zac's eyes. "I'm sorry. I need to stay here." Maybe she could make Zac love her again. He'd fallen in love with her once before, hadn't he? He must still feel something for her.

Brad continued talking, cajoling, his voice fluttering like bats' wings through her head. She swayed.

Zac caught her arm and snatched the phone from her fingers. "Lucy's not feeling well. She'll call back another time."

Brad's voice carried through the line. Zac shifted the phone away from his ear. A brow disappeared beneath the flop of hair that had fallen over his forehead. He pursed his lips before hanging up mid-rant.

Lucy blinked against the blurriness that had returned. Her head was hurting too. Would this ever go away?

"Let's get you to bed," he said gruffly as he led her from the room.

"What—what did Brad say?"

Zac's gaze bounced off her. "Nothing fit for a lady's ears."

Chapter 13

Lucy's feet pounded the boardwalk, and her breaths came in rhythmic puffs. The morning was brisk, the temperature not having yet reached sixty. She was glad she'd chosen sweatpants and a long-sleeved tee. A cool breeze blew in off the harbor, sending chills up her arms, but the sun, well over the horizon, soon chased them away. She drew in the salty tang of sea air blended with the faint smell of decaying kelp. It smelled like home.

Beside her Eden breathed easily, her arms swinging in time with her legs. "Am I going too fast? Let me know if you want to slow down."

"No, it's good. I'm feeling better today."

After walking together Wednesday, they'd agreed to meet every Monday, Wednesday, and Friday. Time really did fly by as they shot the breeze.

She'd already learned heaps about Eden. She had a six-year-old son, Micah, who always had breakfast at her dad's house while she jogged.

She'd started a home-based web design business that must be faring pretty well since she lived in a nice bungalow right outside of town. She and her dad originally hailed from Mississippi, though Eden sounded more like a Yankee. She'd hinted about a trying past but hadn't gotten into it yet. Though Lucy was curious, she could appreciate her discretion.

"How's the job search going?" Eden asked. "Any leads yet?"

"Not a solitary thing." She'd scanned the help-wanted ads again yesterday and made a few calls. It seemed Summer Harbor had very few employment opportunities.

"I wish I could hire you as an assistant. But what am I saying? You're way overqualified for that."

"Listen, at this point I'd be tickled pink to work a drive-through."

Eden smiled. "Well, you won't find any of those around here." She suggested a few places, but Lucy had already tried them. She was running out of ideas—and cash. Her bank account was not what she'd hoped.

"I've got to get some money flowing in." As much as she loved being near Zac all the time, his obvious desire to have her gone took the shine right off of being there. She was underfoot and unwanted.

They passed a small subdivision that was set

back from the shore. The thumping of a basketball carried across the distance, and Lucy followed the sound to a girl of about eleven or twelve. She put up a shot, missed, then dribbled the ball around the driveway court. Lucy had noticed her on their last walk. There was something lonely about the set of her shoulders, the slowness of her motions, and she felt an immediate affinity for the child.

"Who is that?" she asked.

Eden followed her gaze. "Brittany Conley. She was in my vacation Bible school group. Sweet girl. Her mom works over at the co-op."

"What about her dad?"

"I don't know. He's not around, I don't think. I see her over there a lot, shooting hoops. She must love basketball."

Or she had nothing to do, and no one to do it with. Lucy watched the girl put up another shot, her heart squeezing. She knew what it was like to be a lonely kid.

"Is she left home alone? She looks kind of young."

"I don't know, probably. There's a lot of that here. Beau said when he was deputy a lot of his calls were for teens. With single parents or both parents working, they're at loose ends a lot. Especially during the summer. Even good kids can make trouble when they're bored."

Lucy's eyes cut to Brittany again, her sociologist mind hard at work. She wondered about the girl's relationship with her mom, with her dad. Had her dad ever been in her life? Had her mom stayed home with her until a divorce forced her to get a job? Lucy was only speculating. But it was unfortunate how many children suffered because of their parents' decisions.

"So how'd you end up at Harvard?" Eden asked.

Lucy shifted her thoughts back. "It's a long story."

"Well, we're only fifteen minutes into our walk."

"I grew up in Savannah. I was an only child, and Mama passed away when I was young."

"Wow, me too. So your dad raised you?"

"Well, for a bit. Then he—my great-aunt became my guardian. She was pretty old, and she'd never had children of her own. I was only seven, and she didn't quite know what to do with me. She sent me off to boarding school in Alabama as soon as I hit seventh grade."

"Boarding school, huh? Must've been hard to be away from home."

"It wasn't much of a home, really. My aunt had the means to see to my needs, but she wasn't exactly a mother figure."

"You must've missed your parents."

Lucy shrugged. "I made good friends at school. And the teachers kind of became our surrogate parents. We were all in the same boat, you know?"

"Did you go home for summers?"

"Sure enough. But I was always ready to head

back in the fall. I came from a long line of Harvard graduates—my dad being the exception. He flaunted his independence by refusing to go to college at all. Apparently that caused a big upheaval in the family. Anyway, I got good grades at school, and I always scored high on those aptitude tests, so I applied at Harvard and got in."

"Your aunt must've been very proud."

"Proud is stretching it, since she expected no less. So that's how I ended up at Harvard."

"If you don't mind my asking, why aren't you the head of human resources at some Fortune 500 company?"

Lucy laughed. "I can't think of anything more dreary. I like to help people, and I can do that just about anywhere. When I graduated, though, I decided I wanted to do some traveling, see a bit of the country while I figured out what was what. There was only my great-aunt in Savannah, and we weren't close. I just found out she passed away while I was in Portland. I don't even remember getting word."

"Aw, I'm sorry. That must be hard." Eden lifted the hair off her neck. "Were you her heir? I'm sorry. That's really nosy."

Lucy grinned. "Not at all. She was always a big believer in making your own way; she was on the board of a ton of charities, and it was always understood that's where her money would go. But that's okay. I believe in earning my own keep. I've done a lot of things, met some interesting people along the way."

"What brought you to Summer Harbor originally?"

"I was just passing through. I was going to spend one night here on my way up to Lubec. But I stopped at the Roadhouse for dinner, took one look at Zac, and knew I wasn't going anywhere."

Eden's brows hiked up. "That fast, huh?"

Lucy smiled wistfully. "Yes, ma'am. Chemistry galore."

"That must be hard, living under the same roof now. Unless the chemistry disappeared with your memories."

"Oh no. It's still there in spades. Only it's worse now because the feelings are there too, and Zac's built a big ol' wall around his heart. I guess I deserve that though."

"You don't remember what happened at all?"

"I've no clue. I have wracked my brain. You know, I don't even care if I remember all the stuff that happened in Portland—and I know that's awful harsh since there's a man there who was hoping to marry me. But I don't want to remember him. I want things to be like they were before I left. I want to fix this with Zac, and there's no way that's happening if I can't remember what went wrong."

"Is he open to that?"

Lucy gave a humorless laugh. "No. But I can't

help but think . . . Anyway, I'm staying, and he's just going to have to get used to the idea." She drew in a few ragged breaths. "So . . . have you told Beau we're walking together?"

"Mm-hmm."

Lucy waited for more, but only the sound of their footfalls on the boardwalk broke the silence. It didn't take a sociology degree to put two and two together.

Lucy gave a humorless laugh. "Well, I guess that says it all."

Eden flashed a sheepish grin. "Look, you know Beau. He's very protective of his brothers. One's in a war zone, and he's helpless to protect him, so the other's getting laser focus right now. Lucky Zac."

"Lucky me." She didn't want to think about Beau and his grudge. "Zac told me Riley joined the marines. Do they communicate with him much?"

"Yeah, they Skype and e-mail. Riley's not very good about writing back, so it's mostly Skype. It's been hard for Beau to let go. It's times like this, you just gotta trust God, you know? He's got it all under control."

Lucy admired Eden's faith. She just radiated with it. Lucy's own spiritual walk wasn't anything to write home about. Sometimes she felt she was just going through the motions.

"Easier said than done," she said.

"For sure. We try so hard to control things, but it's just an illusion."

Lucy didn't feel like she had any control lately. And honestly, the thought of handing it all over to God made her squirm.

She sucked in a deep breath, stretching her lungs, then blew it out. "So how did you and Beau end up together?"

"Strangely enough, I was just passing through too. We had car trouble, Micah and I, and someone stole all my money. It was winter, naturally, and we didn't have food or a place to stay the night or anything. We had the clothes on our backs and a broken-down car I couldn't afford to repair. I was desperate for a job."

And Lucy thought she had it bad. No wonder Eden was sympathetic to her plight. "What did you do?"

"I showed up on Beau's doorstep, a shivering, desperate mess, looking for a job at the tree farm. He turned me down flat."

"He didn't."

"That's okay." Eden quirked a brow. "I broke into his outbuilding and made myself comfortable."

Lucy laughed.

Eden shot her a wry grin. "Unfortunately, he found us. Although I guess it wasn't unfortunate after all because it worked out. Miss Trudy had just broken her leg, so she needed a caretaker and Beau offered me the job."

Lucy gave her a mock grimace. "And you took it?"

Eden's laugh tinkled like wind chimes. "Somebody had to do it. And I was the only one desperate enough to agree."

"Amazing the decisions we make under duress. And you and Beau just hit it off?"

"It wasn't quite that simple. I mean, of course I was drawn to him right away—have you seen my fiancé? But I tried to ignore it. I had too much going on in my own life, and he was dating Paige. But after a while he broke up with her. We started confiding in each other and, well, you know how that Callahan charm works. Just sucks you right in. Before I knew it, I was head over heels."

Lucy sighed. "Yeah. I know what you mean."

Eden shot Lucy a sympathetic look. "Sorry. I didn't mean to bring you down."

As they entered town, they slowed their pace. Up ahead a jogger approached. Lucy recognized the long, lithe figure of Morgan LeBlanc and bristled at the sight. The woman had made no secret of her crush on Zac. She'd come into the Roadhouse, flirting subtly, even after they were engaged.

Her short honey-blonde ponytail swung behind her, and a few tendrils had escaped, framing her beautiful features. Her generous breasts bounced with each long stride. Lucy's own sports bra was managing her B-cups just fine.

Morgan smiled only at Eden as she passed. "Hi, Eden."

"Hi, Morgan."

Lucy clamped her lips together at the snub.

"That was Morgan LeBlanc," Eden said after she'd passed. "Her daddy owns the *Harbor Tides*."

"I know who she is. She was always flirting with Zac."

"Oh . . ."

Something in Eden's tone made Lucy look her way. Her new friend was biting her lip and avoiding her eyes. "What aren't you telling me?"

Eden lifted a shoulder and gave her a weak smile. "Nothing, really."

Lucy continued to drill her with a look. There was something Eden wasn't saying, and she was going to press until she found out what it was.

Eden darted a glance off her. "Okay. She and Zac might have gone out a time or two recently."

Something pinched hard inside. The thought of him with any woman was enough to drive a stake through her heart. The thought of him with Morgan made her want to jump off the nearest cliff. With ankle weights.

You have no right to be jealous, Lucy Lovett. Hadn't she been engaged to another man only a week ago? Still, it wasn't like she remembered any of that.

"How recently?" Lucy asked.

"A couple weeks ago, I think. I'm sure it's nothing serious."

Morgan had doubtless been thrilled when Lucy left town. The woman reminded her of a stalking leopard, quiet and subtle, with long, sharp claws that knew how to get the job done. She could just imagine Morgan's arms curling around Zac's waist, her lips pressing against his neck. How handy that she wouldn't even have to rise up on her tiptoes.

Lucy sighed hard. "Sometimes I wish the amnesia had wiped out Zac's memory too."

Eden chuckled, giving Lucy a quick squeeze around the shoulders. "Come on, let's head over to Frumpy Joe's. I think we could both use a big plate o' carbs."

Lucy couldn't seem to shake off the dark mood as they walked toward the café. Inside she began burning with irritation over her whole situation. Bad enough she had a brain injury and had lost the only man she'd ever loved. Not to mention the whole town, including Zac's family, seemed to be against her for something she couldn't even remember. She had no money, no job, and, oh yes, the love of her life was dating Morgan LeBlanc.

The diner hushed as Lucy and Eden entered a few minutes later. Lucy felt every eye in the place settle on her as the hostess led them to their seats. An older woman peeked around her friend to gawk at Lucy as she passed. Heat climbed the back of her neck, and she could feel her blood pressure increasing by the second.

Okay, enough of this. She stopped as they reached the corner booth and whirled around, facing the patrons.

"All right, now. That's it." A few more eyes turned her way, but the frustration burning inside outweighed any embarrassment she might feel. "Yes, I ran out on Zac Callahan last year, barely a week before our wedding vows; yes, it was a terrible thing to do; yes, I do have amnesia, thank you very much; and no, I don't remember leaving him. Oh, and yes, I'm still in love with him, but don't you worry, he's not about to trust me again after what I did even though I don't even remember doing it. That about cover it?" Her eyes drifted around the room, boldly meeting the chagrined stares of the customers. She nodded once. "Good."

She turned and lowered herself into the booth across from Eden, her heart racing and her cheeks flooding with heat. Her hands shook as she picked up her menu and opened it in front of her.

The sounds of chatter and the clatter of silverware slowly resumed. Who cared if they were talking about her? At least now they had their facts straight.

Eden lowered her menu, her wide eyes peeking out above it. "I can't believe you did that," she whispered. Her brown eyes sparkled with delight. "That was totally awesome!"

Chapter 14

Saturday mornings were quiet at the Roadhouse. The place had been hopping last night, a Red Sox game on maximum volume, pool games going in the back room, and the jukebox cranking in the background.

Lucy cracked an egg, and it slid into the buttered skillet with the others. Zac was up and about; she'd heard the shower running, heard his footsteps overhead. He was avoiding her. She had to do something, and soon. It was obvious he regretted bringing her back. She couldn't cook enough breakfasts to make it worth his while.

She'd seen the town doctor the afternoon before. He'd given her a clean bill of health, but no assurance that she'd ever regain her memory. Just as well. She wasn't so sure she wanted it back anymore.

She was sliding the eggs onto plates with the toast when the Roadhouse phone rang. Should she answer it or let voicemail pick it up? After three more rings, she picked up the kitchen extension, ready with a greeting. But Zac was already answering.

"Hi, Zac, it's Marci."

"Hey, Marci, how you feeling?"

"Not so good. I have bad news. I went to the

doctor yesterday and found out I have mono."

"Oh boy."

"Yeah. I can't come back until my symptoms are gone. I'm so sorry."

Lucy's conscience got the best of her, and she quietly hung up the extension. Poor Marci. Lucy'd had mono the summer she was nineteen. She'd been down for two months.

Two months.

Zac would be short a server. He couldn't fill in for Marci that long. That meant he'd have to find a temporary replacement. A thread of excitement wound its way through her. This was just the thing to tide her over until she found a permanent job.

She carried the plates out front where Zac was finishing up on the phone. She set the plates on the bar and took a seat across from him.

"Take care, Marci. All right. Bye." He hung up the phone and spared her a tight smile. "Morning."

"Good morning. I made you some eggs."

"Thank you. I think I'll take it upstairs and catch up on the news."

"Zac," she said as he turned to go. "Can we talk a minute?"

He carried reluctance in the rigid line of his shoulders as he set the plate down, not bothering with a seat. "What's up?"

"You know I've been looking for a job. I haven't had much luck. There doesn't seem to be a thing open at the moment."

"Maybe you should just—"

"I was thinking maybe you could use some help around here."

His eyes showed retreat before his words confirmed the notion. "I don't really have any openings, Lucy. I think it might be best if—"

"I know about Marci," she blurted. "I heard her on the phone."

Something in his eyes shifted, making the color turn steely gray. His mouth tightened, and his left eye twitched. "You listened to my phone conversation?"

"I wasn't trying to eavesdrop, honest. I was just answering the phone, but you beat me to it."

"And you couldn't just hang up?"

Guilt pinched hard. She'd already invaded his home, his life. "Sorry."

"This isn't working." He took the plate and turned toward the hallway.

Lucy followed him, her face heating. "I know. I know you don't want me around, but I can't get my own apartment till I get a job, and I can't find anything, so maybe if I could just fill in for Marci until she comes back? By then I'll have another job, but the sooner I get a paycheck, the sooner I can get out of your hair."

Zac turned at the base of the steps, looking down at her with those intense eyes of his.

She was closer than she realized, crowding

him. She took a step back, remembering a day when he would've drawn her closer.

Zac stared down at Lucy's face. She pleaded with her eyes even while she retreated a step. Lord knew at one time he'd been willing to give her anything she wanted. One look, one touch, and her wish was as good as granted.

But not now. He didn't trust her anymore. And he sure didn't want to get sucked back into the vortex of her love.

"This is pointless, Lucy. You could wake up with your memory tomorrow and be on your way back to Portland."

"Or I could never get my memory back, and we could pick up right where we left off." Her eyes widened suddenly. Her fingers touched her lips. A pink flush climbed her cheeks.

Her words sparked his desire. Tempted him like a perfect summer day during lunch rush. He could ignore her, he could avoid her, he could take a flipping bath in denial. But it didn't change the truth. He wanted Lucy more than he wanted his next breath.

Get a grip, Callahan. She left you. She may not remember it, and she may wish it hadn't happened, but nothing he did now was going to change the fact that she had.

Zac tempered his tone. "That's not going to happen, Lucy."

"I didn't mean to say that."

How ironic that he now had everything he'd wanted since she'd left: Lucy back in his life. Lucy still in love with him. Lucy wanting to spend forever with him. And it didn't even matter because it would all be gone the moment her memory returned.

Lucy cleared her throat. "I've been a server before. I have experience. You wouldn't even have to train me."

She'd told him about her waitressing jobs in Boston and Nantucket. He had no doubt she'd been efficient with that amazing memory of hers. But she'd also held a record for dropped trays.

"I know what you're thinking. But I got better."

"You got fired."

Her chin went up. "It was a cutback."

He was shaking his head.

Her eyes pleaded with him. "I'll be the best server you have."

"No, Lucy."

"Come on, Zac. I need a job, and you need me out of your hair. This is the quickest solution I can think of."

"You should go back to Portland."

"And be the center of a media circus? Be the freak with amnesia?"

He palmed the back of his neck. "Lucy, I need my space. You can't just come back here, move in, and start hanging out at the restaurant all day."

Hurt flickered in her eyes before she tipped her chin up. "Well, I can't get out of here without a job, Zac."

"You had a perfectly good job in Portland."

"Well, I don't anymore. It's just until Marci comes back, and then I'll have enough for a deposit on an apartment."

He spun around and paced the length of the bar. He didn't want to look into her pleading blue eyes anymore. Didn't want to feel like he was letting her down. No matter what she'd done in the past, she was in a defenseless position right now. He didn't want her to be manipulated by her ex-fiancé or by other people who didn't have her best interests at heart.

And truth was, he didn't have anyone else he could call to take Marci's place. Tourist season was under way, and he had other responsibilities. Finding and training a server would take time he didn't have.

What would his dad advise? Probably to get Lucy out of his spare room.

The sooner the better.

But she couldn't do that without a job, and this was the only one available. If she was working, he wouldn't see so much of her—not really. They'd both be busy, plenty of people around. That was good.

He couldn't believe he was considering this. He shook his head.

"*Please,* Zac. I need a job and you need a server. You won't regret it. I promise."

She could stinking read his mind. That much hadn't changed. Beau was going to have a cow. But when did Beau's opinion ever keep Zac from doing what he wanted?

When he was directly across from Lucy he stopped, nailing her with a look. He searched her eyes for a hint of a reason to say no. Anything that smacked of manipulation. He wouldn't be played. But she stared back through guileless eyes lit with hope.

He gave a hard sigh. Fine. Whatever. "Just until Marci's back," he said gruffly.

Her eyes sparked, her mouth lifting at the corners. "I'll turn in my apron the second she returns."

"Your shift starts at five tonight and goes till closing."

"I'll be here."

"You need to familiarize yourself with the menu and pricing. There've been some changes."

"I'll have it memorized." She threw herself across the bar and squeezed him around the neck with her delicate arms. "Thank you, Zac!"

He braced himself against the warmth of her embrace, against the sweet apple smell of her, forbidding himself from wrapping his arms around her and drawing her closer.

"You won't regret it," she said as she drew away, her eyes shining with relief.

But that was the thing. He already did.

Chapter 15

The Roadhouse was busy that night. Lucy ran her legs off between the tables and the kitchen. Conversations buzzed in the air, mingling with the noise of the Red Sox game. The pool tables were full all night, hosting rowdy competitions, and the tangy smell of buffalo wings hung heavily in the air.

By eight o'clock Lucy's legs ached, and one of her eyes was blurry. She'd forgotten how physical waitressing was. But she was determined to prove to Zac she was up to the job.

None of the townspeople had been particularly friendly, but she was too busy for small talk anyway. She bustled around refilling glasses and taking orders, keeping a smile plastered to her face until her cheeks hurt.

Seeing that table twenty-three had been seated, she tucked the empty tray under her arm and approached the booth. Her smile dimmed when she recognized its occupants. Beau sat on the aisle, Eden beside him. Across the table his aunt peered at the menu through her readers.

Lucy conjured up a smile as she came to a stop beside the table. "Hey, y'all."

Beau glanced up from his conversation with Eden. His smile drooped, and his onyx eyes went flat as they fell to her apron. "You gotta be kidding me."

Eden shoved an elbow in his gut. "Hey, Lucy. You found a job. That's great. Isn't it, Beau?"

"Fan-freaking-tastic," he muttered, scanning a menu he surely didn't need.

"It's only temporary," she said, focusing on the one friendly face at the table. "I'm filling in for Marci."

Miss Trudy scowled at Lucy over her readers, her lips pursed as if she'd just sucked a particularly sour lemon. The woman was somewhere near sixty, with short silver hair framing a narrow face. At the moment frown lines crouched between her blue eyes.

"Howdy, Miss Trudy," Lucy said. "It's good to see you. What can I get y'all to drink?" she asked before the woman could spear her with that sharp tongue of hers.

Lucy took their drink orders and left to fill them, stopping on the way to fetch Sheriff Colton's empty plate. She rang up his bill, giving him a discount since he was in uniform and since he'd deigned to talk to her. Next she grabbed the Callahans' drinks, dropping off the sheriff's bill before arriving back at their table.

She began taking their orders, grateful her strong memory required no pad or pen.

The sheriff ambled over before she was finished. At six foot seven he towered over Lucy —

and everyone else. The overhead lights gleamed off his shaved head and caught the red in his fiery mustache. He was in decent shape for a man in his late fifties. He was locally famous for his short-lived career with the Celtics years ago before a knee injury forced him to retire.

"Howdy, Beau, Eden." Sheriff Colton placed his hat over his heart and nodded at Beau's aunt. "Miss Trudy."

The older woman gave him a curt nod, suddenly fascinated with the baseball game on the screen across from their table.

"Hey there, Colton," Beau said. "Have a seat. Finish the game with us."

"Well . . ." He eyed the empty spot beside Miss Trudy. "If it's not too much trouble."

Miss Trudy frowned as she scooted toward the wall, and the sheriff lowered his weight onto the bench.

"Can I bring you another Dr Pepper?" Lucy asked him.

"That'd be great. Thank you."

The kitchen was buzzing when she put the order in, and there was a line of people waiting for an inside table. Zac was mopping up a spill on the deck where a few souls were braving the evening chill.

Moments later she turned to a newly seated table, smile ready, only to find Morgan LeBlanc perusing a menu. One of her friends sat across from her.

Lucy's heart sank. Of course they'd be seated at her station. She scooped up the tip from the last diners and forced a smile to her face. "Hey."

Dismay rolled over Morgan's face like a summer fog into the harbor. "You know that word only has one syllable, right?" Her eyes scanned Lucy's apron, then rolled slowly up to Lucy's face. "You're waitressing. How . . . cute."

Lucy tipped her chin up, holding her smile steady. "What can I say? Zac needed my help."

Morgan tilted her head, her eyes narrowing reflectively. "I wonder how long it'll take you to bail on him this time."

Her friend snickered behind a manicured hand.

Lucy bit her tongue. Hard. Then fixed a smile on her face. "Can I get you something to drink?"

"We're ready to order actually," Morgan said. "I'd like the half salad and sandwich combo. Make the salad with extra tomatoes and no croutons, with balsamic vinaigrette on the side. For the sandwich I'd like—shouldn't you be writing this down?"

"I'll remember."

Morgan's eyes taunted her. "I'd like the tuna fish sandwich, toasted, with extra tomatoes and no mayo on whole wheat bread."

Morgan's friend closed her menu and shot Lucy a condescending look. "I'll have the grilled salmon platter with a salad—no tomatoes and extra croutons. Low-fat ranch on the side."

"You get one more side with that."

"What are my choices?"

"French fries, onion rings, baked potato, mashed potatoes, broccoli, asparagus, or coleslaw."

"A baked potato. Sour cream but no butter."

With one last tight smile, Lucy walked away, turned the order in to the kitchen, and went to refill drinks. She stopped by the Callahan table for a few minutes, refilling drinks and trying to get Beau to ease up. Miss Trudy still sported a scowl, bless her heart.

She took another order, helped bus a table, and delivered a couple bills. She finished the salads for Morgan's table and delivered them.

Morgan frowned at the salad. "Is there a tomato shortage I don't know about?"

Lucy dredged up a smile. "I'll bring you some more. Anything else?"

"Order up, Lucy!" someone called from the kitchen.

A few moments later she delivered the extra tomatoes, then returned to the kitchen, staying busy until the meals for Morgan's table were ready.

She slid the plates onto the table between the women. She was relieved when they ignored her, but as she passed by a few minutes later, Morgan flagged her down.

"This bread is stale. And where's the mayo?" She pushed the plate away. "Can you really be that dense?" she asked, mocking Lucy's accent.

Lucy's muscles quivered with the need to slap the sneer off Morgan's face. "The bread was delivered this morning, and there's mayo on the sandwich."

Morgan lifted a finely plucked brow. "Are you saying I'm wrong?"

"I'm saying you're mistaken."

Her friend piped up as she pushed her plate away. "I think there's butter on this baked potato. I can't have butter." She shuddered.

Lucy gritted her teeth. "It's sour cream only, just as you ordered."

"Everything okay?" Zac stopped behind her. Awkwardness descended upon them like ants over a bread crumb.

Morgan offered him a sweet smile. "Oh, Zac, it's fine. Just a minor issue with our orders. Lucy's doing her best, but I'm sure she's just confused, what with that awful head injury and all. Bless her heart." She gave Lucy a pitying glance. "Isn't that what they say in your neck of the woods?"

"I'm sorry, ladies," Zac said, reaching for their plates. "Lucy, can you take care of this?"

"Oh no, Zac," Morgan said with enough sugar in her voice to sweeten a pitcher of iced tea. "It's not a big deal. Really."

"Don't be silly. We'll fix it." He grabbed Morgan's plate and handed it to Lucy. "Won't we, Lucy?"

Heat filled her face. "Of course."

Chapter 16

Zac sank into his office chair and opened the Skype program. Riley was supposed to call in a few minutes. The restaurant was usually pretty slow after lunch, and since it was late evening in Afghanistan, it was a good time to catch up with his brother.

A few minutes later Riley appeared on the screen in his desert fatigues.

Zac still wasn't used to his high-and-tight haircut or the chiseled cut of his jawline. Sometime when he hadn't been looking, his baby brother had grown up.

"Hey, brother," Zac said.

Riley's lips tipped in a crooked smile. "Zac. How's it going, man?"

"Not bad. You look tired."

"Keeping busy over here. But I'm doing all right. How's things around town? Roadhouse doing all right?"

"Ayuh. Same old, same old. Beau and Eden came in last night with Aunt Trudy. Sheriff stopped by the table to flirt for a while. That's always entertaining."

"Poor guy. He ever going to make a move?"

Zac smiled. "Not with all those hands-off signals Aunt Trudy gives him."

"She could do worse."

"That she could."

"Talked to the rest of the family last week." Riley ran a palm over his head. "Heard you're going out with Morgan LeBlanc. What up with that?"

Zac lifted a shoulder. "Just a couple dates. Nothing serious." He'd been hoping for a spark or two, but so far she left him as cold as a February morning. He should give it a little longer. He was just distracted right now with Lucy's return.

"Hard to believe Fourth of July is coming up in a week," Zac said, eager to change the subject.

"No kidding. I lose all sense of time over here. We'll have to schedule a chat before you all stuff yourselves with grilled burgers and hot dogs. Man, my mouth's watering just thinking about it."

"I'll eat one for you."

"Eat a couple for me, will you? I'm stuck with chow-hall fare."

"Looks like you're filling out just fine. Your shoulders take up the whole screen."

"Just remember that when I get home. I can totally take you now. Not that I couldn't before."

"In your dreams, baby brother," Zac said, chuckling, even though he knew it was probably true.

"So . . . ," Riley said. "How's Paige doing? Haven't heard from her lately."

His casual tone didn't fool Zac. Riley and Paige had been best friends for years. But then Riley's feelings changed, and before he got up the gump-tion to do anything about it, Paige started liking their brother Beau. It had all gone downhill from there when Beau and Paige became a couple. Riley had ultimately responded by joining the marines, but only Zac was privy to Riley's feelings. Well . . . Zac and Eden.

"She's doing all right. I thought she was e-mailing you."

"She is. I heard from her a week ago."

"Might help if you e-mailed back."

"I'll catch her on Skype on the Fourth."

Zac considered biting his tongue, then decided life was too short. "Maybe you should say something to her, man."

"Like what?"

"You know what."

"Like, 'Gosh, best buddy, I've fallen in love with you, and I know you don't feel the same way, but will you put your life on hold for me until my tour's up?' Something like that, you mean?"

"You might want to soften it up a little, but yeah."

Riley looked down, his lashes becoming shadows on his upper cheeks. "I've had a lot of time to think over here. A lot of moments when—" He looked up at Zac. "I don't want to have any regrets, you know? But this isn't something to dump on her when I'm six thousand miles away. Maybe I'll have that talk with her when I get home. Ask for a chance to be more than friends. I don't know yet. I'm praying about it."

Zac knew as well as anyone that opportunities sometimes faded quicker than smoke on the open seas. "Why wait, Riley? Why not just tell her now?"

"It wouldn't be fair to her. She finds out how I feel, and she's going to feel guilty that she doesn't feel the same. She worries about me enough as it is."

"You said you didn't want any regrets. What if you regret waiting, huh?"

Riley's gaze sharpened, his lips going in a tight line as he stared intently through the screen. "She seeing someone? Is that what you're saying?"

"No. No, man, not that I know of."

Relief flickered in Riley's eyes, and his shoulders fell. "That's good. Hate to think I'd have to whip somebody's butt the second I hit shore."

Zac smiled. "I got your back, man. You know that."

"Is she—you think she's over Beau? She says she is, but I don't know if she's just telling me what I want to hear. She doesn't want me worrying about her."

"I think she is. She's coming around the family more often, doesn't seem to mind being around Beau and Eden. They were never meant to be, bro. I think she sees that now."

"Yeah, well, I hope—"

A knock sounded as someone pushed his office door open. "Zac, do you know where the—" Lucy stopped on the threshold. "Oh, sorry. Am I interrupting?"

Zac resisted the urge to close the screen. It wasn't as if Riley could see her with the laptop facing the opposite direction. "No, I'm just Skyping with Riley. I'll be out in a few."

"Oh, no hurry. Take your time." She shut the door, and Zac looked back to the screen.

Riley was leaning in, his eyes fixed on Zac. A frown crouched between his brows. "Who was that? Was that—was that *Lucy?*"

Dadblameit. Well, he was lucky he'd kept it from his brother this long, now that all of Summer Harbor knew she was back.

"It *was,*" Riley said. "What the heck, Zac. What's she doing there? Are you nuts?"

"It's not what you think. We're not back together. She has amnesia. She was in Portland, and she hit her head. She's lost the last seven months of her life. Doesn't remember leaving here or her life in Portland."

"What? When did this happen?"

"Little over a week ago."

"And you became involved because . . ."

"She called me. She didn't have anyone else. She was confused and . . . dizzy and stuff. I went and got her and brought her back."

"And no one thought to tell me any of this?"

"We didn't want to worry you."

Riley pitched back against his chair, making a face. "I wish everyone would stop filtering the news for me. I'm capable of dealing with reality."

"Like you don't filter news on your end?" Riley talked very little about what went on in his world.

His jaw flinched. "That's different. Are there any other little tidbits no one's telling me?"

Zac sighed. May as well get it all out there. "Lucy's staying here, in your old room, and temporarily filling in as a server."

Riley's face tipped forward. "What? Zac . . ."

"And she was engaged to another man while she was in Portland. She was running from her wedding when she hit her head."

Riley gave a hard laugh. "Of course she was." He shook his head, still laughing, though there was no humor in it.

Heat crawled up the back of Zac's neck, the mocking laugh running right through him. Hearing the truth out loud made him feel even more of a fool. And Riley's reaction wasn't making him feel any better.

"Knock it off, lover boy. I don't see you doing much better."

Riley's laugh tapered off. He ran a hand over his face. "Yeah, yeah. All right, I'll give you that one. Still, dude. You know you're asking for trouble."

Trouble seemed to be Lucy's middle name. At least where he was concerned.

"This is only temporary. She finds another job, she's out of here." He didn't add that she was planning to go no farther than the nearest apartment complex.

Maybe he was still in denial.

Chapter 17

Lucy turned an order in to the kitchen and stuffed a handful of straws into her apron pocket. Friday nights at the Roadhouse always seemed to be hopping. Zac's new assistant manager, Susan, was on staff tonight, running the place like a well-oiled machine.

When they'd been dating, Lucy had been after Zac to hire management help. He'd always been so busy, running the restaurant six days a week. He'd said he couldn't afford it, but that must've changed in the time she'd been in Portland.

Lucy spied a recently seated table and headed toward it. She felt her shoulders droop as she recognized the honey-blonde hair, the slim shoulders, and the classically beautiful profile.

Not again.

There were other servers, other stations, for pity's sake. What was it with the woman? Was she trying to make Lucy's life miserable?

Drawing a deep breath, Lucy tucked the empty tray under her arm and approached the table.

Morgan's blonde hair tumbled to her shoulders in spiral curls, and her makeup was flawlessly applied. She wore a little black dress that was riding up high on her long legs. The tiny white sweater she wore over it didn't quite hide her cleavage.

Overdress much?

Lucy gave a tight smile. "Can I get you something to drink?"

Morgan's eyes scrolled down Lucy's dowdy shirt and apron. Lucy fought the urge to cover the ketchup stain over her left hip.

"I'm just waiting for Zac. He'll be down any minute."

Lucy felt a pinch in her chest. "I'll check back after he arrives then."

Morgan tossed her hair over her shoulder. "We're not staying *here*." Morgan pulled out a compact and checked her perfect red lips. "He's taking me to the Oyster Bistro."

Lucy's smile faltered as her heart squeezed. That's where Zac had taken her on their first date. He'd kissed her for the first time after dinner.

"You've heard of it." Morgan snapped the compact shut. "It's in the Hotel Tourmaline on Folly Shoals. You have to take the ferry to reach it. I do hope we make it back before the last run." She arched a brow. "But if we don't . . . oh well. I'm sure we'll find *something* to do."

"Morgan."

At the sound of Zac's deep voice, Lucy's eyes swung to him. She clutched the empty tray to her chest.

"Did you get my text?" Morgan's voice was as smooth as velvet.

"Ayuh . . ." His eyes darted between Lucy's and Morgan's. "I was supposed to pick you up."

"I was out running an errand with Daddy, so I had him drop me here," Morgan said as she stood, towering over Lucy in her stilettos.

The heels also brought her much closer to Zac's height. He wouldn't even have to stoop when he kissed her good night. His eyes caught on hers just then, and she felt the betrayal like a sucker punch.

She wrenched her eyes away. "I—I have an order to pick up." She scooted away on trembling legs, the heat of Zac's stare on her back.

This had to be the longest evening of her life.

Lucy threw back the covers, rolled over, and stared at the darkened ceiling. Even the bustling Friday night crowd hadn't kept her mind occupied. Every moment she'd wondered what Zac and Morgan were doing. Were they at the Oyster Bistro yet? Were they sitting in a quiet corner or on the outdoor patio under the white twinkle lights? Was he holding her hand under the table? Was he noticing the way her eyes glinted green in the candlelight?

She checked the clock for the hundredth time. He should be back by now. The last ferry ran at ten o'clock, and it was almost eleven. Was he kissing her good night at her door right now? Or maybe they were steaming up the windows of his truck. Maybe she'd invited him inside.

Lucy groaned, closing her eyes against the thought. She had no rights to Zac. He was free to take Morgan out, free to make out in his truck, free to—

No. She wouldn't go there.

She had to stop this. What good did it do to torture herself? He wasn't hers anymore. She wished she could turn back time all the way to the beginning and have a second chance. She remembered the night he asked her out like it was yesterday.

It had barely been a week since she'd first seen Zac Callahan behind the bar, chatting with some guys, but it seemed like a month. In the meantime she'd scored a job at the visitor center and found herself a nice little apartment not far from town.

The Roadhouse was fairly empty on this Monday night. She scanned the rustic restaurant, her eyes stopping at the bar, where once again Zac stood, chatting with a few patrons. He wore a plaid button-down, rolled up at the cuffs. Like last time, he sported a five o'clock shadow, and she wondered if he knew just how sexy he looked.

She walked that direction, glad she'd worn her favorite jeans and the lightweight sweater that matched her blue eyes perfectly.

She found a stool at the quiet end of the counter —taking care as she climbed on—and perused the laminated menu. She knew the exact moment Zac spotted her. The skin on her arms tightened and heat flared up inside, prickling at the back of her neck. She'd never been so aware of a man before. It was as if an invisible cord connected them.

She didn't look up until he stood directly in front of her.

The smile he gave her should've been illegal worldwide. "Georgia . . ."

Lucy offered a saucy smile despite the niggle of disappointment. "Ah. I see you've forgotten my name already."

He withdrew a rag from his pocket and swiped the counter in front of her. "I never forget a pretty lady's name."

She wasn't letting him off that easy. She raised her brows and tilted her head, waiting expectantly.

Just when she thought he was going to leave her hanging, his lips twitched and he slid her a look. "Lucy Lovett, sociology major, Harvard graduate, adorable dimples, endearingly clumsy, with a long list of ways in which she embarrasses herself."

Her heart did a slow roll, and something fluttered inside. Her smile faltered.

"I just happen to like nicknames," he said. "And that sweet Southern drawl of yours."

She shifted on the stool, recovering. "Now, see . . . that's just not fair. You've got a cute little nickname for me, and I don't have one for you."

He pocketed the rag as the corner of his mouth kicked up. "You'll have to work on that."

Lord have mercy, she did love that deep voice of his. She folded her arms across the still-damp counter. "Turns out I might just have the time for that. I came by to thank you for the job tip. Your aunt Trudy hired me today."

His smile widened. "Well . . . congratulations. You'll be sticking around awhile then."

"Fair warning—you might be seeing a lot of me. The center's just down the beach, and a girl has to eat someplace." She gave her shoulders an exaggerated lift.

"I think I could stand to see your pretty face in here now and again."

"Is that so?"

He brought her a sweet tea on the house without asking what she was drinking. She turned down his offer of food, having had a late lunch.

He was different from so many other men she'd met in her travels. He looked her in the eyes when she talked, like he was really listening. And he must be; he'd remembered every detail from their conversation a week ago. He was confident, comfortable with himself, but he didn't wear it with arrogance like so many other handsome men.

He waited on customers, and she noticed his easy way with people. His employees seemed to respect him. She watched out of the corner of her eye as he helped a new employee with the credit card machine. He was patient and soft-spoken no matter how many times she messed up. He was a good boss.

Her lips lifted as he slipped behind the bar.

He brought her a refill and seemed in no hurry to go, leaning his elbows on the counter. The movement brought him closer, and, mercy, he was even more handsome at eye level. His deep-set eyes stared back, a fathomless gray color. A lock of hair flopped carelessly over his fore-head, and her fingers twitched to feather it back.

"So . . . Lucy Lovett." His eyes twinkled, silver sparks igniting something inside her. "I think you should go out with me."

She raised her eyebrows, reaching for her fresh tea. "You do, do you?"

"I do."

Her lips twitched as she sipped her drink. She took her time, swallowing slowly and folding her arms on the counter opposite him before meeting his gaze.

"And why's that?" she asked.

"Well . . . as you said, it's not fair that you're the only one with a nickname. Only way to fix that is to spend more time with me, get to know me, so you can come up with something fitting."

She'd already come up with a nickname, but she wasn't about to admit it just yet. Especially since his piercing gray eyes were about to melt her into a puddle.

"Well, that's a mighty good reason, Zac Callahan."

"So how 'bout it? Got plans this weekend?"

She brought her dimples out to play. "It just so happens I'm free as a bird."

That Friday night he picked her up at her new apartment. She wore her kelly-green sheath dress that was fitted but not tight. She paired it with silver heels that were low enough to walk about in.

She opened the door, looking up at him with a ready smile on her face.

Lord a-mercy. They didn't grow them this tall in Savannah. He wore a black button-down that accentuated the color of his hair and hugged the broad curves of his shoulders. It was tucked into a fitted pair of khakis.

"Hey there." She took a deep breath, trying to quell the low hum of excitement that moved through her.

"Hey, Georgia." His eyes took a quick tour of her outfit, and she caught the flicker of male appreciation. "You look beautiful."

"Not so bad yourself, Boss," she said, trying out the nickname.

He gave a crooked smile, and those silver sparks in his eyes flashed in approval.

They took the ferry over to Folly Shoals and got a quiet table at the Oyster Bistro. Conversation flowed with normal first-date information.

Zac was twenty-seven, and he'd been born and raised in Summer Harbor. He was six foot five and had gotten his height from his great-grandpa. His mom was gone, and his dad ran the family Christmas tree farm outside of town. He had two brothers: an older brother, Beau, who was a deputy sheriff, and a younger brother, Riley, who was a lobsterman in the warm months and farm help during the winter.

Zac had gone to a local college, majoring in business management, but he hadn't finished. A slight flush colored his cheeks as he admitted this, endearing him to her even more. He was confident but unassuming about his restaurant, as if it were commonplace for a twenty-seven-year-old to own a successful business.

He teased her about her accent, and she teased him right back about his. She liked it—the way he dropped his *r*'s and sometimes added them back in where they didn't belong.

After dinner they strolled the island's quaint downtown area and stopped for ice cream. They sat on a bench as the sun sank low over the harbor. A salt-laden breeze teased the tendrils alongside her face.

"You have to try this." Zac held his cone toward her.

He'd tried to talk her into the maple walnut, but she'd settled on a dish of mint chocolate chip with sprinkles—jimmies, he called them.

She angled her head and tried to take a delicate bite, but the ice cream was harder than she expected. The force of her bite knocked the scoop off the cone, and it toppled downward.

Right into his lap.

She sucked in a breath, and her stomach clenched hard. Her eyes met his startled gaze. "Oh no." She reached for the scoop, then realized it had landed in an awkward spot.

"Oh, gosh. I am so sorry."

He shuddered beside her.

Her hands fluttered helplessly before she scrambled for her napkins. Leave it to her to ruin a perfect evening. *You are such a klutz, Lucy Lovett!* Her gaze flickered reluctantly to his face.

His eyes glinted with amusement, and the corners of his lips twitched. He shook with silent laughter. As their eyes met, a laugh escaped him, lighting up his whole face. He scooped up the ice cream bare-handed and tossed it into the nearby trash can.

Her shoulders relaxed, her lips turning up of their own will. She bit back her own laughter.

"Here," Lucy said sheepishly as she handed him her napkins.

He wiped off his hands and dabbed at the spot on his khakis.

"I'm sorry," she said, but laughter bubbled out with the words.

"I see that."

"I can't believe I did that."

"You know you're going to have to walk in front of me on the way back to the ferry."

She put her hands against her heated cheeks. "I am so clumsy."

The remnants of laughter still sparked in his eyes and played on his lips as he reached toward her and dabbed her nose with a napkin.

Oh, great. She'd gotten ice cream all over both of them. Heat suffused her face.

He tossed the napkins, then turned back to her, their eyes aligning. The humor faded bit by bit as his eyes drifted over her face. "You are so adorable."

Her heart turned over in her chest, and her cheeks went hotter under the intensity of his warm, smoky eyes.

His gaze dropped to her mouth, making her breath stutter.

He came closer, leaning in until his lips touched hers. They were cool and faintly sweet. And soft. So soft. They moved against hers, slow and savoring. That familiar low hum moved through her, and her heart rate doubled in speed. The world reduced in size until it was only him and her, hot breath and cool lips, giving and taking.

He drew away too soon, his eyes catching and holding hers.

"Sorry," he whispered. "I couldn't wait."

"I'm glad."

The mood shifted after that. He held her hand on the way back to the ferry. Her hand felt small in his. He made her feel special and protected, and she knew it wouldn't take much at all to fall for him. She was already falling bit by bit every minute she spent with him.

You're in deep trouble, Lucy.

Their conversation focused on simple things. The color of the sky, the brevity of summer, the shortening of the days. At her doorstep, he kissed her good night, and the feel of his lips made everything unravel inside her.

A long while later he drew away, their warm breaths mingling between them. "I'm already half crazy about you, Georgia," he said softly. "You know that, right?"

Her smile started inside and traveled to her lips. Yes, she was definitely in deep trouble.

They traded numbers and began texting, and they went out again the next weekend. She stopped by the Roadhouse every few days for lunch. She'd dated before. Had seriously dated a man in Boston. She'd broken up with him though, just before she'd taken a job offer in Nantucket. She'd decided she didn't love him like she should.

But Zac . . . Zac she could love too much. She knew it before their first date had ended. And the more time she spent with him, the more she knew it was true.

Sometimes the feeling brought a tremor of panic. The memory of being abandoned. The urgency to flee. But she pushed the feelings away, determined to enjoy the moments, wherever they might lead. She couldn't seem to help herself.

They'd only had four dates when they became exclusive. She loved everything about him. But sometimes she held things back from him, and she didn't quite know why. When he asked about her father, she told him he'd died. She let him believe that was how she'd ended up under her great-aunt's care. When he asked if she'd ever been in love, she told him yes. But she didn't mention that she'd left Noah for a job elsewhere.

When he told her he loved her, she pulled him close and kissed him deeply, letting her actions speak the words she couldn't seem to say.

The sound of a door closing pulled Lucy back to the present. A loud click, then footsteps going down the hall and up the stairs. Zac was finally home from his date.

The shift from wistful memory to harsh reality was a jarring one. She closed her eyes, wanting to hang on to the wispy edges of the memory for just a little while longer.

Chapter 18

Lucy settled back in the chair and closed her eyes as an evening breeze swept past. The metallic smell of fireworks mingled with the salty tang of the sea. She'd crashed the Callahans' Fourth of July party—though, technically, Eden had invited her.

She'd skipped the family barbecue at the farm-house since she was working, but joined them on the Roadhouse deck after closing. They sat in a half circle around a large table, facing the harbor, waiting for the fireworks show. Miss Trudy sat on one side of her, Zac next. Those two were chatting about the farm. Eden was on her other side.

Paige, Beau's ex-girlfriend and Riley's best friend, had hung out with them for a while before joining her friends down on the beach.

Lucy had always liked hanging out with the Callahans. Maybe it was because she was an only child, or maybe it was the sociologist in her, but it fascinated her to watch the give-and-take between the brothers. There was a different vibe now with Riley gone. An obvious hole in the Callahan family. They must miss him keenly on nights like tonight.

On the other side of the deck railing, people clustered on the sand with blankets and coolers, waiting for the show. The fireworks barge sat out in the harbor with a smattering of other boats, their white stern lights reflecting off the water. In the pauses between the sounds of firecrackers and bottle rockets, chatter and laughter carried through the night air.

In the corner of the balcony, Beau helped little Micah hold a sparkler. The glow cast a golden light on the boy's olive-skinned face and made his dark brown eyes gleam. He was adorable, with his headful of black curls.

"Beau's really good with him," Lucy said to Eden. "You'll make a wonderful family."

Eden glanced at her son and fiancé, smiling as she watched the pair. "If you'd told me last year I'd be engaged right now, I would've said you were crazy."

"You're the crazy one, I think. Crazy about Beau Callahan."

Eden sighed. "I really am. He's . . . everything my late husband wasn't. Antonio was . . ." She shook her head, pressing her lips together. "I guess we just do the best we can and trust God with the rest. Life will always have troubles. It's what shapes and molds us and makes us into the people He wants us to be. As hard as my marriage was, I'll never regret it because I wouldn't have Micah otherwise. Besides, everything that happened led me to Beau, and I've never been so happy."

"I'm glad. You deserve it. And so does Beau—even though he thinks I'm the devil."

Eden snorted. "He does not. He's been friendlier tonight, you have to admit. He even asked you how work's going."

"I'm guessing it was that elbow you put in his rib."

Eden waved her away. "Beside the point."

The popping sound of firecrackers went off down the beach, and a firework sizzled through the air. A small bloom of red flared. Zac slipped back inside saying he needed a refill.

"Look!" Micah pointed. "It's starting."

"Those are just warm-ups, bud," Beau said. "We've still got a little time before the big show."

"Evening, all." Sheriff Colton approached from the beach in full uniform, so tall he was almost at eye level with them. He perched a foot on the bottom step and pulled off his hat as his greeting was returned.

"All quiet out there, Sheriff?" Beau asked.

"Aw, a couple scuffles, but nothing major. Some kids drinking underage, shooting off illegal fireworks. Called their parents, put the fear of God into 'em."

"Let me know if you need a hand," Beau said.

"We should be all right." His gaze swung to Miss Trudy. "Looking forward to the show, Trudy?"

"I'm sure it'll be just dandy." The woman

crossed her arms over her sweater and squirmed in her seat.

"Things pretty busy over at the visitor center?" he asked.

" 'Bout the usual."

"I ran into Rusty and Belinda Davis over in Ellsworth," he said. "They're expecting a grand-baby any day now."

"Already have half a dozen."

"Four, they said. This'll be their first boy though. They're excited."

"Good for them." Miss Trudy scooched back her chair. "Excuse me. I'm going to the ladies' room."

The sheriff shuffled in the sand, twisting the brim of his hat before setting it on his head. "Well . . . I'd best get back to it. You all take care driving home."

"Poor guy," Eden whispered as he walked away.

"He sure seems sweet on Miss Trudy." Lucy spoke quietly, even though the woman had gone inside.

"Too bad she doesn't return his feelings. He gets all red and flustered . . . it's painful to watch. She's always so short with him."

"Well, she's kind of a crusty lady. Maybe that's her way of flirting."

"I don't know. Sometimes I wonder if some-thing happened."

"Like what?"

Eden shrugged. "Like maybe she's holding a

grudge or something. I've tried to prod but she shuts me down. He must've done something to rile her up so much."

"I don't know, but I wouldn't want to be on her bad side—any more than I already am."

"She's more bark than bite. You should see her with Micah when no one's watching. She's practically a teddy bear."

Lucy gave a wry smile. "I'll take your word for it."

"How are you feeling? Anything coming back to you yet?"

"My symptoms are gone, but nothing's come back. Not a single memory." She sighed. "Maybe it'll never come back."

"Is that what you want?"

Lucy made a face. "Well, it's no fun being in love with someone who wants you out of his life."

She felt the weight of Eden's stare. "I'm sorry. That must be hard."

Another sizzle sounded, and a small white firework spread in the sky. On the corner of the patio Micah's sparkler fizzled out, and he begged Beau for another.

"Zac went out with Morgan Friday," Lucy said quietly. She wasn't sure why she brought it up. Thinking about it only made her heart ache.

"I heard. I also heard she came by first to rub it in your face."

"Where'd you hear that?"

Eden shrugged. "Small town. Not much gets by.

154

Just ignore her. She thinks she's all that just because her daddy runs the newspaper. Far as I can tell, she doesn't do anything but paint her nails and lie out in the sun."

"He took her the same place he took me on our first date. The same place we had our first kiss."

"Wow. I'm sorry. I don't know what he sees in her."

"Other than her mile-long legs and double Ds?"

"Please. She has nothing on you. And if it's any consolation, it's not like there's a whole bunch of restaurants to choose from around here. You go on a few dates, you've pretty much exhausted your options."

"True enough."

They went quiet as Beau sank into the seat beside Eden and slipped his arm around her. "Almost time."

Eden laced her hand with Beau's as she gave Lucy a long, measured look. "Know what you need? You need a guy. Someone to take you out and get your mind off"—she seemed to check herself—"things."

"Oh no, I don't—"

"What about Nick Donahue?" Eden said.

"What about him?" Miss Trudy asked as she came out onto the deck, Zac on her heels.

"Nothing," Lucy said.

"We're fixing Lucy up," Eden said at the same time.

• • •

Zac pulled the patio door shut and swatted at a mosquito hovering near his face. Eden's words were a sucker punch to his gut.

"Nick hasn't dated anyone since Paige," Aunt Trudy said. "Comes from good stock."

Now she thought of something positive to say. Zac dropped into his seat, pressing his lips together.

"Isn't he a doctor?" Lucy asked.

"Pediatrician," Eden said. "I took Micah to see him for his annual checkup. He's great with kids."

Wasn't it about time for the fireworks? Zac took a big gulp of his soda.

"What do you think, Beau?" Eden asked. "You know him better than I do."

"He's a nice enough guy. He was a couple years behind me in school, so I don't know him well. He's smart. Paige had nothing bad to say about him."

"Did they go out for long?" Lucy asked.

No doubt she didn't want to step on Paige's toes. Zac squirmed in his seat.

"Only two or three times," Miss Trudy said, no doubt happy for Lucy to be interested in anyone other than him. "They fit better as friends, she said. But I can see the two of you hitting it off."

Zac bit his tongue. He had no dog in this hunt. They'd been over a long time. He wanted her to move on.

156

Then why does your stomach feel like it's on a wooden roller coaster?

"I can too," Eden said. "He's kind of quiet and unassuming, but in a reflective way, not to mention he's not exactly hard on the eyes."

Zac's mind formed an image of Nick and Lucy together with their matching brown hair and kilowatt smiles. The man in the image slipped his arms around Lucy and pulled her close until their bodies came together.

Zac smacked a mosquito on his arm. The sound carried across the patio.

"That settles it then," Eden said. "I'll introduce you at church."

Swell. He could hardly wait.

Chapter 19

Zac ducked into his office, a niggle of guilt worming through him. He'd been helping a new kid bus tables when Morgan had arrived with a girlfriend in a cloud of perfume. He'd given her a polite nod and a smile and pretended—yes, pretended—he was too busy to stop and say hello. But it was a Tuesday night, and the restaurant was half empty. Who was he kidding?

Ever since their date Friday at the Oyster Bistro, he'd known this was coming. He had to tell her it wasn't working. All he could think of as he sat across from her at the candlelit table was Lucy. It felt like he was sullying the memory of their first date.

The conversation had flowed so easily that night. The more things he'd learned about her, the more he'd wanted to know. Her charming drawl and spirited inflections . . . he could've listened to her talk all night.

Their time at the harbor lingered in his mind as well. That scoop of ice cream falling into his lap. Her face cloaked in dismay. The dab of ice cream dotting the tip of her nose.

The kiss. Making him fall more deeply than he'd ever fallen.

He paced his office, filled with too much energy to sit. He had a perfectly nice, attractive woman interested in him. She was attentive and fun. She could hold an intelligent conversation about local politics and business management. He hadn't even had to stoop down the one time he'd kissed her.

So why did he find himself missing the way Lucy used to look up at him with those big blue eyes? The way she fit snugly into his chest when he held her? The way he could rest his chin on the top of her head?

He laced his fingers behind his neck. What was wrong with him? She was driving him crazy, that was what. And he was hiding in his office like a little girl.

Butch up, Callahan.

He left his office and turned down the hall, the barely there noise of the weeknight filtering down the hall. Rain pattered quietly on the roof, and thunder rumbled in the distance.

A familiar voice caught his ears as he neared the doorway to the restaurant. A Southern drawl. But it wasn't Lucy's voice. He slowed his steps at the mouth of the hallway, listening.

"Well, I see how *y'all* might be confused," Morgan was saying in an exaggerated Southern accent. "But I said I wanted a Dr Pepper, and this is clearly not Dr Pepper."

"And this lemonade doesn't have enough ice," another voice said. "Really, is there a shortage or something?"

"I'll be right back," Lucy said in a tight voice.

A moment of silence passed, but Zac waited.

"She's such a dimwit," Morgan said.

Zac's muscles tensed, his eyes narrowing on the sliver of booth he could see from his vantage point.

"I don't know what he ever saw in her. You're so much prettier."

"And she's so short. I mean she's practically a midget."

Their tinkling laughs ran right up his spine.

"I'll bet she's faking all that amnesia stuff," Morgan said. Her voice went Southern again. " 'Oh, Zac, I'm so helpless and needy. Please rescue me so I can have purpose and meaning in my *lahf* again!' "

He ground his teeth together, forcing himself to wait. Heat crawled up the back of his neck and settled there.

"I can't believe he's letting her stay here," the friend said. "And work here. We've got to do something."

"Oh, don't you worry about that. Pretty soon she's going to have her hands so full, he'll be plenty eager to see the back of her fat behind."

"What do you have up your sleeve, Morgan LeBlanc?"

A moment of quiet ensued, and Zac heard the quiet *thunk* of drinks being set down.

"It's about *tahm,*" Morgan said.

"Did you actually get it right for once?" the friend asked.

The heat behind his neck had spread down his limbs and out his pores. He'd heard enough. He slipped around the corner, adjusting his face into a pleasant mask.

"Everything okay, ladies?" His gaze drifted between them. Lucy's face was drawn, her eyes tight with emotion.

"Oh, it's fine," Morgan said. "Lucy just made a teensy mistake, but it's all good."

"Oh, terrific. Glad she's taking care of you." He looked innocently at Morgan. "So you don't think she's a dimwit after all?"

He watched with morbid pleasure as the blood drained from her face. The smile faltered on her red lips, and her eyes darted to her friend's.

He felt the weight of Lucy's gaze but continued staring at Morgan as if expecting an answer.

"I—Zac . . ." She chuckled. "We were only kidding."

"Like you were kidding about ordering the Dr Pepper?"

A bright flush that had nothing to do with makeup flooded into her cheeks. "I don't know what—"

"I think both of you need to leave."

Morgan settled a hand over her heart, a look of innocent shock coming over her features. "What?"

"Patrons who don't respect my employees aren't welcome." He nailed Morgan with a look. "Leave."

An awkward pause ensued before Morgan drew herself up straight and extricated herself from the booth, her friend following suit.

Morgan turned to him with a lift to her chin, but her heightened color ruined the effect. Zac stared into her brittle green eyes, wondering how he'd ever thought her pretty.

"You just made a terrible miscalculation," she said.

"I beg to differ."

"Let's go, Morgan," her friend said.

Morgan's perfect nose flared, then she turned and left in a wake of cloying perfume.

Lucy's lips were parted as her eyes swung to him. "Thank you." She sounded a little dumbfounded.

He opened his mouth, so many things on the tip of his tongue. He held them all back, merely gave her a smile and touched her on the arm as he passed. He would've done the same for any employee.

Keep telling yourself that, Callahan.

Lucy pulled the tips from her apron pocket, straightening the bills. Thirty-eight dollars. It had been a long, slow night. The rain pounding the roof overhead made her drowsy, and she fought a yawn as she headed to the bathroom to wash up.

Her feet ached and her back screamed, but as she washed her face, she smiled, remembering the way Zac had stood up for her.

Oh, how she wished she had it on tape so she could watch the color drain from Morgan's face again and again. And the look on her face when Zac kicked her out—priceless.

Good riddance. Lucy wouldn't be seeing her around here anymore. The thought lifted her lips even more.

Just as quickly, her smile faltered. She wouldn't be here to see Morgan anyway. Zac had caught her in the kitchen just before closing to say that Marci was over her illness and returning to work tomorrow.

He'd given her a crooked grin after he'd delivered the news. "You made it—didn't even drop one tray."

She didn't tell him about the one she'd dropped when he'd gone to the bank last week. Dropping trays was the least of her worries. She had no job now. No reason to spend time with Zac. No excuse to catch little glimpses of him as he worked the front or managed the kitchen. The thought put a pinch in her chest.

A crack of thunder sounded and the room went dark. She waited a minute, clutching the washcloth in her hand, to see if the lights would flicker back on. When the moment passed without incident, she peeked out the door. The rest of the downstairs was dark too. Pitch black.

Zac had already headed upstairs to his apartment. If he was already in bed, he wouldn't know they'd lost electric. She wondered if he had a generator. Or if there was something he needed to do to protect the food in the walk-in.

She padded out of the bathroom and down the hall, feeling her way with a hand on the wall. She couldn't see a single thing.

Thunder boomed overhead and rain pummeled the roof. Hopefully it wasn't prone to leaks. As it was, the parking lot was going to be—

Oompfh. She ran smack into a wall, bouncing backward.

Strong hands steadied her. "Whoa."

Her hands landed on the firm wall of his chest.

"You okay?" he asked.

"Oh my. I was—I was just coming for you."

"I was checking on you." His voice sounded deeper in the dark somehow. The warmth of his hands seeped through the sleeves of her shirt. One of his fingers slid along her skin, awakening every cell.

"Do you—do you have a generator?"

"No."

"What about the food?"

"It'll keep. The juice'll probably be back on by morning. Might want to throw another blanket on your bed. There's an extra in the chest of drawers."

"Good idea."

Silence stretched between them, tension hovering around them. His hand flexed on her arm, and her pulse jumped. She'd always been so aware of him. But it seemed like it had been so long since he'd touched her. And after the way he'd stood up to Morgan tonight, she was having warm feelings—dangerous feelings—toward him.

"Th-thanks again for what you did tonight. With Morgan."

"I'm just sorry I didn't see it earlier."

"It's not your fault."

She wished she could see his face, his smoky eyes. His breath fluttered her bangs, and the movement sent a shiver skittering down her arms.

He cleared his throat. "There's a, ah, flashlight in the kitchen. And candles."

"All right."

Neither of them moved. His spicy scent wrapped around her like a warm embrace. She should remove her hands from his chest, but the slow rise and fall was comforting somehow.

Her fingers clutched at the soft cotton. The muscles beneath it tensed.

Oh, how she'd missed being close to him. Missed the way she fit into him so perfectly. His touch was as familiar as an ocean breeze, his kiss as necessary as her next breath.

He couldn't be immune to her, could he? He'd always been so quick to respond to her kisses, often taking over in a flurry of passion. She'd missed that so much. Seven months couldn't have erased his desire for her. His love for her.

Her heart pounded in her chest, but the darkness made her bold. She stepped closer until she could feel the heat of him against her. Her hands moved up the solid wall of his chest, and his heart thumped against her palm.

She worked her way up to his broad shoulders. The tips of her fingers tingled with want. His neck was warm and sandpaper rough, his pulse strong and quick. The stubble on his jaw prickled against her palms.

"Lucy . . ."

His voice was thick, filled with emotion, though whether it was encouragement or caution she wasn't sure. Maybe he wasn't either. Maybe it didn't matter.

She pulled his face toward hers, stretching up to him like a tulip toward the sun. His breath teased her mouth for an instant before their lips met.

Ah, sweet heaven. She'd missed the familiar fresh and minty taste of him. His lips were as soft as she remembered.

But they were not pliant. They were not moving. Not one bit. His jaw had grown hard under her palm. His hands gripped her arms tightly.

He's not kissing you back, you imbecile!

Her heart buckled. She drew back, glad for the darkness as heat climbed her neck, flooding into her cheeks with mortification.

Way to go, Lucy. Throw yourself at a man who doesn't even want you.

"I'm sorry," she said on a thready breath. "I—I shouldn't have—"

He pulled her into him, and his lips were on hers.

Her heart lurched in a moment of confusion. Then her legs went soft, and her fingers trembled against his neck. He demanded a response, and she gave it gladly, heady with the familiar dance. Her mouth parted on a breath, and he took full advantage.

She slid her fingers into the softness of his hair, tugging. He wrapped his arms around her waist, drawing her closer until the warmth of his chest seeped through her shirt.

How had she made it these seven months without this? He was her rock. Her home. Her soul mate. Warmth pooled deep inside in a space that had been cold for too long.

She sensed a change, some subtle shift in his kiss, a tensing of his body. And then he pushed her away.

Zac dropped his hands, stepping back. His mind waged war with his heart, and his heart waged a war with his ribs. He was pretty sure his heart was winning both battles. It had never pounded so hard. Her kiss had sucked him right in. He'd held his own for all of two seconds before he'd dragged her back for more.

Way to hold out, Callahan.

He was glad he couldn't see her face. See the hurt he knew he'd find there. He was glad she couldn't see his either. His cheeks must be flushed with desire, and his eyes would give away his every thought.

And man was he having thoughts.

Their ragged breaths filled the space between them, mingling with the heavy cloud of tension.

"I shouldn't have done that," he said finally. Was that his voice, all thick and husky? Lord, what she did to him. He'd never wipe the memory of her from his lips.

"Why not, Zac? Why can't we—?"

"No, Lucy. I know you think you love me, but—"

"Don't tell me how I feel."

"—you're confused."

"Apparently so are you." Her voice rose above the patter of rain.

Well. She had him there. He palmed the back of his neck, a long, slow breath leaving his body. "This is too hard."

"It doesn't have to be."

He stepped back, putting distance between them before his hands did something he hadn't given them permission to do.

"Yes, it does. We're over, Lucy. It was your decision to end things, not mine. Time didn't stand still while you were gone. I've moved on." Maybe if he said it with enough conviction, she'd believe it. Maybe they both would. "When your memory comes back—"

"*If* my memory comes back."

"Even if it doesn't . . . I don't trust you now. You left me high and dry, and it was hard, Lucy. It took me months to even—" A hard knot formed in his throat, and he swallowed past it. "I'm not going there again. Maybe I'm still attracted to you, and maybe I'll always care about you on some level, but it can't go any further than that. It just can't."

He brushed past her, feeling his way down the hall and toward the kitchen. He tried to ignore the way his legs quaked. The way his heart shuddered. The way every piece of him still screamed to go back and take her in his arms again.

Chapter 20

Lucy lay in bed listening to the patter of rain on the roof. She'd been lying awake for hours, the memory of Zac's kiss lingering like a stolen dream. She would've been lying here with a smile, but for the way it had ended. The hurtful things he'd said.

Now she only felt rejected. And the roots of those emotions sank all the way to her core, roping around her, strangling.

Lucy's mama had been a beautiful woman, full of energy and laughter, who smelled of flowers and sunshine from tending her beloved garden. Lucy's favorite flower was the starflower with its vibrant blue petals and honey-sweet smell.

"This one represents courage," her mother had said one day as they gardened together. She ran her fingers through the tiny flowers. "It's beautiful and sweet smelling, and you can even eat it."

Lucy wasn't sure about eating flowers. But one

spring morning when she was fretting over an upcoming math test, she found a starflower in her bowl of Cheerios.

"For courage," her mom said with a wink.

With a little giggle, Lucy ate the tiny flower. She was surprised by its subtle, pleasant flavor—and by the A she got on her test later that day.

Another starflower appeared later that summer when she had her first dance recital. On the night of the big event, she sashayed across the stage, not missing a single beat.

The starflower soon became her favorite tradition.

Lucy also had tea parties with her mom and grand balls where they danced around the living room while her dolls looked on with adoration. The days only got better when her daddy came home from work. Sometimes he even came home early because he was his own boss.

Her parents were so in love. They snuggled on the sofa, sharing private smiles and quiet whispers. Sometimes Lucy would walk past them, close enough for Daddy to snatch her up and draw her into the hug. She would giggle and curl up between them, feeling so safe and loved.

They took weekend trips to the beach and stayed at seaside hotels. They looked for shells every morning and built sand castles in the heat of the afternoon. They returned home on Sunday nights, sun-tired and happy.

Shortly past her sixth birthday everything changed. Her mom became awful sick. Much later Lucy learned it was a rare brain tumor that had made her so ill. They spent hours at the hospital where her mom lay as white as the sheets. Lucy watched her chest rise and fall, listening to the beeping and whirring of the machines.

Until all of it stopped.

Everything afterward was sad and bewildering. She kept asking Daddy when Mama would come home. Looking back, she realized the pain her questions must've caused him. But death was the kind of permanence a young child couldn't comprehend.

The house on Oak Street was no longer filled with laughter and music. Daddy wandered from room to room with bloodshot eyes, a cigarette often trembling between his lips. He forgot to turn on lights. He slept in the spare room, the door of her parents' bedroom remaining shut at all times.

He often left Lucy with Mrs. Wilmington, their next-door neighbor—an elderly woman with a lot of rules. Lucy cried when he left her there in the mornings. What if he went where Mama went? What if he stayed away too? There weren't enough starflowers in the world to give her the courage for that.

When her dad stopped long enough to settle on the couch, Lucy would walk slowly by. But he didn't snatch her off her feet anymore. He didn't draw her into hugs or find that ticklish spot at her side.

The weeks and months after her mama's death passed in a lonely blur. There was an overwhelming heaviness that Lucy later learned was grief's calling card. It rolled in like a heavy fog, sinking into everything it touched.

Then one Friday when Lucy was seven, she got off the bus. A cold rain was drizzling from a cloudy gray sky. She was supposed to stay with Mrs. Wilmington until Daddy got home. But his blue car was in their driveway, so she headed that way instead.

Happiness swirled inside. Daddy had been coming home late, especially on Friday nights. Sometimes Mrs. Wilmington tucked her into her own bed and stayed until he came home. He was always quiet in the morning, and Lucy knew he wouldn't be fit for talking until after his second cup of coffee, but by then he had to leave for work.

But tonight she wouldn't have to stay with Mrs. Wilmington. Maybe Daddy would help her with her penguin project. Maybe they could go out for ice cream later like they used to.

She shuffled through the piles of decaying leaves that carpeted their yard. They used to make huge piles by the porch. She'd jump into them until there were chips of leaves stuck so deep in her scalp that Mama would have to help wash her hair.

She passed the remnants of her mama's garden. Weeds had choked out most of the flowers, and decaying leaves covered the rest. Lucy tried to picture the garden the way it used to be. Tried to picture Mama as she climbed the porch steps, but all she could remember was soft brown hair and blue eyes. These days her mama seemed like a ghost from her past, and she disappeared more and more every day. Lucy was afraid that someday she wouldn't remember Mama at all.

She pushed the thought away before the big, dark fog could swallow her up. Daddy was home, and it was going to be a happy night. The front door was unlocked, and she pushed it open. The house was dark and quiet, the smell of cigarette smoke hanging in the air.

She slid her backpack to the floor and kicked off her ballerina flats. She heard floorboards creaking overhead, so she dashed up the stairs.

"Daddy?" she called.

The door to his bedroom—his new one—was open. He was standing by the bed.

He turned as she approached. "Lucy . . ." His thick eyebrows pulled close. "What are you doing here? You're supposed to go on over to Mrs. Wilmington's."

Her face fell at his scolding tone. "But you're here."

Her eyes dropped to the suitcase on the bed. It

was filled with clothes. A lot of clothes. Lucy wondered if the lid would even shut. She remembered their trips to the beach, and a wonderful feeling swept over her. Daddy was taking her to the beach! She suddenly couldn't wait to escape this dark, quiet house.

"Are we going to the beach?" She bounced up and down on her toes, her body unable to stay still.

"What? No." He took his cigarette from the ashtray and put it between his lips, his jaws going hollow as he sucked on it. He blew out, the smoke swirling into the air.

"Where we going then? Can we go camping?" Delaney, her friend from school, went camping all the time in the summer. Was it too cold to camp?

Daddy stubbed out the cigarette and closed the suitcase lid. His face wore the same sad frown it had worn for months. His movements were fast and jerky as he worked to close the suitcase. He seemed to have forgotten she was even there.

A cold chill swept up her spine. Her heart lurched, and her legs suddenly felt like a rag doll's.

She crawled onto the bed and got in front of him. "Daddy? Where we going?"

He struggled with the latch, opened the suitcase, stuffed in the clothes, then shut it again, but it still wouldn't latch. The bed bounced with his efforts.

"Daddy?"

He reached for the cigarette again, but it was nothing but a smoking stub. He patted his pockets, scowling.

"Daddy?"

He jerked his face toward her, as if just realizing she was still there. His frown deepened. "I told you to go next door."

"But—but aren't we going on a trip?"

"Not *we,* Lucy." He pushed at the clothes, tucking and shoving, then closed the lid, a far-away look in his eyes. "I have to get away. I need a break." He pushed the latches, and they closed with a snap of finality.

Her eyes burned as she watched him heave the suitcase from the bed. She followed him down the steps, her legs working fast to keep up. Mama had gone away, and now Daddy was going too.

She followed him to the car, where he shoved the suitcase into the trunk. There were other things in there too. Boxes of things. His coffeepot and books and the dishes she used to have tea parties with.

Her chest was so tight she couldn't breathe. Her heart felt like it might explode, and a scream clawed for escape.

Daddy shut the trunk with a loud *thunk.*

She grabbed him around his waist, burying her head into his side. "Take me with you, Daddy! Please!"

He picked her up, and her frantic heart settled

as she buried her face into his neck, breathing in his familiar smell. Her arms wrapped around his strong shoulders and held tight. He wouldn't go without her. Of course he wouldn't.

He began walking, but she closed her eyes, telling them to stop leaking. He was taking her with him. Maybe they were moving to the beach, and she wouldn't have to live in their dark, quiet house anymore. She wouldn't have to stay with Mrs. Wilmington or fall asleep without Daddy.

She bounced in his arms as he went up steps. At the knocking sound she opened her eyes.

The door opened, and Mrs. Wilmington reached for her.

Daddy's words rang in her ears. *"I have to get away"* . . . *"I have to get away"* . . . *"I have to get away."*

Lucy's head snapped up. Her grip tightened around her dad's neck, her heart going on that wild race again.

Daddy pulled at her arms as he spoke to Mrs. Wilmington. "Here. You have her number." His voice was like a robot's.

She clung tight with her arms and legs. He couldn't leave her here. They were a team, she and Daddy. He'd said so.

"Let go, Lucy."

"Daddy, no! Take me with you!"

He pulled until her arms lost their grip. "I can't, sugar. I just can't."

Mrs. Wilmington pulled her into her arms.

Lucy fought. She kicked, she pushed. But the door shut, and Daddy was walking away.

She fought with renewed strength. Sobs welled up in her chest, fighting for release. "Daddy!" she screamed until she was sure he had to hear her.

Something stirred Zac from his sleep. His eyes opened in the darkness, and it took a moment to orient himself. He was on his office couch. The electricity had gone off.

Lucy. The kiss. He exhaled, palming his aching eyes.

Sleep had been elusive. The memory of her lips on his had tortured him until after two, and without electricity the upstairs had cooled quickly. It had been after three when he'd finally grabbed his blankets and headed to his office where it was warmer.

He must've fallen asleep, but what had awakened him? The sound came again, a voice. Distress.

Lucy.

He jumped from the sofa and moved for the door. He was down the hall and pushing through her door before he could blink. He stopped on the threshold, his heart battering him from the inside out.

Moonlight spilled through the sheer curtains, revealing the shadowed lump of Lucy's body in the center of the bed. She twitched and squirmed. The bedsheets rustled, and her ragged breaths punctuated the silence.

A nightmare. He entered the room, telling his heart to chill. "Lucy."

She thrashed, her legs kicking out. "Daddy!"

His heart squeezed at the torment in her voice. He stepped closer. He didn't know much about her dad—her mom either, for that matter—only that they'd passed away. Lucy hadn't talked much about her childhood.

He eased up to the bed and set a hand on her shoulder. "Lucy."

"No, Daddy!"

"Lucy."

She stilled, her shoulder tensing. Then she pulled away from him, and his hand fell.

"You were having a nightmare."

Her breaths came again in quiet rasps. Every cell in his body wanted to reach for her. Wanted to drag her into his arms and tell her it was okay.

"I'm okay." Her voice was thick with emotion.

If he reached out, he knew he'd find her cheeks wet with tears. But she was huddled on the far side of the bed, and after the kiss they'd shared earlier, touching her was the last thing he needed to do.

He should ask her if she wanted to talk about the nightmare, but she'd already slipped too far under his defenses. It wasn't good for either of them.

"Sorry I woke you." Her voice sounded more controlled this time. She relaxed into the bed. The covers rustled as she pulled them back into place.

The air was as cool in here as the office. "You warm enough?"

"Of course. You can go on back to bed now; I'm just fine."

He knew the brave face she wore even if he couldn't see it. It was the one she'd worn every time he'd asked about her childhood. The one she'd worn when they'd wheeled her away for her MRI. When he'd left her at her apartment in Portland. She wasn't fine. Not even close.

It took everything in him to ease away from her bed. "All right. Good night then."

"Night."

He slipped out the door, pulling it almost shut, wondering how long he could keep Lucy Lovett from sinking back into his heart.

Chapter 21

Lucy squinted against the morning sun hanging over the harbor. A few lobster boats were moored there, mere silhouettes, their short masts like skinny fingers pointing heavenward. The smell of burning wood hung in the air, combined with the briny scent of the sea. Overhead, a seagull sailed on the wind, releasing a high-pitched, mournful cry.

Lucy turned down the planked walk leading toward the visitor center. She'd already tried every other place in town, and she'd heard from Eden that Miss Trudy wanted to cut back on her hours at the center. She was set on making this happen.

She'd returned from her jog to find power restored at the Roadhouse. Unfortunately, her memories of the night before had also been restored. She wished she could forget the way Zac had pushed her away. Wished she could forget the nightmare of her dad's abandonment. The two events blurred together, blending into one.

She had to get out from under Zac's roof. And to do that, she needed to find herself a job.

The visitor center was a shack just off the boardwalk. Its shingles had been weathered by wind and sand, but a fresh coat of white paint trimmed out the building. The sign over the door read *Visitor and Natural History Center*, and the one beside it announced the hours.

The screen door opened with a familiar squawk, and Lucy stepped into the space that had been hers for a year and a half. Miss Trudy was over by the trail map with a couple who looked as if they'd stepped right off the page of an L.L.Bean catalog.

Lucy wandered over to the brochure rack and began straightening the pamphlets. She spotted a few new ones. Beau's Christmas tree farm, featuring fall activities; a new tour company offering day-trips on a lobster boat; and a brochure advertising the activities and events on Folly Shoals. She situated that one beside the ferry schedule and moved the dining guide over by the day-trip pamphlet.

"Get your hands off my brochures, missy."

Lucy turned and faced Miss Trudy. "I was just straightening them. There are a few new ones."

Miss Trudy pursed her lips. "Well, you *have* been gone awhile."

She wasn't going to make this easy. "Yes, ma'am." Her eyes drifted over the room. It was tidy enough. Miss Trudy was sure enough doing a great job with the center. But Lucy had the inside scoop.

"You needing a bus schedule?" The woman reached past Lucy, pulling a pamphlet and handing it to her. "There's one leaving Bangor tonight. I'm sure we can get you up there in time."

Lucy winced. "I know I left you in a lurch before. I'm awfully sorry."

Miss Trudy's eyes pierced hers. "I'm not the only one you left in a lurch."

Her skin tingled at the back of her neck, and her feet itched. No, she wasn't running. She'd already run from here once, then she'd run from Portland. At some point a body had to stay put. And this was the only place she had friends. Well. People who used to be her friends.

Lucy put the pamphlet back. "I have a lot to make up for and a lot of people to make amends with. I'm asking for a second chance. I don't have anywhere else to go."

"What about that fiancé back in Portland?"

"He's nothing but a stranger to me."

Miss Trudy crossed her arms.

"I came by to see if you'd be willing to hire me again. I hear you're wanting to cut back your hours, and I've got nothing but time on my hands."

The woman's eyes narrowed.

"I'm already trained, and I'm willing to take whatever hours you can give me."

Lucy forced herself to hold still under Miss Trudy's unnerving scrutiny. Maybe she'd made a mistake or two, let a few people down. But could she really be held accountable for something she didn't even remember doing?

"Give me one good reason why I should even think about hiring you again."

Lucy drew a deep breath, the one reason already on her tongue. "Because I can't get out from under Zac's roof until I have a job. I've already tried everywhere else—and I do mean everywhere."

Miss Trudy scowled, her nostrils flaring. "And you want to be rid of him again, is that it?"

Lucy remembered the kiss last night. She could still feel his soft lips on hers. Still taste the minty freshness of him on her tongue. Still feel the solid strength of his chest against her.

"No, ma'am," she said on a soft breath, blinking against the burn behind her eyes. "I just—I just think it might be best. For both of us."

Miss Trudy studied her long and hard. "I heard about that little show you put on at Frumpy Joe's. You trying to win everyone's sympathy?"

"No, ma'am."

"He should've left you in Portland."

Shame swelled inside, and Lucy withered as heat rose into her cheeks. She could pretend she wasn't responsible for her actions all she wanted. But it had happened, and she'd hurt Zac. She deserved to be left behind.

"Yes, ma'am." She forced herself to hold Miss Trudy's direct gaze.

A long moment later something shifted in the woman's brittle blue eyes. She pursed her lips. "Be here at ten in the morning, not a minute later. You'll work the weekdays, and I'll take the weekends."

A breath escaped her lungs as a smile forced its way onto her lips. "I'll be here." She backed toward the door before Miss Trudy had a change of heart.

"I'll leave an extra key under the flowerpot. Don't lose it."

Lucy pushed open the screen door. "I won't. Thank you!"

"And you leave my brochures where I put them," Miss Trudy called as the screen door slapped against the frame behind Lucy.

"Yes, ma'am," Lucy returned, unable to quell the smile on her face as her pace quickened on the walkway.

Lucy Lovett was officially employed. Next up on her agenda: apartment hunting.

Chapter 22

The following Sunday morning Eden called out to Lucy on the sidewalk outside the chapel. Lucy turned and waited, drawing her sweater tighter. She'd never gotten used to Maine's morning chill.

Once she'd caught up with Lucy, Eden scooted her son off to class. "Have you heard about the article?" Eden asked.

"What article?"

"Your story was on the *USA Today* blog this morning. Paige saw it and called."

Lucy's pulse jumped even as dread tightened her chest. "What did it say?"

Eden dug her phone out of her purse. "I didn't really give it a thorough read, but the gist is that you're a runaway bride with amnesia and that you went missing—you didn't tell me you were Audrey Lovett's great-niece."

"It didn't seem important," Lucy said. "I can't believe it's in the national news."

"It's only one website," Eden said. "It probably didn't even make the actual paper."

"I surely hope not." Lucy rubbed her temple. She didn't like the idea of her private life displayed for all the world to see, especially when she was feeling so lost.

Eden had pulled up the article on her phone, and she held it out to Lucy. It was short and spelled out the basic facts.

"Leastwise they don't know where to find me." Lucy handed the phone back when she finished the article.

"I'm sure it's just a fluke."

Throughout church Lucy worked to stay focused on the message. It was about perfect love casting out fear. That scripture had always been a mystery to her. But she couldn't focus on what Pastor Daniels was saying. All she could think about was the article. She couldn't imagine why she'd be news to anyone.

After church she followed Eden down the aisle, pausing whenever her friend stopped to introduce her to someone. The townsfolk seemed to be softening toward her—or maybe they felt guilted into being friendly simply because they were in church.

"Nick's over by the drinking fountain." Eden tugged her along. "I'll introduce you."

Lucy wasn't really in the mood to meet a potential date, but she had to get Zac out of her head somehow.

She scanned the foyer as they neared, her eyes

settling on a handsome man leaning against the wall. He had short brown hair, a clean-shaven face, and he wore a button-down with khakis, a black belt circling his trim waist. She recognized him from when she'd lived here before.

"Look, Eden, I'm not sure about—"

"Hey, Nick," Eden said as they approached.

He straightened, his eyes smiling before his mouth. "Eden, how you doing?" His gaze moved to Lucy.

"This is Lucy Lovett. You might remember her from when she lived here before."

He held out his hand. "I do. Nice to see you again, Lucy."

"You too." His handshake was firm, his smile kind. He wasn't much taller than she was, but then, she did have on three-inch heels.

"I hear you've been in Portland."

She gave a wry grin. "So I hear."

He chuckled. "Good that you have a sense of humor about the whole thing."

Eden touched her arm. "I have to go grab Micah from class. I'll call you later."

Don't leave me, Lucy said with her eyes, but Eden either didn't read the plea or chose to ignore it. With a final wave she shuffled down the hall toward the classrooms.

Lucy turned back to Nick, cognizant of the awkward tension weaving through the space around them. "So . . ."

He smiled, his brown eyes twinkling. "That wasn't obvious at all."

"Not one iota."

"I like the way she thinks though."

"Listen, Nick—" Lucy shifted, and as she did so, her purse slipped from her shoulder. It thumped to the ground and fell to the side, spilling its contents. "Whoopsie." She stooped down.

"I've seen you around the Roadhouse," Nick said after he'd helped her gather the things. "You working for Zac now?"

She couldn't blame him for getting the lay of the land. No doubt there were all sorts of rumors flying about. "Um, I was just filling in for one of his servers. I'm working at the visitor center now, and I'm getting my own apartment right soon so I won't be staying at the Roadhouse anymore. Zac and I aren't, um, involved any-more . . . ? In case you were speculating. Although to be completely honest, I'm kind of still hung up on him, though I guess I burnt that bridge, but even so, I'm really not looking for a relationship." She pinched her bottom lip as heat suffused her face. "I reckon I'll stop talking now."

He gave a warm laugh. "I like you, Lucy. We should hang out sometime. As friends."

Lucy sagged with relief. "I'd like that."

They made plans for the following Saturday. He had a nice smile and warm brown eyes. If there was anything she needed in her life, it was more friends.

Lucy pointed a family of five to the brochure rack, pulling a few activities she thought might be of interest to them. They were from Georgia, and their accents reminded her of home. She talked to the woman for twenty minutes while her husband studied the trail map of Acadia National Park.

Once they were off, Lucy straightened up the brochures. The phone rang, and she swept across the room, feeling happy and productive. She loved interacting with people and helping them use their time wisely while they visited the area.

"Summer Harbor Visitor and Natural History Center, how can I assist you?"

"May I speak with Lucy Lovett, please?"

"This is she."

"Hi, I'm Frank Whisman from the *US Enquirer*. I wondered if you might have a few minutes to answer some questions."

Lucy's stomach sank to her toes. "What? No, I don't think so."

"Is it true that you can't remember being engaged to Brad Martin?"

"I don't—no comment." She hung up the phone, her hand trembling. What was he from? The *US Enquirer*? He must've seen the *USA Today* article yesterday. But how had he known where to find her?

188

Lucy jumped as the screen door squawked open, but it was only a couple of hikers wanting information on the Blackwoods Campground. After going over the wall map with her, they left with a handful of brochures.

She took a short break, grabbing a sandwich at Frumpy Joe's. The afternoon flew by as she took phone calls and helped customers. The game warden stopped in and introduced himself, and by five o'clock Lucy's stomach was growling.

She was beginning to turn off lights when the screen door opened. She turned with a ready smile, but the men slipping through the door didn't look one bit like tourists. The first fellow was somewhere in his twenties. He wore a suit and a Colgate smile as he approached. An older man followed. Lucy's heart plummeted when she spotted the camera perched on his shoulder.

"Lucy Lovett?" the man with the teeth asked. "I'm Ethan Everson with *Celebrity Tonight.*"

Lucy's feet froze to the floor. "I'm afraid you'll have to leave."

"I just have a few questions. How do you feel about—?"

"I'm not answering any questions." She walked to the door, but they didn't follow. The camera was pointed her way, the light indicating he was filming. "Y'all need to get out now, you hear?"

"Just a few moments of your time—"

"Get going." She pushed open the screen.

He gave a sympathetic smile. "This is a public building, Miss Lovett."

"And it's closing time. Read the posted hours on your way out."

"Is it true you don't remember running from your wedding?"

"If you don't leave, I'm calling the sheriff."

"Do you remember your relationship with Brad Martin? What brought you to Summer Harbor?"

She walked toward the phone and snatched up the extension.

The reporter held up his hands. "All right, all right. If you change your mind, I only need a few minutes of your time." He held out a business card.

Lucy pressed her lips together, glowering, the phone in her hand.

He gave a tight smile and set his card on her desk.

She breathed a sigh of relief when the men left. She closed the door behind them, watching through the small window. She'd expected them to get in their vehicle and go, but they stopped at the end of the wooden walkway and made themselves at home.

Great. Terrific. There was no back door. She'd have to pass them on her way out, and she'd walked to work this morning. They'd follow her all the way back to Zac's.

Or she could wait them out. Do a bit of

paperwork and catch up on the new inventory Miss Trudy asked her to process, some gift shop items. It was almost suppertime. Surely they wouldn't tarry long.

Lucy got busy with the new T-shirts and trinkets, keeping occupied until the sun set low on the horizon. She peeked out the front window and what she saw made her heart seize in her chest. More people, seven or eight of them, more cameras and equipment.

No.

Stupid paparazzi. What right did they have to trap her here?

She had a mind to call Sheriff Colton. But before she touched the phone, reality took hold. They were on public property. They weren't doing anything illegal.

She should've set off when it was just the two men. Now she'd have to get past a whole gaggle of reporters. Maybe she should just answer their questions and be done with it. They'd go away and tell their story, and it would be over.

But would it really? Or would it only stir more interest? It was hard enough to work out her own feelings on her memory loss without a bunch of strangers sticking their noses into it. She couldn't deal with this right now. She just wanted to be back at the Roadhouse in her little room.

She picked up the phone and dialed.

Zac peeled from the lot and took a right out of the parking lot, clenching his teeth. Beside him Lucy clamped onto the armrest. The parasites had followed them to the parking lot, and a quick check in his rearview mirror showed some of them getting into their cars.

He turned left onto Tipsy Avenue and made a hard right into the alley behind the stores.

"Buckle up," he said.

Lucy complied, then turned in her seat. "I don't see them."

"We'll go around the block just to be sure."

"Why are they doing this?"

"How long were they there?"

"An hour or so? There was only one crew at first. They came into the center and started firing questions at me. It was all I could do to get them to leave."

Anger flushed Zac's face with heat, and he held back a growl. Scumbags. He had half a mind to go back there and slug a few of those pretty boys.

He made a left onto Jackson Street, checking his rearview mirror. "I think we lost them."

He made another left on Bayberry, heading back toward the Roadhouse. "It's only a matter of time before they find where you're staying though."

"Then they'll be hanging out in front of your restaurant. Zac . . . I'm so sorry. You've done nothing but come to my rescue." She turned toward the passenger window. "And I've been nothing but trouble."

He wasn't sure he was supposed to hear her whispered words. His chest tightened. Maybe he'd stepped up for Lucy, but he hadn't exactly been the welcome wagon.

"I'm not worried about the restaurant. I'll contact Sheriff Colton, and he'll make sure they mind their manners." He turned into the Roadhouse parking lot to find a smattering of the usual cars and trucks.

He pulled into his spot and shut off the engine. "But in the meantime it's not going to be much fun for you."

Chapter 23

Lucy waved Eden over to the corner booth at the Roadhouse. The place was moderately busy, a baseball game on the overhead TVs and a game of pool under way in the back room. The savory smells of clam chowder and buffalo wings lingered in the air. Zac was stuck in the kitchen after one of his cooks failed to show.

Her friend gave a sympathetic smile as she slid into the booth. "How long are those guys going to be out there?"

It had been three days since the reporters had

turned up in town, but they'd kept their distance since Sheriff Colton stopped by.

"They don't seem in a big hurry to leave. Maybe I should just go on out there and make a statement. Maybe if they got what they wanted they'd leave me be."

"Don't say a word to those vultures. They'll just twist everything you say, and next thing you know you'll be pregnant with your alien lover's child."

Megan stopped by their table and took their orders.

"I can't even go jogging without being harassed," Lucy continued after Megan left. "I can't run to the post office or get things for my new apartment. I'm trapped. I'll bet I'm really all the gossip now."

"I'm not going to lie; that's pretty much true. On the bright side, people are more sympathetic toward you. I overheard one of Zac's staff giving them what-for outside. He told them to get lost and—this is a quote—'stop hassling one of our own.' "

Lucy blinked. "Is that so?"

"And when Miss Trudy and I passed them yesterday in front of the visitor center, she gave them an earful. I practically had to drag her away."

The thought warmed her. Maybe everyone here didn't hate her after all. "I hope they get going soon. Poor Zac's been running me to work and back every day, and they're blocking his establishment. This isn't fair to him."

Eden's gaze drifted around the restaurant. "It doesn't seem to be hurting business any. And he wouldn't be doing it if he didn't care."

Lucy couldn't think about him caring. He'd made it clear he wanted nothing more to do with her. He was just too softhearted for his own good. Too softhearted to leave her at the reporters' mercy, too softhearted to leave her at her own mercy after the concussion. She had to stop confusing compassion with love.

"Maybe you should think about staying here at the Roadhouse until they're gone," Eden said.

Lucy's eyes met Eden's. She'd told her friend about their kiss and the way Zac had pushed her away. Even now, the memory of his rejection made her want to curl up in a corner.

"No," Lucy said. "I need to get out of here. For both our sakes."

Eden gave her a heartfelt smile. "You still don't remember anything?"

"Not a single thing. I wish it would come back though. All of it. Then maybe I'd be as over Zac as he is over me."

Eden tilted her head, giving Lucy a thoughtful look. "Did you ever think that maybe God brought you back together for a reason? I mean, amnesia . . . what are the chances? Maybe it's all part of His plan to get you two back together."

"Well, if it is, He failed to inform Zac. It takes two to tango, you know."

"Maybe he's just not listening for the music. We should pray about that. Or, as my daddy says, 'time to wear out the knees in those jeans.' "

Lucy smiled through the prick of guilt. When was the last time she'd really prayed about anything? Maybe that was how her life had gotten so out of whack.

Eden looked as if she wanted to say something, but their drinks arrived and the moment passed. They made small talk once their food arrived, glancing at the TV whenever the crowd cheered or gave grunts of disapproval. Their server passed by with a seafood platter, and the tantalizing aroma wafted her way.

As Megan brought the bill, Nick entered with a couple of friends. He waved at Eden and Lucy as they ordered drinks, then they proceeded to the poolroom.

Awhile later, Eden glanced over Lucy's shoulder. "He keeps looking over this way."

"He's probably trying to figure out what the media find so fascinating."

Eden smiled, rolling her eyes. "Yeah, that's exactly what his expression is saying."

Lucy's new phone vibrated in her pocket. She paid the bill, then checked the screen.

It was from Nick.

Up for a game of pool?

She glanced at Eden, who was fishing her wallet from her purse, then typed I'm really bad at pool. Hopeless.

And that was no joke. She could never seem to get the cue to balance right on her fingers. It inevitably slipped, ruining her shot.

A few seconds later another text arrived.

I'll teach you.

When Lucy looked up, Eden was eyeing her with a knowing look. "He's texting you, isn't he?"

"He invited me to play pool. But I don't know. It's a little weird, you know, with Zac here and all."

"I haven't seen Zac since I've been here. Besides, he's been perfectly clear where he stands."

Even the gently delivered words were a kick in the gut. "True enough. Besides, Nick and I agreed we'd just be friends."

Eden nudged her foot under the table. "Go play. Have fun. I have to pick up Micah anyway before he completely wears out my dad." She scooted out of the booth. "Call me if you want to talk."

After Eden left, Lucy drained the last of her iced tea and headed toward the poolroom. Nick introduced her to his friends, and they set up a game. Nick broke the balls, sinking two solids.

When it was her turn, he helped her choose a ball that was close to the corner pocket. She bent over to line up the shot.

"Wait, wait, wait," Nick said. "You're too close to the table. Scoot back." He tugged her away from the table. "Okay, you want your hands like this." He leaned over her, his arms coming around her. "Spread out those fingers. There you go."

His voice was low in her ear, his hands over hers on the cue. "Okay, a nice, smooth stroke. Let's do it together. Nice aim, here we go . . ."

They pulled back the cue and brought it forward. *Crack.* The cue ball kissed the six and shot off at an angle. The ball rolled across the felt and dropped into the corner pocket.

"I did it!"

He backed away as she straightened, giving her a high five and a half smile. "Awesome, Lucy. You got the touch. Okay, now line this next one up. Which one you going after?"

"The four?"

"Great choice. Line it up. Spread your fingers. Yeah, that looks good. Now give it a nice, even stroke."

She pulled back the cue and followed through. The cue ball touched the four, but the ball bounced off the corner of the pocket.

"Nice try, nice try." Nick squeezed her shoulder.

Nick's friends beat them the first and second

games. Nick continued to give her pointers, and by the third game Lucy was on fire. They won the game hands down. She could tell even Nick was impressed by her progress.

She lost all track of time. So much so that she was caught off guard when some of the lights in the dining room went off. She was surprised to see the restaurant empty and one of the staff turning chairs up onto the tables.

"Closing time," Zac growled on his way past the room. He looked like he'd been ridden hard and put away wet.

Was he just tired and ready to close, or was he vexed that she was spending time with Nick? Well, he couldn't have it both ways. Either he wanted her or he didn't. And he'd made it perfectly clear that he didn't.

She said goodbye to Nick and his friends. Zac had gone into the kitchen, and she wasn't yet tired, so she finished stacking the chairs on the tables.

When she was finished, she peeked out the front window. The reporters had given up for the night. She should get the mail. Her ATM card and new credit card were supposed to arrive any day. She was down to her last twelve dollars, and she didn't want to have to borrow money. She already owed Zac far too much.

As she neared the front door, Zac came through the kitchen pushing a mop and bucket, his eyes drifting around the room. "Thanks for putting up the chairs."

"You're welcome. I'm going to get the mail."

"All right."

The night was cool, a fresh breeze skating over her skin. She crossed her arms against the chill and drew in a deep breath of tangy sea air. Crickets chirped in the nearby grass. She crossed the gravel lot, her shoes crunching on the pebbles.

A car door shut, drawing her eyes to the lone car in the parking lot, a dark sedan. A man walked toward her, crossing a puddle of light.

Her steps faltered as he walked between her and the Roadhouse, trapping her.

A cold shiver of fear washed over her skin. "I'm not giving a comment, so you need to be on your way."

He stopped in a puddle of light, a wrinkle creasing his brow. "Lucy—"

"I mean it. I'll call the sheriff if you don't leave now."

"You don't even recognize me, do you?"

Lucy shifted, her gaze taking in his short wind-blown hair, his perfectly oval face, his dark eyes. He was dressed for the office, his tie loose as if he'd tugged on it.

"Lucy . . . it's me. Brad."

Somehow hearing he was her ex-fiancé didn't make her feel one iota better. She tightened her arms across her stomach. "What are you doing here?"

He walked toward her. "I was worried about you. You haven't returned my calls."

She'd made the mistake of giving him her new phone number after he'd called Zac's line repeatedly.

Brad had gotten within a few feet of her. She stepped back. "I know, I'm sorry. I just . . . Things are a little crazy right now. I'm trying to settle in and figure things out."

"You don't remember me at all?"

She looked at his face now that he was closer. The security light made harsh angles of his nose and cheekbones. Gleamed off his high forehead.

She shook her head. "I'm sorry."

"I can't believe you don't—" He shook his head, frowning. "We were *engaged*," he said as if that fact trumped her traumatic brain injury.

"I don't even remember moving to Portland. I know it's a lot to take in, but I can't help it."

His eyes moved to her hand, and his lips tightened. "You're not wearing my ring."

"We're not engaged anymore. I—I'll give it back."

"You should come back home. I can help you remember."

But she didn't want to remember. Not him or Portland.

But remembering would mean she wouldn't

be stuck on Zac anymore. It would put her out of her misery. If she remembered, would she go through with a wedding with this man she didn't even hold a warm thought for now?

He stepped forward. "I can help you, Lucy. I'll be patient with you, and I'll help you deal with the reporters. They won't bother you in Portland. I'll make sure of it."

Her eyes zeroed in on his as a knot tightened in her belly. "It was you."

"What was me?"

She took a step back. "You alerted the media. You told them where to find me."

He held his palms up. "Hey. I had nothing to do with—"

"Why would you do that?" Her voice crescendoed.

He walked toward her, a resolute look on his face. "I didn't, Lucy. I came by earlier and heard some talk at the café. That's all."

She didn't know what to believe, but her feet stopped as her back hit the mailbox.

Zac pulled the mop from the bucket and slopped it across the floor. His hands worked on automatic, his mind replaying the moment earlier when he'd barreled out of the kitchen. When his eyes fell on Lucy in the poolroom. Nick bent over her, his body too close, one arm around her, the other over her hand on the back of the cue.

Zac's muscles had gone tight, his jaw aching as

his teeth clenched together. For a brief second he imagined picking up the guy by his collar and britches and tossing him like a bowling ball down the front walkway, straight into the reporters.

Strike.

Instead he patiently mollified an elderly customer, giving him 50 percent off his tab, his eyes only drifting to Lucy again when her laughter rang out. He glowered at Nick as he gave her a double high five, practically turning the moment into a hand-holding session.

Every time he glanced over at the poolroom, his blood pressure soared. Lucy seemed to be having a great time, laughing and chatting as if she hadn't a care in the world. And it didn't take much to see that Nick was smitten with her. He hardly took his eyes off her long enough to get a shot in.

She'd distanced herself from Zac after their kiss, not that he could blame her. He'd pushed her away first. Right into Nick's arms, apparently. Did she really like him? Zac couldn't find fault with him, and that really rankled.

Well, he's in for a rough ride. Getting tangled up with Lucy Lovett was a lot easier than getting untangled. He was living proof.

Zac swished the mop across the floor. He should be glad she was moving on with a guy like Nick. That was exactly what needed to happen. She thought she was still in love with Zac, but she really wasn't. She'd moved on when she'd left

Summer Harbor, her heart just didn't remember. Maybe she wouldn't get her memory back at all. Maybe Nick was just what she needed to get over him for good.

The thought poked like a hundred burrs into his stomach. He jammed the mop back into the bucket. *Either you want her or you don't, Callahan. Make up your mind.*

But it wasn't that simple. Nothing about Lucy was simple.

But it was good. Or it had been, once upon a time. So good he could hardly stand the thought of her with someone else.

Which was why she needed to get out of here ASAP. Her apartment would be ready next week, and the moment couldn't come soon enough. As much as he hated the thought of putting her out there with those parasites still in town, he had to let go—really let go—of her. She wasn't his responsibility anymore. She was an adult, albeit one with a minor brain injury. She could tak care of herself.

He glanced at the front door. She still wasn't back from getting the mail. She'd been gone too long. A tight fist coiled in his gut when he thought of those reporters. Surely they were tucked away at the hotel by now. They wouldn't hassle her, not after Sheriff Colton had warned them.

He dropped the mop and went to open the front door. His eyes fell on two figures across the parking lot by the mailbox, just outside a beam of light.

The man reached out, taking hold of Lucy's arm. Lucy squirmed away, but his grip held.

"Hey!" Zac bolted off the porch. "Let go of her!"

The man turned, glowering at Zac, not relinquishing his hold. "I'm her *fiancé*."

"I don't care who you are—get your hands off her." His strides made quick work of the distance.

The man's hand fell as he neared, no doubt gauging Zac's size and realizing Zac had him by a head.

Lucy's face was white and tense. She stepped away, her hands shaking.

For the second time tonight Zac wanted to pummel somebody.

The man threw his shoulders back, trying to act bigger than he was. "Who are you?"

"Zac Callahan, and you're standing on my property. I expect you to rectify that real soon."

Bozo stepped beside Lucy. "We have some things to settle. This is really none of your business."

Zac homed in on Lucy. She was pinching her bottom lip. Her pale face glowed in the moon-light.

"Lucy, you want to talk to this guy?"

Lucy's eyes toggled between them, settling on Zac. "No," she whispered.

"That's it, pal, you're out of here."

"Come on, Lucy . . . ," the guy wheedled.

But Zac grabbed the back of his collar and walked him toward the only car in the lot. "You're not welcome back here. If she wants you, she has your number."

The guy pulled away, and Zac let him go. He walked toward his car, tossing a sneer over his shoulder after he opened the door. "I'll be back."

"At your own risk, buddy."

Once he left, Zac guided Lucy back inside. She was shaking, and he didn't think it was from the chill in the air.

He pulled a chair from the table and turned it over. "Sit down. Did he hurt you?"

"No, I'm fine." Lucy sank into the chair.

He perched his hip on the table. "What'd he have to say?"

She shrugged. Some of her color had returned. "He wants me to come back to Portland. I think he may have alerted the media."

"To get you to go back with him?"

"Maybe. I don't know."

"I don't like the guy," he said, then wished he'd kept his mouth shut. Lucy might think he was jealous. And that wasn't it. At least, he didn't think so.

"He's probably just hurt after—everything that's happened."

Zac didn't buy it. There was something in the guy's eyes. Something ruthless and hard. If

Zac's fiancée had gotten amnesia, he'd like to think he'd be patient and concerned rather than trying to force his own will down her throat.

And he hadn't liked the look on Brad's face when he'd made that parting threat. Was he capable of danger? He'd grabbed Lucy, and for no apparent reason other than he didn't like her answers.

Between the reporters and Brad, the timing of Lucy's leaving couldn't be worse. He clasped his hands on the back of his neck, closed his eyes in a long blink. He couldn't believe he was about to say this.

"Maybe you should stay here awhile longer."

Lucy popped to her feet. "No."

He blinked at the speed of her reply. "You see the look on his face? You might've been engaged to him, but you don't know anything about him, Lucy. Maybe he's got a violent streak. Maybe that's why you didn't go through with the wedding."

Lucy shook her head.

"He's not going to give up, and if you're alone in an apartment, what protection will you have? Plus you've got a horde of reporters following you around town."

Lucy crossed her arms, piercing him with those blue eyes. "I'm not staying, Zac."

"Don't be so stubborn."

She lifted her set chin. "This isn't working out —for either of us. I'm leaving next week, and that's all there is to it."

He watched her go, her slender shoulders stiff, and sighed. When Zac wanted her to leave, she insisted on staying, and when he wanted her to stay, she insisted on leaving. That was just the way it had always been with Lucy.

Chapter 24

Lucy dabbed on pink lipstick and pressed her lips together. After fluffing her hair she stood back and surveyed her image. Subtle makeup enhanced her eyes and colored her cheeks, and tousled waves fell over her shoulders. She looked all put together in her pale blue sundress. But inside she was conflicted. She was going out with an awfully nice fellow, but the man she really wanted was right here.

And he wants nothing to do with you, Lucy Lovett. So just get over it.

She capped her lipstick and left her room. She'd wait for Nick on the front stoop. Maybe Nick was just a friend, but it was still awkward. And if she was honest, she had to admit that Nick was awfully flirty for a friend.

Oomph! She bounced off Zac's muscular chest as he exited his office.

He steadied her with his hands. "Sorry."

His fingers burned through the light sweater,

heating her arms, and his familiar spicy scent wrapped around her like a warm hug.

He lifted his hands abruptly as if he'd been burned.

"My fault." She'd been flying down the hall, her mind elsewhere.

His eyes swept her body, a glimmer of male appreciation registering in his eyes. "You look nice."

Her cheeks heated. She clutched her purse to her stomach. "Thank you."

He impaled her with those stormy gray eyes. "Got a date tonight?"

She cleared her throat. "I'm going out with Nick. We're taking his boat over to Folly Shoals for supper at the Seafood Shack, then we're going dancing at the Hotel Tourmaline. There's some kind of shindig going on over there. I didn't really pay much mind to what it is exactly, but I wore my dancing shoes." She kicked up her foot, giving a chuckle that sounded as nervous as she felt.

Hush up, Lucy.

He gave a tight smile. "Well. Sounds like a good time. Have fun."

"I reckon I will."

He let her precede him down the hall. Her legs were shaky from the brief encounter.

"Lucy . . . ," he said.

She turned as she reached the busy dining room. Had she heard something in his voice?

Regret? Longing? She looked into his eyes, searching. They held her hostage for a long moment. Her heart beat up into her throat, and her chest tightened with want.

Something flared in his eyes, something warm and hopeful. But just as quickly, it was gone. "Nick's a nice guy. You should give him a chance."

Heat scorched her cheeks as though he'd just slapped her. She blinked against the burning behind her eyes as something dark pooled in her belly. Nothing like the man you loved pushing you off on someone else.

But even as the thought formed, something else swelled deep in her belly. Something that felt heaps better. Something red and determined and just a little bit peeved.

"You're right, Zac. You're absolutely right."

Chapter 25

Lucy sneaked away from the Roadhouse early the next Monday, meeting Eden by the marina for their jog. The reporters had yet to show up, but she'd tucked her hair under a ball cap anyway.

"So . . . ," Eden said as they ramped up to a brisk walk. "Don't keep me in suspense. How'd your date with Nick go? I noticed he sat with you in church yesterday."

A salty breeze blew a tendril across Lucy's face, and she swept it back. "It wasn't a date, but it was really nice." She injected some enthusiasm into her voice. "We had a lot of fun. He's a good dancer, and we never ran out of things to talk about. We have some of the same interests, and he's got a real good sense of humor."

"And . . ."

"And . . . that was it. He was great. It was nice."

"Nice."

"What? There's not a thing wrong with nice."

Eden spared her a look. "Nice is how it feels to kick off your heels after church on Sundays. It's what your friends say about a bad haircut. It's what—"

"All right, all right. I don't know what you want me to say. Nick's just a friend. I'm in love with Zac. That feeling's not going to go away anytime soon." She gave a wry grin. "Unless my memory comes back. And then, apparently, it'll disappear faster than a hot knife through butter."

"Sorry, didn't mean to push. I just hate seeing you like this. There aren't any sparks at all with Nick?"

"Not really. I mean, maybe something could come of it someday. They say the best relationships start as friendships, right?"

She remembered the instantaneous spark she'd had with Zac. She'd wanted to fall into his smoky-gray eyes and drown. She felt a pang of loss.

"Sure."

Their conversation slowed as their pace picked up. Zac had been nowhere to be found when she arrived home from her date. She'd tried to have a good time. Maybe too hard. Nick had been a little flirtatious, and she didn't want to lead him on. Had she not been clear enough about being friends?

Her eyes caught a flash of blue, and she saw Brittany Conley swinging on her front porch. Lucy lifted a hand and got a wave back in return. She'd run into the girl riding her bike downtown before the media had shown up. They'd talked a few minutes about basketball. Brittany hadn't made the school team, but Lucy encouraged her to keep practicing her skills.

Awhile later, they slowed to a walk as they entered town again, catching their breath. Lucy shelved her hands on her hips, breathing through a hitch in her side. Her endurance was improving. She was only a little more winded than Eden.

"I have about a half hour," Eden said. "Want to grab breakfast at Joe's?"

"Sure." The center didn't open until ten, and the longer she stayed away from the Roadhouse the better.

"Beau told me your ex-fiancé paid a visit a few days ago."

"It was really peculiar. I felt kind of intimidated by him. I was awful glad when Zac came out and shooed him off."

"Is he still in town?"

"I'm not sure. He hasn't come around anymore. I'm going to mail the engagement ring back to him. Maybe he'll leave me be then."

"Maybe you should reconsider that new apartment. Just until things settle down. Beau said he threatened to come back."

"I think that was just his pride talking." She didn't want to think about that today. "So what about you . . . any wedding plans yet?"

"Oh!" Eden said as they turned toward the diner. "I can't believe I forgot to tell you. We set a date yesterday. August sixth of next year."

"Isn't that just something! Let me know if I can help with the planning."

"We're going to keep it pretty simple. I already had the big white wedding, and it didn't work out so well."

"I'm surprised you're going to wait a whole year. You and Beau seem like you can't get enough of each other."

"Oh, we can't. And while a part of me can't wait to start our happily-ever-after, the saner part of me knows I need time. My first marriage was so difficult."

"You've alluded to that. Is it hard to think about getting hitched again?"

"Not in the way you think. Beau's so different from Antonio. He was controlling and emotionally abusive. I still kind of chafe at restrictions.

Even prudent ones. I lost myself for a few years, and I'm still finding my way back."

"You seem so independent and confident," Lucy said as they reached Frumpy Joe's. "I'd never guess that you struggle with something like that."

Eden tossed Lucy a saucy smile as she held open the door. "Fake it till you make it."

The sound of talking and clinking silverware rose as they entered the diner, and the heavenly aromas of bacon and syrup teased her nostrils. Lucy's stomach let out a hearty growl as they made their way to an empty booth in the back.

Margaret LeFebvre was in the third booth. Lucy hadn't seen the owner of the Primrose Inn since she'd tried to apply for the desk-clerk position. When their eyes met, she gave Lucy a warm smile.

Mildly surprised, Lucy returned the smile. Mrs. Parker and her daughter Millie said hello to them as they passed. Both of them.

Maybe the town really was warming up to her. The thought lifted her mood.

Charlotte Dupree approached as soon as they slid into the corner booth. Her dyed red hair was Southern poufy today, and her charm bracelet tinkled as she set down two glasses of water. "I thought you girls could use a drink. I saw you jogging by. Know what you'd like?" Her eyes warmed as she smiled at Lucy. "Our Belgian blueberry waffles are on special—I know you're partial to those."

"Oh . . . why, sure, that sounds just divine." Lucy closed her menu and took a long drink as Eden ordered. Had she stepped back in time? Why was everyone being so cordial?

As soon as Charlotte left, Lucy nailed Eden with a look. "Is it just me, or is something awful strange going on?"

"Now that you mention it . . ." Eden leaned over the table and lowered her voice. "Mrs. Miller keeps looking back here. We'll ask Charlotte what's going on. If anyone knows, she will. News flies around this place like a pinball through a machine."

When Charlotte brought their coffee by, Eden snagged her arm. "Hey, Charlotte, is there something going on we don't know about? Everyone's kind of acting funny."

Her eyes toggled between the women, settling on Lucy with a sympathetic smile. "I guess you haven't heard. There's an article in one of those gossip rags that just hit the stands."

Lucy's stomach hit the floor. "What kind of article?"

"A stupid one, that's what kind." She patted Lucy's shoulder. "Don't you worry. I sent Joe to the Shop 'n' Save this morning to buy up every copy, and we pitched them in the Dumpster." She gave Lucy a final pat before she walked away.

Eden was on her phone. "I'm looking it up now."

"This can't be good." Wasn't her life in enough turmoil? Why did anyone even care what was going on with her?

"Okay, I found it." She winced. "Oh boy."

"What?"

Eden shifted to Lucy's side of the booth, and they read together.

Audrey Lovett's Niece
Seeking Solace from Lovers

It seems Lucy Lovett, look-alike great-niece of sixties icon Audrey Lovett, has plenty of company since she ditched her fiancé and allegedly acquired amnesia four weeks ago. It has since come to light that she has not only one, but two former fiancés, both of whom she jilted at the altar.

Since her jaunt to Summer Harbor, Maine, she's been keeping company with her most recently jilted fiancé, Brad Martin, while shacking up with her formerly jilted fiancé, Zac Callahan. And if that's not enough action for Lovett, she's also dating handsome local physician Nick Donahue.

It seems amnesia may be the least of Miss Lovett's problems—if she even has amnesia at all.

A quiet squeak exited Lucy's throat. They'd not only dragged her name through the mud, they'd made Zac and Nick look like her playthings. Heat climbed her cheeks, making her glad she was facing the corner and not the diner full of customers, all of whom had no doubt *read this humiliating article!*

Eden scrolled down to the pictures that accompanied the article. One of Zac walking her into the Roadhouse, hand on the small of her back. One of her and Brad in the Roadhouse parking lot, his hands on her shoulders. Somehow the photo looked like a tender moment instead of the altercation it actually was. And one of Nick as she'd hugged him goodbye Saturday night.

Those vermin were stalking her! And everyone in Summer Harbor must think so badly of her now. She grabbed the menu and fanned her face.

Eden set her hand on Lucy's clenched fist. "Nobody believes these stupid tabloids anyway. At least Charlotte bought up all the copies . . ."

"She can't buy up all the copies in the whole country. And it's online for anyone to see." She gave Eden a pained look. "They made me out to be some kind of—"

"Don't say it."

Lucy dropped her menu, pinching her lip. "But everything they said was true. They just spun it all to make it sound bad, and they suggested I don't even have amnesia! Do they think this

217

is some kind of game? Why would I do that?"

Eden rubbed her hand. "They're just trying to sell their sick magazine, honey, that's all."

"Why didn't I just give them a stupid statement?"

"That only would've given them more things to twist around. Nobody's going to believe you're the girl they made you out to be. Not anybody around here." Eden's eyes squeezed in a wince. "At least everyone's being nicer to you . . . They're sympathetic. This is a good town. Good people. They'll stand behind you. You'll see."

Lucy had to pull herself together. There was nothing she could do about the article except hold her head high the way Mama had taught her.

When the owner returned with their meals, Lucy pinned a smile to her face. "Charlotte, thank you ever so much for confiscating the magazines. I so appreciate your kindness."

"Why, of course, honey. You enjoy your food now."

Her appetite was gone, but she forced herself to eat. Eden tried to distract her with wedding talk, but Lucy had a hard time focusing. When they were almost finished eating, the bell above the diner tinkled.

"Oh no," Eden said, looking over Lucy's shoulder.

Lucy turned around. Two of the reporters had just entered.

Wonderful. A public showdown. Just what she

needed—more publicity and gossip. Lucy shrank in her seat.

"I don't think they know you're here. They're probably just here for breakfast."

Maybe she could leave without drawing their attention.

Who was she kidding? It was a one-room diner with fifteen booths, and the cap she wore wasn't magic.

"I'm afraid we're all full up." Charlotte's raised voice carried across the diner. "You'll have to eat elsewhere."

"There's two open booths right there," one of the men said.

"Those are reserved," Charlotte said without looking. "You'd best get on out of here."

"Now, listen—"

"No, you listen. You and your kind aren't welcome here. Not for breakfast, lunch, supper, or so much as a slice of pie. If I see you in here again, I'll take my broom to you. Now scram!"

Lucy peeked over her shoulder. Charlotte held up her broom, a stormy look on her face.

The men glowered at her as they left, but the patrons gave Charlotte Dupree a quiet round of applause. A pleasant feeling swelled inside Lucy's stomach.

Eden put a hand over hers. "What'd I tell you? Keep your chin up, Lucy Lovett. You've got a whole town standing behind you."

Chapter 26

At the tap on the door Zac looked up from the employee schedule he was working on.

"Come in."

Megan entered. At least he thought it was Megan from what he could see behind the gigantic wildflower arrangement she carried. "Delivery for Lucy. Where you want me to put it?"

Zac's lips pressed together. So Nick was giving it the old full-court press. Unfortunately for Nick, Lucy was allergic to daisies.

"Put them right here. I'll give them to her when she gets home."

Did you really just say "home"?

He scratched behind his ear. He loved having her here. He hated having her here. He didn't know how both could be true, but they were.

After Megan left, he returned to the work schedule, juggling the staff around, cognizant of child-care schedules, night classes, and second jobs. The sweet, cloying scent of flowers was a constant distraction.

Reaching out, he turned the vase until he found the envelope. It only had her name. He wondered what Nick had written, then he scolded himself. It didn't matter. She needed to move on. They both did.

She'd handled the gossip-rag ordeal with her shoulders back. The events of the past month would've knocked a lesser woman to her knees, but Lucy was strong. He was proud of her. She had a job and was getting her new apartment tomorrow. He still thought she should stay, given the circumstances, but that was her decision. She was a grown woman.

And not his.

His eyes drifted to the flowers, narrowing as they focused on the envelope. He was tempted to throw the whole thing in the trash. She wouldn't be able to keep them in her room anyway.

Not cool, Callahan.

Rising from his seat, he moved the flowers to the floor in front of his desk where he wouldn't have to look at them. He worked through the rest of the afternoon, catching up on paperwork, filling out a workers' comp form, and running out to the front to put out fires. Not literal ones, thank God.

Later a tap on his door made him check the time. He'd had his head down for two hours straight. He rubbed his neck as he called, "Come in."

Lucy peeked through the open door, looking prettier than any woman had a right to, with her wide blue eyes and flawless skin.

"Hey." Her sweet Southern drawl made two syllables of the word. "Megan said there was a delivery for me today." Even as she said the words, her eyes fell to the flower arrangement on the floor. "Oh!" Her dimples appeared as she entered the room, bringing her appley scent with her.

He tried not to let her hopeful smile get to him. "Don't get too close. Unless you're looking to have a sneezefest."

"Well, I have to read the card, now, don't I?"

Of course she did. He watched as she slid the card from the envelope, bracing himself against the little secret smile that would curl her lips. But as her eyes scanned the card, her lips fell. Some emotion tightened the corners of her eyes.

She stuffed the card into the envelope, struggling to get it back in. Her hands were trembling, making her efforts difficult. Her motions became more frantic.

"Hey." He propelled himself to his feet, rounding the desk. "What's wrong?"

She gave up on the card, clenching it in her hand. "Nothing."

"Is it from Nick?"

"No."

He frowned, a new thought occurring, one he liked even less. *Brad.* "Let me see."

He reached for it but she hung on tight. "Come on, Lucy." He snatched it from her grip and pulled at the cockeyed card. His eyes scanned the words.

Can't wait to see you again. All my love, Brad

Lucy crossed her arms over her chest, tilting her chin up in that familiar display of bravery.

Even if he hadn't noticed the glimmer of distress in her glassy blue eyes, he would've seen right through it.

"I don't understand," he said. "Why are you upset? Because he says he's coming back?"

"I'm not upset." She tilted her lips in a smile, but she couldn't erase the troubled look from her eyes.

"Your hands are shaking, and you're sucking all the oxygen out of the room. Talk to me, Lucy."

She held his gaze for a long moment, then she slowly crumbled. Her shoulders fell and her lips quivered. She rubbed her nose. "I don't know. I don't know why I'm upset."

He waved the card. "There's nothing ominous here. Did something happen today? Did you remember something?"

"*No*. And I'm getting mighty tired of being asked that question."

"Then why did you react like—?"

"I don't know! I just read the words and a shiver went up my spine. I had a bit of a scare. It doesn't make any sense. I'm just being plain silly."

He studied her. Lucy was a lot of things, but she wasn't silly or irrational. "No, you're not. Maybe you don't remember, but some part of you remembers something. You gotta trust your gut."

She palmed the side of her throat, threading her fingers up into her hair. "I don't want to see him anymore."

"You have to tell him that."

"I did!" She rubbed her nose.

Zac frowned. A niggle of worry squirmed in his belly. Maybe she hadn't been firm enough. Maybe she'd tried to spare his feelings with her Southern diplomacy.

Lucy reared back. *"A-choo! A-choo!"*

Zac sighed. He grabbed the arrangement and took it out of the office. He threw open the metal back door and took great satisfaction in heaving the flowers into the alley Dumpster, vase and all.

When he returned, Lucy was in the hall, blotting her eyes with a tissue. *"A-choo!"* She sniffled. "You could've given them to someone else."

Her eyes were getting bloodshot, the tip of her nose turning a delicate pink. And still she was the prettiest thing he'd ever seen.

There was a man harassing her and a group of reporters stalking her. He envisioned her alone at the Misty Mountain apartment complex, set back off the road in the middle of nowhere. No security, no friends nearby. What would stop a man who wanted her badly enough? Did Brad really only want to win her back? Zac had a hard time believing that.

Lucy dabbed the corners of her itchy eyes. She couldn't even describe the feeling that had come over her when she'd read the card. It made no sense, but she couldn't deny the shiver of fear and the heavy feeling that had closed in around her.

"Lucy," Zac said. "I think you need to reconsider that apartment."

A different kind of feeling settled in her stomach. A different kind of fear. The kind that involved her heart. The kind that made the walls of her chest close in.

Did it mean anything that Zac was fretting over her? Or was it just his kind heart at work?

And why on earth does the distinction even matter, Lucy Lovett?

"We've been through this," she said.

"I know it's not ideal. But just until things settle down. Until Brad goes away and stays away. Until the reporters crawl back into what-ever hole they came out of."

"Some of them went home already."

"But some of them are still here, and they're still stalking you. And who's to say Brad isn't doing the same thing?"

The thought sent a shiver up her spine. She rubbed her palm over the tight muscles of her chest.

"I'm not trying to scare you, but I don't trust him. There's something about him, and you obviously feel it too."

He was right, she knew that. Logic said it was safer to stay here. But her heart begged her to leave, even while she fell headlong into those smoky-gray eyes.

She shook her head.

"Then what about leasing something else? Something in town where it's not so—"

"I can't afford that."

"Well, you can't afford to take risks either. We don't know this Brad or what he's capable of. Just for a few weeks, Lucy. You know I'm right."

He was making sense. It was the reasonable thing to do. It wasn't like she was sharing an apartment with him. They were on separate floors, for heaven's sake. She could stay in her room when she was home.

Home. First off, Lucy Lovett, you have to stop thinking like that.

"You know it's the smart thing to do. I'll keep to my own space, and you can keep to yours. We're both adults. We can handle it. Shoot, haven't we handled it for a month already?"

Had they? She was still in love with him, and he still had the power to hurt her with a mere look. Even now the way he was looking at her, like he really cared about her, was tugging at her heart, making her hope.

And nothing but pain lay that way.

She wrenched her eyes away. She just wouldn't look at him. Wouldn't go near him. How much longer could this Brad guy try to hang on? He lived and worked three hours away. She wasn't some grand prize that he'd pine away for her for the rest of his days.

"All right." She stared at her pink toenails through the peep-toed heels. "I'll stay awhile longer. Thank you for your hospitality, Zac." She turned and left before he could respond.

She'd just have to get it through Brad's head that it was over between them. The reporters would get bored with her soon enough, and then she could resume her life. Somehow the thought didn't inspire the hopeful feeling she'd expected.

Chapter 27

Lucy's phone rang later that evening as she was rehanging the clothing she'd packed for her move. She checked the screen and saw Nick's name.

"Well, hey there, Nick." She dredged up a tired smile.

"Hi, Lucy. How was your day?"

"Not too bad. The center's getting pretty busy. I hardly had a moment to rest, but that's the way I prefer it."

"Summer's in full swing. We're supposed to have great weather this weekend. I was thinking we should take advantage of it. Take a hike out to Echo Lake, pack a picnic or something."

"Why, that sounds like a wonderful idea." She wondered if they could manage to get away without being followed. She pulled her shoes from the box and lined them up at the bottom of her closet.

The closet.

"So, guess who has a half day off tomorrow?" he asked. "I thought I could help you move into your new apartment."

She stopped, her nude Kate Spade sling-backs dangling from her fingers.

"I could even run you to Portland to get your stuff out of storage. You know, do the big move all in one day. How's that sound?"

"Oh, Nick, I . . ."

"I know we've only just met, but I figured you could use the help. Plus I happen to have a buddy with a trailer."

She squeezed the phone. "Nick . . . I'm not moving. Not yet. There's just . . . a lot going on with the reporters and such. I'm sure you saw the article in the tabloid yesterday—everyone did. They're stalking me."

"There are only a few of them now, right? They'll probably be gone within a week."

"I know, but . . ." Boy, she hadn't wanted to get into this with him. "It's not just the reporters. It seems my ex-fiancé—um, Brad—" *How sad that you have to clarify.* "He hasn't quite given up on things. I mean, it's totally over between us, but as you know, he visited over the weekend and—"

"Yeah, I saw the picture." His tone bordered on sarcastic.

"That wasn't what it looked like at all. He—he kinda scared me. Then today he sent flowers."

"He sent you flowers?"

"I told him I don't want to see him anymore, but he's not taking no for an answer."

"Lucy . . ."

"I don't want any more to do with him."

"So you're depending on your other ex-fiancé for protection."

There was nothing ugly about his tone, but the words put a pinch in her chest anyway. Guilt? "That's not fair," she said softly. "It's not the way the article made it sound."

He exhaled long and slow. "I wasn't judging, Lucy. And I know better than to believe some gossip rag."

"I'm sorry. The article didn't show you in a good light. You must be taking a lot of heat from your friends."

"How can you even know how you really feel about this Brad when you can't remember your relationship? You were about to marry him."

"I left him before the wedding."

"Look . . . Lucy." He sighed into the pause. "I think this is just too much for me. I like you; you're a lot of fun. But you've got a lot going on right now. You can't help but be confused."

"I'm not confused." Why did everyone think that? She knew perfectly well what she wanted. Who she wanted.

He just didn't want her back.

"But I did tell you I wasn't ready to date—that I just wanted to be friends."

"You did. But if I'm honest, I was hoping things might change. I like you."

She dropped the shoes to the floor, pushing them into line beside the others. She'd been afraid of that. She should've listened to her gut.

"Bad timing," he said.

She sighed. "I'm sorry if I misled you."

"You didn't. But maybe we should just give things a rest for now. You've got a lot going on, and the last thing you need is another complication."

That was the truth if ever she'd heard it. She gave a humorless laugh.

They wound up the phone call a few minutes later, and Lucy took the last of her shoes from the box. Truthfully, Nick was never going to be anything more than a friend, because her heart was already spoken for.

Chapter 28

Zac pushed a table to the stage area with the others, then grabbed a mike and stand from the storage closet. He was serving as the sponsor and host of the firehouse fundraiser. The volunteer squad had moved from the old, outdated fire station and needed equipment for their new building. Paige had volunteered to head up the event. It was for a good cause.

Speak of the devil . . . she returned from his office where she was stashing the ladies' picnic baskets until auction time. Since it was a blind auction, they were trying to keep the baskets' owners anonymous, but inevitably some of the couples would cheat.

Paige had already set up tables for two all over the beach, in the square, and on his deck. Once couples had their baskets, they'd retreat to their own romantic lunch.

"Looking great, Zac," Paige said. "Sara and Lauren are stationed out front to receive the baskets."

"Think we need more tables up here?"

"We can always add more if we have too many baskets. I hope we do. We need a good turnout to raise all that money."

He slid the mike into the stand. "It'll be great. You know the town'll come out in support."

Beau entered with Eden and Aunt Trudy. After they traded greetings, they helped Zac shift tables around.

"So . . . ," Paige said a few minutes later. "Whose basket are you bidding on, Zac?"

"Oh no. I'm not bidding on anything."

Paige shelved her fists on her hips. "You have to bid. You're the sponsor."

"Exactly. I'm doing my part already."

"Which means you have to set an example. Bid often, bid high."

He narrowed his eyes at her. "The last time you said that, I ended up having lunch with Myrtle Franke."

"Who is a perfectly nice woman," Aunt Trudy added.

He shot her a look. "She pinched my butt. Twice."

Beau snickered, covering his mouth when Zac glowered at him.

"I'm sure she didn't mean anything by it," Aunt Trudy said. "She's eighty-some years old, for heaven's sake. She gets a little confused."

"Confused, my—"

"You should bid on Miss Trudy's basket." Eden gave his aunt a look. "She's got deviled eggs, pulled pork sandwiches—"

"La-la-la-la-la," Paige said, putting her hands over her ears. "I don't hear a thing."

"—and apple pie," Eden finished. "I know you like apple pie."

"But I—oh yes," Aunt Trudy said. "Bid on my basket, Zac. Maybe I'll be spared yet another awkward luncheon with the sheriff."

"Well . . . I suppose." He hated to disappoint Sheriff Colton, but Paige was probably right about his setting an example. "All right. I'll do it."

Eden clapped her hands together, beaming. "It's settled then. I'm going to go see if Lucy needs help with her basket."

Ah, yes, Lucy and her basket. Wouldn't it be fun to watch Nick and who-knew-who-else battle for lunch with his sweet Southern girl?

He squeezed his eyes closed. *Not yours anymore, Callahan.* He heaved a sigh and went back to arranging tables, trying to ignore the fist that tightened around his heart.

Lucy leaned back in her chair as Beau handed off an auctioned basket and Sara Porter handed him another. He was doing a great job as emcee. The place was standing room only, and the smell of coffee lingered in the air, mixed with a hint of male desperation.

There were only several baskets left. There'd been a lot of laughter, teasing, and poking as the men bid against each other just to rile up their friends. Beau played along, making it even more entertaining. She'd initially thought the picnic auction was too old-fashioned to fly, but it was turning out to be a hoot. So fascinating to watch the interactions and dynamics of the townspeople at work.

Dylan Moore held the top bid so far. He'd paid ninety dollars for Paige's basket. Even if Lucy hadn't recognized the insulated cooler, she would've identified its owner by the twin flags of color on Paige's face as the handsome Dylan bid with confidence.

"This next beautiful basket is sure to be a

winner," Beau said into the mike. "It features fried chicken, potato salad, and, mmm, mmm, chocolate cream pie. My favorite. Unfortunately for you fellas, this one's all mine. I'll start—and end—the bidding with a crisp fifty-dollar bill. Thank you very much."

Eden beamed at her fiancé as a chorus of boos sounded.

"Beau!" Paige scolded from her spot against the wall.

He gave her an exaggerated shrug as he handed off the basket.

"Moving on . . . ," Beau said with a wily smile. "Ah, what have we here?"

Lucy's pulse kicked up at the sight of herbasket. What if no one bid on it? She'd be so humiliated.

Beau read the label. "Pulled pork sandwiches, deviled eggs, and apple pie! Looks like some lucky winner's about to have a tasty meal. Let's start the bidding at ten dollars. Who'd like to start us off?"

She surreptitiously scanned the room, heat climbing her cheeks, as the silence seemed to draw on forever.

Zac raised his hand. "Ten dollars."

Her heart flopped over. She stared at his profile. Why was he bidding on her basket? Maybe he didn't know it was hers. But he hadn't bid on any others. Her head snapped to the front, her cheeks burning.

"Twenty!" Eddie from the garage shouted.

Beau held up the basket, sniffing. "Smells awfully nice, fellas. I think you can do better than that."

"Twenty-five," Zac said.

"Thirty!"

Zac pressed his lips together.

"Thirty-five!" someone behind her called.

"Look at that pretty ribbon," Beau said. "If the lady's gone to all that trouble on the outside, imagine what's in store on the inside. Not many baskets left, guys. Better open up your wallets."

"Forty," Zac said.

Lucy pinched her lower lip as her heart found a new gear. What was going on? Had he changed his mind about her? About them?

"Forty-five!" Eddie said.

"Fifty," called the voice in the back.

Zac slapped his hand on the table. "One hundred!" He turned, giving Eddie and the other guy a flinty look.

The crowd applauded the generosity and the entertainment.

"Going once, going twice . . . sold to Zac Callahan for one hundred dollars!"

Zac worked his way to the front through the gathering crowd to grab Aunt Trudy's basket. She'd probably want to go to the square and sit under a shade tree. Just as well. He wanted to be far away from Nick and Lucy. Nick had only paid thirty-five dollars for the pleasure of her company. Cheapskate.

Zac reached for the basket decorated with a ruffly white ribbon. The corner of a red-and-white checkered cloth peeked artfully from the lid. He took the basket out of the throng and scanned the mob for his aunt while the crowd began to dissipate. He found her in the far corner with Beau and Paige. Sometimes being a head taller than everyone else came in handy.

As his aunt's eyes caught his, he lifted a hand and started her way, nearly barreling over . . . Lucy.

He braced her shoulder, then stepped back. "Sorry." Why'd he always seem to be bumping into her?

"No problem." She stood in his way, shifting, her eyes darting off his, looking adorably uncertain.

"Well . . . ," he said.

"Well."

He lifted the basket. "I should go get Aunt Trudy."

"We should probably eat on the deck."

They spoke at the same time.

It took a moment for her words to register. *We should probably eat on the deck.*

This was . . . Lucy's basket?

His eyes searched Lucy's, hoping for some mistake. Lead filled his stomach, and it dried to a hard, heavy lump during the long moment that passed. He was going to kill Eden. And Aunt Trudy.

Lucy's smile fell, her lips parting. The light in her eyes slowly dimmed. "Oh."

"This isn't—?"

She gave a wobbly smile. "You thought—no, it's mine."

"Oh."

Her wobbly smile crumbled, and she looked away.

"You don't have to—"

"We should probably—"

They spoke at the same time.

"—eat on the deck," he finished. "The reporters."

"Right. Okay."

He ushered her out the patio door, blinking against the sunshine. How did he get himself into these messes?

Eden and Aunt Trudy, that's how.

It's just lunch. He could sit across a table from Lucy and carry on a casual conversation. *It's for a good cause,* he repeated to himself about a dozen times.

He chose a table near the railing and set the basket on one of the seats. No one else had chosen the deck, but there were several tables in view on the beach, one situated on the flat rocky outcrop. A young couple from church was making the climb toward that one.

Lucy whipped out the tablecloth, and the breeze pulled at its corners. Her cheeks were flushed, and she bit the corner of her lip.

He was such an idiot. He'd hurt her feelings. Again. He helped her spread the tablecloth. "I'm sorry about—"

"It's all right." Her eyes darted off him.

"I thought it was—"

"I know. It's fine." She gave a brave smile as she smoothed out invisible creases. "It's just lunch, and for a good cause. They raised a fortune for the new firehouse. And I have to admit it was amusing to watch Sheriff Colton battle for Miss Trudy's basket."

Zac had wondered why the sheriff hadn't been bidding against him on Aunt Trudy's basket. He had thought the man was confused about which basket was hers. Turned out he'd been the confused one.

"Marshall gave him a run for his money." Sheriff Colton's face had turned three shades of red, each one darker than the one before it. His bid alone had netted the firehouse over a hundred dollars.

"Who's the guy who won Paige's basket? Dark hair, sturdy build . . ."

"Dylan Moore. He's a fourth-generation lobsterman." Zac hadn't missed the looks he'd given Paige or the flush on her face. Lord, he hoped nothing was blooming between them. He didn't think he could stand to see Riley's heart broken again.

The tablecloth smoothed, Lucy reached for the food, and he helped her unpack it. The eggs were nestled in a special container, and the pulled pork was kept warm in a stone dish, separate from the bread. Fresh bread from the deli. She'd gone to a lot of trouble, and not for him.

"Was there a mix-up with Nick?" he asked. The guy had bid on someone else's basket.

She lowered herself to the seat across from him. "Nick and I are just friends."

"Oh." His stomach lightened somehow, emptying of all the lead that had filled it before. Some-thing tightened in the vicinity of his heart.

No. No, no, no. This is not good, Callahan.

They tucked into their food. The pork was delicious, tangy with a hint of spice. The deviled eggs seasoned to perfection. Maybe she'd hoped to meet someone new. Someone who would love her back.

"This is good, Lucy. I'm sorry you went to all this trouble."

Her eyes turned to his, and those twin pools of blue caught him like a riptide. He couldn't think of a better way to drown. A breeze swept across the table, carrying her appley fragrance his way. She smelled even better than the BBQ pork. Way better.

Her shoulders sank as her tension seemed to

drain away. "It's no trouble, Zac. You've done so much for me. I know you didn't ask for all this. I've been nothing but an inconvenience and you don't owe me a thing, much less a place to lay my head." Her lips worked wordlessly for a moment, then tipped in a little smile. "You're a good man, Zac Callahan."

His heart fluttered in his chest. *Fluttered.*

She was too generous, considering how he'd been pushing her away since she got here.

He cleared his throat. "Have you heard, ah, anything from your ex-fiancé?"

She blinked, then picked at her sandwich. "Um, no. Not since the flowers. I sent the engagement ring back."

"That's good. Maybe that'll get through to him. I noticed more of the reporters left." He took a swig of the bottled peach tea. "Did they let you out of your apartment lease?"

"They're holding it for another month. Awful nice of them."

"The Ferrises are good people. You think a month will be long enough?"

She gave him a desperate look. "Gosh, I hope so. Surely he won't harass me longer than that."

He eyed her as she bit into her sandwich, remembering the sheer desperation he'd felt when she'd left last year. He'd tried everything he knew to find her. He'd told himself he wanted answers, but he knew now it was more than that.

He wanted her back. And if he'd had any way of reaching her, he would've tried for way longer than a month.

"We'll have to see how it goes," he said. "How's the job going?"

"Just fine. I like working with people, helping them plan out their vacation, make proper use of their time."

"I'm sure you're good at it." He wiped his mouth. "You think you'll ever use your sociology degree?"

Her eyes found her plate. "I don't know." She bit her lip, her gaze flickering up to meet his. "Sometimes I think about opening some kind of community center one day . . . Someplace kids could go to after school and during the summer. So many families have both parents working these days, and that leaves kids at loose ends."

"What kinds of activities would it offer?"

"Oh, a basketball court would be ideal, and maybe Ping-Pong tables. Maybe an area where they can play board games or work a puzzle, watch a movie and whatnot. A quiet corner for homework." Her eyes lit up as she talked. "I'd love to have adult volunteers to serve as mentors and have it be a real place of connection, you know?" Her eyes fell away from his, color blooming in her cheeks. "That's probably silly."

He leaned forward. "Not at all. You've seen the teens that loiter around the Roadhouse. And the sheriff's always complaining about kids making trouble. They're good kids, but they've got too much time on their hands. A community center sounds like a great idea. You should do it."

She snorted. "Oh, sure. I'll just run over to the bank and borrow a million or two."

"You shouldn't—"

A voice carried to the deck. A loud one. He tilted his head, listening. It was coming from around the corner, in the shade of the Roadhouse.

"Well, maybe you shouldn't have left me!"

"It was the NBA, Trudy. I was just a farm boy. How could I turn down an opportunity like that?"

Lucy's eyes widened as they met and held Zac's.

"You promised me!" Aunt Trudy said. "But I should've known better than to believe anything you say, Danny Colton."

"Me? You married someone else the second I left!"

"I don't have to sit here and listen to this."

"Well, then, by all means! That'll only leave more for me."

"If I leave, I'm taking my basket with me!"

"I paid for that basket."

"Fine. Here you go then!"

A pause ensued. Lucy's eyes widened.

Zac winced. He had the feeling the sheriff was now wearing Aunt Trudy's lunch.

The splash of water kissing the shore and a

long seagull calling out were the only sounds filling the silence.

"Oh boy," he said.

Lucy leaned closer. "They used to date?"

"First I've heard of it."

"She never told you?"

"Nope." How had he not known this all these years? Gossip alone should've assured he would know.

Lucy's eyes took on that dreamy quality. "And now he wants his first love back. Oh, that's so romantic. We have to do something."

Zac held up his palms. "Oh no. I'm not getting in the middle of that. And before you stick your feet in that mess, I should remind you he's wearing a potato salad bib about now."

Lucy's lips twitched, and Zac found it difficult to tear his eyes away. No way was he playing matchmaker with Aunt Trudy and the sheriff. He had plenty of worries just trying to manage his own love life.

Chapter 29

Lucy barreled through the reporters and up the Roadhouse sidewalk, ignoring the questions. Her blood pulsed through her veins like floodwaters, and her jaw hurt from gritting her teeth all day.

The tangy smell of buffalo wings assaulted her nose as she entered the restaurant. Several tables had filled for supper, and a country tune blared from the jukebox. She scanned the room and found Zac behind the bar, stocking glasses.

She made a beeline for him and slapped her palms on the counter. "You have got to talk to your aunt."

Zac turned, eyebrows disappearing beneath his bangs.

"Well, hello to you too. How was your day?"

"I'll tell you how my day was. It was just like yesterday. And the day before. And the day before that. Your aunt practically follows me to the bathroom. She's on my case about the brochures and the wildlife displays—which, by the way, I am not even responsible for. She's usurping my authority with the customers and going behind me with that infernal white rag of hers, cleaning everything I just cleaned. She is driving me flat crazy!"

Zac tweaked a brow, one corner of his lips twitching.

"Do not smirk at me, Zac Callahan. You have to do something. Ever since her tiff with the sheriff, she has been insufferable!"

"More than usual?"

She nailed him with a look. "I cannot take another day."

"She'll be fine. She's just upset. Be patient with her."

Patient? Lucy's eyes narrowed on his admittedly beautiful gray eyes. "I have been patient all week. I have done everything she's asked of me and I have done it with a smile; nonetheless, she bites my head off at every turn."

He set a stack of glasses on the ledge. "What am I supposed to do about it?"

"Talk to her. Talk to Sheriff Colton. Do something!"

"Lucy . . . this is none of our business. We should stay out of it."

She reached over the bar, knotted his shirt in her fist, and pulled him in. "Do. Something."

His widened eyes locked with hers.

The spicy scent of him wrapped around her. As if someone released a valve, the anger drained right out of her. Her breath tumbled out. Her muscles relaxed, her shoulders fell.

Something flared in his eyes, something that made her pulse flutter. Everything inside her softened, going as mushy as melted butter.

His breath kissed the skin of her forehead, stirring every cell to life. Her legs trembled beneath her, making her balance precarious.

She relaxed her grip on his shirt and smoothed out the wrinkled cotton. "Sorry. I guess I got a little carried away."

The corner of his lips kicked up, drawing her attention, and she watched as his mouth formed the words. "She's a complicated woman."

Lucy just nodded. Her throat had closed up.

Her fingers itched to run along the scruff of his jaw, to sweep across his plump lower lip.

"She's got a good heart though," he said softly. "She doesn't mean to hurt anyone."

"I know that, I just—" Wait. Were they still talking about Miss Trudy?

She wrenched her eyes from his lips, only to settle on his eyes. She wasn't sure which was worse. All she knew was she wanted him to keep looking at her that way. She wanted his mouth on hers more than she wanted her next breath. She wanted his arms around her, his ring on her finger. The plain gold one she'd never gotten to wear.

The one she'd never wear. He'd probably sold it at the pawnshop the minute she left town.

Sadness flooded through her at the thought. Her legs went so weak they couldn't hold her. She eased back onto a stool, her eyes still locked with his.

"Phone, Zac!" one of his servers called.

She hadn't even heard it ring.

Zac took a step back. "I'll talk to my aunt."

"Thank you," she muttered, wishing for the anger back. Because now an aching emptiness had settled deep inside, and there was nothing she could do about it.

Zac gave two sharp raps on his aunt's screen door and eased it open. "Knock-knock."

The savory smell of meat loaf lingered in the

air, and a reality show played on the TV. The screen door slapped shut behind him.

Aunt Trudy frowned up at him from the recliner where she was knitting up a storm. "What do you want?"

"I just stopped by to see my favorite aunt."

"Humph."

"Where's Beau?"

"He's out with Eden, probably scheming up ways to get me out of this house so they can live together in perfect harmony."

He settled on the sofa. "Now, Aunt Trudy, they love having you around."

"That's what they say now, but I know how it is. A couple newlyweds aren't going to want an old widow hanging around."

"You aren't old, and you're the one who got them together in the first place, with all your mistletoe mischief."

"Well, I didn't think it'd lead to this!"

He smothered a smile. "To what? Your nephew happier than the day is long? Come on, Aunt Trudy, this has got to stop."

"I don't know what you're talking about." Her needles waved at dizzying speeds.

"I'm talking about you and Sheriff Colton."

Her lips flattened as she sent him the look of death. "What in heaven's name does that man have to do with anything?"

He tilted his head, giving her a look. "I overheard your argument Saturday. My table was just around the corner from yours."

The needles stopped. Her lips went lax, the corners of her eyes tightening. Just as quickly, her fingers went back to work, her lips pursing.

"Why didn't you ever tell us you'd dated the sheriff?"

"It was a long time ago."

"Not so long ago that you're over it."

"Don't be ridiculous. Of course I'm over it."

"Are you?"

The needles clacked together, her fingers moving quick and sure. If anything, her pace had picked up. Her face paled, and the frown between her brows grew more prominent.

He leaned closer and put his hand over hers, stilling her. "Aunt Trudy . . . were you in love with him?"

She looked up, something he'd never seen before shining in her blue eyes. Vulnerability.

His heart softened. "Why doesn't anyone know?"

She shook her head, her eyes falling to the fuzzy blue square. "Daddy didn't approve of him. His father was the town drunk, and his family was dirt poor."

"You went to school together."

She gave a sharp nod. "He was on the basketball team and about to lose his playing privileges senior year because of his grades. I tutored him in math and . . . one thing led to another."

"And no one knew?"

She said nothing for a good minute. But just as Zac was beginning to think she'd shut down, she started talking.

"No one knew except my best friend, Annabelle. We sneaked around that first summer. My mama was bedridden by then, and I cared for her full time. Then Danny started college in the fall. I don't think he even would've gone if it hadn't been for me. He wanted Daddy's approval, wanted to take me out publicly. I missed him so much when he was gone, but I waited for him. I lived for his summer breaks. He was doing so well on his basketball team, and just when I thought he was finally coming home to me, he got drafted by the Celtics."

"He left you."

"Oh, I was furious. He hadn't even told me he'd been hoping for a basketball career. I was stuck at home with my mama, and then there was . . . well, none of that matters now."

He curled his hand around hers. "But it does. He's here now, and there's nothing standing in your way."

She swiped a finger under her eye. "It's too late for us. There's more, things I'm never going to tell you, so you may as well give it up. I married your uncle Tom, and I don't regret it for a minute."

But she still loved Danny Colton. She didn't have to say it. It was right there on her face. Zac thought of how antagonistic she was toward the man. It was only a defense mechanism. She was trying to protect her heart.

"He hurt you."

"I meant what I said, Zac Callahan. It's too late for us. There's too much water under the bridge. But you . . ."

He reared back. "What about me?"

Her sparse brows hiked above her readers.

"Lucy?"

"Don't act all surprised. You know the two of you are meant to be. You need to stop this foolishness and just give in before it's too late. Look what happens when you wait too long, make too many mistakes. Next thing you know, you're fifty-nine years old and alone, that's what. You Callahan men, you only love once, so don't blow your second chance. Stop being so stubborn and put yourselves out of misery."

Zac was numb as he drove home awhile later. Shell-shocked. He couldn't believe Aunt Trudy was pushing for Lucy. She wasn't an easy woman to win over. It was enough to give him pause for thought.

Was he being stubborn, keeping Lucy at arm's length? Was he doing what Aunt Trudy was doing? Building a wall around his heart so Lucy couldn't hurt him again? Was there anything wrong with that?

Or maybe there was a better question: Was

pushing her away in their best interest? Lucy loved him . . . or thought she did.

He remembered the kiss they shared when they'd lost electricity. He could still feel her lips against his, feel her heart beating against him. He hadn't needed to see into her eyes to know she wanted him. He could feel it in her touch, in her kiss.

She'd distanced herself after he'd pushed her away, and things hadn't been the same since. But tonight . . . the way she looked at him after she grabbed his shirt and pulled him close. Despite her recent distance there was something there. He wasn't the only one trying to protect himself.

What if he did give them another chance? What if he found the courage to let her in again? His stomach clenched at the thought, fear warring with desire.

What if he lost his heart to her again, only to have her memory return?

Who are you kidding, Callahan? She's had your heart all along.

Besides, it had been over five weeks, and she hadn't retrieved a single memory. Maybe it was never coming back. In which case he'd be a fool to let her go. What they'd shared had been special. Maybe it didn't even matter why she'd left him. Whatever had caused that decision was gone. In the past. Lost, perhaps forever, to Lucy and to him.

If things continued as they were, she'd eventually fall for someone else. He'd lose her forever like Sheriff Colton had lost Aunt Trudy. Was he willing to risk that?

His grip tightened on the steering wheel. That was the question. He just needed to figure out the answer.

When he got home, he took the back stairs to his apartment. He would let his staff close tonight for a change. He couldn't seem to shut off his mind or sit still, so he put in an hour on his weights, pushing himself to the limits. Afterward, muscles aching, he was still teeming with energy, so he went for a run in the cool night air, praying as his feet pounded the boardwalk.

What should I do? Show me the way.

The quiet night and the briny smell of the ocean soothed his troubled spirit.

When the Roadhouse came into sight, he slowed his steps, cooling down. He hit the shower, his mind still spinning with indecision, and threw on a T-shirt and shorts. He'd hoped the exercise would wear him out, but instead it had only energized him.

His hair was still wet on his nape when a tap sounded at his door. When he opened it to find Lucy looking up at him, he froze. In the shadowed hall her eyes were the deep blue of the harbor.

Her dimple made a brief appearance. "Sorry to bother you. The band's getting ready to leave, and they want to know if they're still on for next weekend."

He watched the words form on her lips. She had such nice lips. Like a Cupid's bow and a delicate shade of pink. They could be so soft and pliant and giving.

"Zac?"

He blinked, wrenching his eyes from her lips only to fall back into her sea-blue eyes. "Ayuh. They're on the schedule."

She blinked, her long lashes making shadows on her porcelain skin. "All—all right. I'll let them know."

When she turned to go, he felt a cord stretching between them, pulling at him. His feet wanted to follow her. His arms ached to gather her close. His lips yearned to say the words he'd clung to for so long.

But something held him back. "I'll be down in a minute to close up."

"It's pretty much finished," she said over her shoulder. "I'll make sure it's locked up. You deserve a night off."

"Thanks."

As vulnerable and confused as he was feeling, that was probably for the best. It wouldn't help to send mixed signals when he still didn't know what the heck he wanted.

He shut the door and resumed pacing, Aunt Trudy's words playing like a recorder in his ear.

"Look what happens when you wait too long, make too many mistakes. Next thing you know, you're fifty-nine years old and alone."

He didn't know all the mistakes his aunt had made. But years from now, would he look back on tonight and know that doing nothing had been the worst mistake of his life?

His stomach twisted hard. That thought packed a punch. Deep inside, the truth hit home. Lucy was the love of his life. He'd known it from the moment she'd first perched up on that bar stool, nearly falling off, when she'd blushed so adorably. Wasn't what they'd had worth a second chance? Wasn't it worth the chance of heartbreak?

He believed everything happened for a reason. Maybe all this—Lucy's concussion, her move back here—maybe all of it had happened so they could be together again. A second chance. Wasn't that what he'd wished for, what he'd prayed for, for months after she'd left?

God had thrown this opportunity into his lap, and what had he done? Pushed it away. Pushed her away. What an idiot. How long did he really think he could resist her anyway? He'd always been a helpless fool when it came to Lucy.

What are you waiting for then, Callahan?

What *was* he waiting for?

He headed for the door, his long strides making quick work of the space. Now that he'd made up his mind, he couldn't get to her soon enough. He took the stairs and started down the hall toward Lucy's room, but was drawn instead toward the dining room by a country jig that was blaring from the jukebox.

The room was empty save for Lucy, who was turning chairs up onto the tables. The floor hadn't been swept or mopped yet, and judging from the quiet kitchen, everyone else was gone for the night.

Lucy finished the table and sashayed toward the next one, stopping to wiggle her hips to the beat. She did a little spin, and her toe caught on a chair leg. She pitched forward, catching herself. Then she straightened and added a little shoulder shimmy to cover.

His lips tilting, he leaned against the threshold, content to watch her in full Lucy mode.

The song ended with a couple of hearty beats, which she accented with a dramatic hitch kick that shook the nearby tables.

Even as his lips twitched, the backs of his eyes burned. Lucy. His Lucy. He still loved her. So much.

She reached for another chair as the soft strains of "Hope You Get Lonely Tonight" filled the room.

Lucy's movements slowed as she swayed to the music, her body moving in time with the song's rhythm. Her lips moved to the words, her expressions stage-worthy. Between chairs she threw in a shuffle followed by a sexy little hip swivel. The tune transitioned to the chorus, and she waltzed to the next table, spinning.

She mesmerized him. She owned him. How was it he was the last one to know?

She did another little spin and, as she came to a stop, her eyes swept over him. They came back in a double take. The expression fell from her face as her mouth snapped shut. Her hands stilled on the tabled chair. A pretty pink flush climbed her cheeks.

His breath caught in his lungs. A wave of tension stretched taut between them, tugging. This time he didn't fight the pull.

Chapter 30

Lucy froze, her eyes stuck on Zac as she rewound the last minute or so in her head. That saying, *Dance like no one's watching,* caught in her head. Only they were. He was.

Boy, was he. The look in his eyes made it hard to breathe. Her pulse raced, and not from the dancing.

He moved toward her, his steps bringing him closer and closer. He was looking at her in a way he hadn't in so very long.

She couldn't tear her eyes away.

His feet shuffled to a stop when he was a breath away. The music faded away and silence filled the gap. Tension wove around them, its sticky threads pulling at her.

"I'm done fighting this, Lucy," he said in a low rumble.

Her breath escaped as her heart rate accelerated. A low hum moved through her body, bringing every cell to life. She shouldn't need him so desperately. It was dangerous to her well-being. Her eyes dropped to the collar of his T-shirt.

She didn't know if she could take another rejection. Her heart was still mending from the last time he'd walked away.

His fingers lifted her chin until her eyes met his again. She clung to the smoky need she saw there. The heart wanted what it wanted. And hers wanted him. So badly.

"Come here, Georgia." He lowered his head until his tantalizing breath fell on her lips. He hovered there for an excruciating moment before his lips met hers. Soft and careful, like she was a precious treasure.

He continued to kiss her, and she gave back move for move. Her arms roped around him and he gathered her close, lifting her to her tiptoes. Her lips moved against his, want coursing through her veins like fire. Her fingers threaded into the damp hair at his nape.

His strong arms felt like heaven's embrace, and she was lost. His kiss was a warm summer day after a cold, hard winter. It was a tall glass of ice water after a long run. It was a soft bed after an impossible day.

His lips parted hers, and she absorbed his moan as his arms tightened. She pressed against him, couldn't get close enough. He made her feel complete, and she hadn't felt that in so long, not since she'd last been in his arms. She could get a job, get a place, get a life, but it wouldn't be complete without Zac. She'd known it all along, down deep inside. She'd tried to convince herself otherwise, but she'd only been fooling herself.

He was her home.

He pulled back until their ragged breaths mingled between them. "I miss you, Lucy. I want you in my life. Let's try again."

The look in his eyes nearly melted her into a puddle. She'd waited weeks to hear those words, and they were like the sweetest melody in her ears.

"I want that so badly," she said. "But what—what happened? What changed?"

He rested his forehead against hers. "It was Aunt Trudy. I went over to talk to her about the sheriff. She's so sad. I don't want to live a life of regret. If I let you get away, it'll be the biggest mistake of my life."

Her eyes burned, and she swallowed hard. "Well, aren't you the sweetest thing."

"You're the only girl for me, Lucy Lovett."

"Kiss me." Her face burned at her boldness, and her eyes found his collar again.

He tipped her chin up until her eyes met his. He lowered his head, brushing her lips slowly, as if he were savoring every moment. She was savoring it too. Could hardly believe she was getting this second chance. He set his hand on her face, his fingers threading into her hair.

This was happening. It was really happening. A curl of joy unfurled in her stomach, making her feel so many wonderful things. Her mind spun with euphoria.

But then troubling thoughts burst in like unwelcome guests into her home. Thoughts of her life in Portland, of her vexing ex-fiancé, of her desertion, which she couldn't even remember. Seven and a half months of her life—a blank slate.

She pushed the worries firmly from her mind. If they could put the past behind them, everything would be just fine. It had to be. She couldn't bear the thought of losing him again.

Chapter 31

Lucy's eyes popped open. Daylight flooded into her room. A breeze pushed at her curtain, skating over her skin, pebbling her arms with goose bumps. A lingering spicy scent clung to her skin.

Zac.

Memories of the night before came surging to

the surface, and a tingly heat spread through her like wildfire.

After the kiss they'd gone up to his apartment and talked awhile. They'd watched a movie, making out whenever the mood struck. And it had struck plenty. She ran her fingers across her swollen lips, across the tender skin on her face where his stubbly chin had rubbed. Her lips tilted in contented pleasure.

Her heart gave a roll at the memory of his hungry eyes, his gentle hands, his pliant lips. But even as butterflies frolicked in her stomach, another feeling lingered just below the surface—the dark expectancy of dread.

What if he woke up this morning and regretted it? He'd been pushing her away for weeks. He'd had one conversation with his aunt, and now everything had changed? But nothing had really changed. She still didn't remember why she'd left before. Her memory could still come back, and everything could change.

Zac would remember that now. Morning had a way of bringing that kind of clarity.

Her muscles clenched at the thought, and a knot tightened in her belly, strangling every last butterfly. A noise sounded outside her door. She cocked her head, recognizing the clanking of the mop bucket. They'd never gotten around to sweeping and mopping last night.

She got out of bed and headed for the shower,

her legs all trembly at the thought of seeing Zac again—and not in a good way. She felt more vulnerable than ever.

Under the showerhead she gave herself a talking-to. She had to pull it together. She had to go out there like nothing had happened the night before. He'd be relieved, and they could both move on.

Something pinched inside at the thought, but she ignored the feeling. She'd see if she could get into her new place, maybe even today. The sooner the better. This wasn't working. How could she be so close to the man she loved and deny herself? It was a fool's mission.

After her shower she dressed in her favorite white shorts and a billowy blouse. She took her time with a minimal amount of makeup, dried her hair straight and fluffed it up. She needed all the confidence she could get.

She stilled her quivering lip. *Chin up, Lucy Lovett. You can do this.*

The ache in her heart belied the thought. She left her room, her legs quaking despite the brave façade she wore. When she walked into the dining room, Zac was taking the chairs from the tables. It was like a reversal of last night only with a different ending. Much different.

He looked up, smiling.

She returned his smile, looking away before she got caught in his gaze. "Morning, Boss. I'll make us something to eat." She headed for the kitchen.

"Already did."

She turned back just before she hit the swing door.

He nodded his head toward the bar where he'd set a covered plate and a tall glass of orange juice.

Something inside warmed and softened. "Oh. Thank you."

No, no, no. This didn't mean a thing. It was probably a guilt gift so his rejection would go down more easily.

She made her way to the stool while he continued pulling the chairs down. She couldn't get a read on him. Of course, it didn't help that she couldn't seem to look him in the eye.

She felt the heat of his gaze on her back as she chewed. The eggs and bacon tasted like cardboard in her mouth and seemed to lodge in her throat. She ate quickly nonetheless. The sooner she was done, the sooner she could give them both some space. She'd go straight to the apartment office and beg them to let her in today.

She shoveled in the last bite of eggs and stood, gathering her plate and glass. "Thank you for breakfast. I'll just take these to the—"

"Lucy . . ."

The slow strains of a country ballad began, and Lucy's eyes shot to Zac.

He stood over by the jukebox, an enigmatic

smile tilting his lips. "Come here." His voice was as thick as honey.

Her breath caught in her throat. She looked at him sideways. "What?"

He held out his arms in an invitation to dance. "Just come here."

"It—it's nine o'clock in the morning."

"I've been waiting weeks to dance with you, and I'm not waiting a second longer."

Her feet—traitorous little things—moved toward him without the permission of her brain. She tried to look away, but it was too late. He'd already sucked her in and held her prisoner.

She stepped into his arms and he took her hand, moving her in the slow box step they'd done so many times before. Despite their height difference they moved effortlessly together, as if they were one. His hand burned into the small of her back like a brand.

Okay, so he hadn't changed his mind. But he would. Right? Her mind warred with her heart, fear making her rigid. She dragged her eyes to the second button of his shirt.

"So . . . what's going on between Miss Trudy and the sheriff? I mean, their argument . . . did she clear up what happened between them?"

"Turns out they were high school sweethearts." His voice rumbled low. "Her daddy didn't approve, so they sneaked around. She was stuck at home with her sick mama when he got drafted by the Celtics."

"So he left her." She knew all too well what that felt like. The thought put a hard pit in the center of her stomach.

"She's still angry about it."

"It's a long time to hold a grudge."

"Have you met Aunt Trudy?"

She understood how the woman felt. By the time she'd been old enough to track down her father, she hadn't even wanted to. And then it was too late. Even so, she had no regrets. Why would she want someone who'd deserted her when she needed him most?

The song reached a crescendo as the final chorus played. Their bodies moved together flawlessly, his legs brushing hers. When his hand moved on her back, her eyes found his of their own volition. They held for a long, poignant moment.

His eyes dipped down to her lips, and she instinctively wetted them.

No, Lucy. You're not going to kiss him. Be strong.

The battle waging inside agitated her. She lowered her eyes to his shirt. "I'm getting a crick in my neck." She winced at her Miss Trudy tone.

He bent at the knees, tightening his arms around her, and lifted her off the floor without missing a beat. They were eye-to-eye now, their bodies pressed together, barely swaying.

"Now you're going to get a crick in your back." The words came out too breathy to serve as the scolding she'd intended.

She braced her hands on his wide shoulders. Her pulse fluttered as their breaths mingled between them.

His lips said nothing, but his eyes said plenty. She couldn't get away from them now. She was close enough to see the flecks of charcoal and a hint of green. Close enough to see the want darkening them.

The final notes played out, sweet and touching. Zac stopped moving and held her there a long moment.

His eyes searched hers. He loosened his hold, his belt buckle scraping her belly as he eased her back onto her feet.

He kept his hands at her waist, loose enough to allow her to flee, but her feet were frozen to the floor.

"Do you regret last night?" His voice was a low rumble in her chest.

"Yes. No. I don't know. I don't rightly know, Zac, I'm just—I'm afraid." She bit her lip. She hadn't meant to say all that. She didn't want him to know how vulnerable she felt. That made her even more afraid.

He tipped her chin up, and she soaked in the confidence shining in his eyes. "I'm not going anywhere, Lucy. I don't regret last night. I don't regret it at all. The only thing I regret is letting you walk away from me last time."

The words loosened the knot inside just a bit. Relieved the tension in her shoulders. Tears burned behind her eyes, and a lump formed in her throat. His face blurred as she stared at him.

"Is that what you needed to hear, baby?" he said on a soft breath. "Because I mean it. You don't need to be afraid."

She nodded, hating the tear that broke loose and trickled down her face. He swept it away with a thumb, lowering to drop a sweet kiss on her lips. The briefest of touches.

He hovered above her, their breaths mingling for a long moment, their eyes meeting. "I'm not going anywhere," he whispered.

Then he kissed her again. Her hands slid up the solid wall of his chest and wrapped around his neck. How did he know just what to say? She wasn't sure, but her legs quaked with relief. He didn't regret last night. He wasn't leaving her. That was all that mattered. The rest of it—the stalking reporters, the bothersome ex-fiancé—would go away soon enough. Then there'd be just her and Zac, picking up right where they'd left off.

Chapter 32

The next week rushed past for Lucy. The warmth of August lured campers and hikers from across the country, and they all seemed to stop at the visitor center for directions and information.

On Wednesday child celebrity Felicity Turner was arrested in Los Angeles for driving under the influence of drugs. The reporters left to chase the national story, leaving Lucy smiling all day.

Zac pulled her into his office when she got home that evening. He gave her a long, slow kiss that made her wish she still worked at the Roadhouse.

"Let's go out Saturday night and celebrate your freedom," he said when they came up for air.

She gave him a mock scowl. "There's a poor girl out there who's headed for rehab, you know."

"And there's a pretty girl right here who deserves her privacy." He took her face in his hands and gave her a quick kiss. "Let's go to the Lobster Hut. You love it."

"I don't even remember it."

"We only went once. Your taste buds will still appreciate it."

That wasn't all her taste buds appreciated, she thought, as he drew her into another kiss.

· · ·

On Saturday Zac led her inside the restaurant with a hand on the small of her back. She thrilled to his touch, no matter how brief. The tempting aroma of seafood filled the air. The restaurant was energetic with the sounds of happy conversation and hearty appetites.

A few minutes later the host led them to the last empty table, a small one with a beautiful view of the harbor. The ambience was casual and the décor eclectic. No two chairs matched, but the red-checkered tablecloths pulled everything together. Lobster buoys and hurricane lamps hung from weathered gray beams that stretched across a wavy tin ceiling.

She picked up the glossy single-page menu. "It smells good. I'm so hungry I could eat a wet mule."

"Get the lobster." He winked. "It's better than mule."

When the server approached, they ordered their drinks and meals and settled back in their chairs to enjoy the view. A seagull perched on a piling outside the window, staring at them with its dark, round eyes. Another swooped in and snatched a nugget of food from the pier.

Zac took her hand, pulling her attention back to him. He swept his thumb over her knuckles. She'd never tire of the way he looked at her. The way he touched her.

"I'm so glad those vultures are gone," he said.

"It'll be nice to not have to sneak around anymore. It's a little hard to blend into the community when I'm being tailed by a horde of reporters."

"Hopefully they got their fill."

She thought of the articles they'd published that had put her in such a bad light. Her cheeks heated at their insinuations.

He squeezed her hand. "Hey. None of that now. You haven't done anything wrong."

He was right. She decided to shake off the mood. She returned the squeeze. "This is a celebration, and that's exactly what we're going to do. Now if I can just get Brad to go away."

His brows creased. "He's still bothering you?"

She pulled the paper from her straw and stuck it into her iced tea. "He texts sometimes."

"He has your new number?"

She winced. "I gave it to him early on when I felt bad for him. I still feel kind of guilty. I mean, I did leave him at the altar with no explanation. Of course he doesn't understand why, and I can't even help with that."

"That's right, you can't help him. So there's no sense in worrying about his feelings. He's harassing you, and that's not okay. How often do you hear from him?"

"A couple times a day, maybe?"

His eyes went tight. "A couple times a day?"

"I stopped answering. And I never pick up

when he calls. I did tell him I was with you now. I mean—" She pinched her lip. Zac hadn't said anything about being exclusive, and now she realized she'd been presumptuous. Heat crawled into her cheeks. "I mean, not that we're, you know . . ."

He threaded his fingers through hers, his eyes piercing hers, going smoky. "Yes, we are *you know*. As far as I'm concerned, you're the only woman in all New England."

Her heart gave a tug. Her eyes drifted over his straight nose, his sculpted cheeks, his scruffy jaw. He was so handsome. And he was hers.

Mine.

"Miss Trudy will be mighty dismayed to hear that," she said.

The corner of his lips tugged upward. "Relatives excluded."

Conversation flowed effortlessly as they waited for their food. They talked about Riley, who'd Skyped the night before, and about a new band Zac was thinking about adding to the Roadhouse's schedule.

Before she knew it, a huge lobster platter was set in front of her. Zac had gotten the shrimp scampi, and the garlicky dish smelled amazing.

"I think you'd better use this." Zac picked up the plastic bib with the image of a big red lobster and held it out.

"You're so right." She leaned forward, and he

brushed her hair to the side, reaching around her with the plastic ties. She felt a tiny sting as a piece of hair got caught in the tie.

A memory flashed in her mind: Zac tying another bib around her neck. He'd gotten her hair caught in the knot, and he'd had to retie it. The image was so vivid her heart thumped wildly in her chest.

She grabbed his hand, squeezing tight. "I remember something!"

His eyes zeroed in on hers. "What?"

"I remember being here before. We sat over there." She pointed toward the far corner.

Something flashed in his eyes. He finished the tie and sat back in his chair. "That's right."

She froze, waiting for more. And it came. It was two weeks before their wedding. They hadn't spent much time together in the days leading up. Zac had brought her here to make amends. He'd been distant, moody recently. Withdrawn. He'd been busy, he said. But with the wedding quickly closing in, she'd been worried he was getting cold feet.

Her eyes stopped on the lobster cracker by her plate as another memory surfaced. Her eyes shot to his. "A piece of my lobster flew onto the lap of the lady next to us."

The corner of his mouth turned up. "She wasn't too happy."

"I remember!" That was good, right? It felt

good, getting back another piece of her life. It meant she was on the mend. She could move forward, with Zac.

• • •

Zac watched with mixed emotions as a myriad of feelings washed over Lucy's face. He remembered that night as if it were yesterday. He'd been under so much stress. He was still grieving the loss of his dad; one of his cooks had just quit, leaving him to pick up the slack; and he was trying to help Beau get the Christmas tree farm ready to open for the season. Add one full-time server off with a broken leg, plus an upcoming wedding, and he had a disaster in the making.

He'd given his fiancée precious little time, and he knew that wasn't right. She was the best thing in his life. How many times had he wondered, after she'd left, if it was his own fault? Had he chased her away? Had she simply tired of his dark mood?

"I can't believe I remembered something." Her eyes lit with excitement, and a smile revealed both dimples.

"That's great, Lucy. Really great." A heavy weight settled in his chest.

They tucked into their food, but the shrimp scampi had lost all appeal. He swallowed past a fist-sized lump as two questions traveled his mind in relentless circles: Would the rest of her memory come back? And if it did, would she still want him?

Chapter 33

Lucy took her mail out to the deck. The week-night was slow at the restaurant, and she had the space all to herself. She'd left Zac in the kitchen dealing with a late bread delivery. They were both having busy weeks, and Zac had suggested they spend the upcoming Saturday evening together.

"I'll plan it," he said. "Just be ready at five and wear something comfortable."

On the deck she kicked off her heels, and her feet practically sighed in relief. The evening was beautiful, the sinking sun stealing the warmth of the day. A salty breeze blew in off the sea, pushing her hair over her shoulders.

She tore open the first envelope, her credit card bill. She looked at the balance. Ugh. She stuck the bill back in the envelope. A Nordstrom flyer, addressed to her, attested to her expensive taste in shoes. Her eyes caught on a pair of emerald Gucci sling-backs with a silver buckle. Her pulse gave a leap at the sleek design and glossy leather. Gorgeous!

Remembering her credit card bill, she gave a hard sigh and set the flyer on the table. She passed on a political brochure and a credit card offer. The last envelope was from an investment firm. She slid a finger under the flap, her eyes on a seagull that swooped near the deck, hoping for a crumb.

"Sorry, little guy, not allowed." Zac had signs posted, but that didn't stop tourists from feeding the birds.

She pulled out the slip of paper and unfolded it, reading. Her eyes narrowed on the words. On the information that followed. On the numbers.

What?

Her heart pounded in her chest as she reread the statement, checked the name at the top. Looked at the number again. She glanced at the letterhead. The investment firm was located in Savannah. She punched the number into her phone, but it was after five. She doubted they were still open.

"B&D Investments."

"Hi, um, may I speak with"—she checked the bottom of the statement—"Allen Foster?"

"Name, please?"

"Lucy Lovett."

"Oh, Miss Lovett. Just a moment. I'll put you right through."

Had the woman's voice warmed when she'd said Lucy's name? Lucy looked over the statement while she waited. All those zeros . . . She blinked, and they were still there. The paper shook in her hand.

"Lucy," a male voice said. He sounded older, maybe in his sixties. "It's so good to hear from you. How are you?"

"Thank you, um, Mr. Foster. I'm—I guess I'm doing just fine."

He gave a warm chuckle. "Allen," he corrected. "I thought we settled that a long time ago."

"Yes, well, the thing is Mr., uh, Allen, I don't exactly remember that conversation. Or lots of other conversations." She explained her injury and the memory loss she'd been coping with.

"Oh, you poor dear! Is there anything I can do?"

"Well, actually, there is. I got a statement in the mail from your firm. Am I to understand I have money invested with you?"

"Oh my . . . I'm not certain how much you remember. Are you aware that your great-aunt, ah . . ."

"Yes. I know she passed on. I don't remember it, but I read about it in the paper."

He tsked. "I'm so sorry. What a wretched way to find out. But yes, your aunt Audrey left you a healthy sum, and you invested the majority in the market. I'd be happy to review your portfolio with you if you'd like."

"But—but she always said she was giving everything to charity. She didn't believe in leaving money to heirs. She said it made for spoiled and entitled children."

"She didn't want you counting on the money, that's all. She wanted you to make your own way and have your own goals. You did. You have."

"But her estate . . . her home and . . ."

"All settled. You handled that months ago."

"Oh. I feel so silly." How did she not remember any of this? She rubbed her temples as if it might make the memories reappear.

"Not at all. The brain is a perplexing organ. Would you like to go over your portfolio tonight? I have a dinner appointment in half an hour, but I'd be happy to call you afterward."

Her mind was reeling, mostly with all those zeroes. "Would you mind sending me the information in the mail? I have a feeling I'll need to see it all in black and white."

"Of course."

She gave him her current address so it wouldn't be forwarded and hung up the phone. Still staring at the number on the bottom line, she headed inside and found Zac in the back alley signing off with the bread guy. She waited by the back door until he was finished.

A minute later exhaust fumes filled the air as the truck pulled away.

Zac turned, a smile tipping his lips when he caught sight of her. His eyes narrowed as they studied her face. "What's that secret little smile all about?"

She blinked, still trying to believe it was true. "I have money." Her voice sounded as dazed as she felt.

Zac pulled her into his arms. "That's good,

because you've worked up quite a tab, young lady. All those sweet teas are adding up."

She braced her hands on his arms. "No, Zac. I mean I have *money*. A lot of it."

He tilted his head, studying her, his fathomless gray eyes questioning.

She held up the statement. "I got this in the mail from an investment firm, and I just called. My aunt left me everything. *Everything.* Apparently I settled up the estate, I just don't remember it." She handed him the paper.

He took the statement and looked it over, his eyes widening when they hit the bottom line. "Holy moly. That's a lot of zeros."

"I know, right? Can you believe it?"

His eyes found hers again, searching. "What do you think about that?"

"I don't know what to think. It's so new." What did a person do, coming into sudden money of that kind? She was used to clipping coupons and saving for apartment deposits and shopping for bargains.

"I don't know who that Lucy Lovett was—the one in Portland. I'm so confused."

He tipped her chin up. "She was the same Lucy that's standing right in front of me. She had a sweet Southern drawl, a special way with people, and a big heart."

His words warmed her from the inside out. She gave a wry smile. "And a big bank account apparently. No wonder I could afford that apartment."

Zac placed a kiss on her forehead and pulled her into his arms. "It's just money. It doesn't change who you are. And hey . . . now you could open

that community center you were talking about. Wouldn't that be something?"

The thought made her chest squeeze tight. She *could* open a community center. The thought of providing a safe place for people, for kids, to connect made her heart race. She saw it as a gathering place. She'd love it if it could be free for the community—and now she actually had the money to pull it off.

She settled into his embrace, letting her hands drift over the hard muscles of his arms. She breathed in his spicy scent, savoring the smell of him. The feel of him.

She snuggled deeper into his arms. She could stay like this forever. In Summer Harbor. In his arms. She could start her community center and keep her little room in the Roadhouse. Maybe she could afford the biggest home in Summer Harbor and a yacht the size of Rhode Island, but that didn't mean she had to have it.

That pair of emerald-green Guccis, though . . . those were all hers.

Chapter 34

The next morning while Lucy was working she missed a call from Brad. She was relieved that he'd left no voicemail, but a few minutes later a text came in.

> Can't we at least talk? I need to hear your voice and know you're okay. I need to see you. I miss you. Please call me back.

A niggle of fear wormed through her veins. Her senses went on heightened alert. She cast a look out the screen door of the visitor center as if he might appear on the stoop.

Stop it, Lucy. You're being melodramatic.

He'd been her fiancé, after all. Maybe he didn't know when to quit, but some part of her must've loved him and trusted him in order to have accepted his proposal.

Later that afternoon she locked up the center, anticipating seeing Zac. She'd gotten in the habit of hunting him down in the restaurant and greeting him with a kiss. She loved seeing the heart-stopping smile that curved his lips when he caught sight of her.

The day was beautiful and sunny, not a cloud in the sky, as she began the short walk home.

When she'd nearly reached the end of the center's walkway, her eyes caught on a familiar figure silhouetted at the end. Her footsteps slowed. She mentally went through her options, from calling Zac to turning back to the center.

But she was overreacting. They were in public. A family frolicked on the beach not far away, and cars crawled past on Main Street at the required thirty miles per hour.

Brad straightened as she neared. A gust of wind swept his hair off his high forehead. "Hi, Lucy."

"Brad. What are you doing here?"

"You look nice."

"You shouldn't be here. I told you I'm with someone else now."

"You wouldn't answer my calls or texts."

"Because I'm with someone else now."

He held up his palm. "I don't want to argue. I just want to talk. Did you walk to work? Can I give you a lift?"

She stepped back, crossing her arms. "I don't think so. We don't have anything to talk about, Brad. I still don't remember why I left the wedding, so there's really no point—"

"I'll walk you home. Is that okay? We can talk on the way."

It was a public boardwalk. She really couldn't stop him from walking alongside her, and maybe if she let him have his say, he'd finally leave her be.

"I suppose so." She turned onto the boardwalk and set a quick pace.

"Guess I'd better talk fast, huh?" A hint of bitterness coated his tone. "Look, Lucy, I've been doing a lot of thinking, and I'd like a second chance."

She opened her mouth, but he cut her off.

"I know you're seeing that other guy, but you were engaged to me. You fell in love with me, and if you hadn't bumped your head, you'd still be in love with *me*."

"I'd already left you by the time I bumped my head. There must've been a good reason."

"You were just getting cold feet. You'd been a little nervous. If things had gone differently that day, I would've come and found you, and we would've talked it out, and we would've been married before the day was over."

"I'm not so sure about that. But it doesn't matter anyway. That's not what happened. I can't change the fact that I bumped my head or lost my memory or the fact that I've fallen for someone else. I'm sorry, but I just don't love—"

"Don't say it. Please don't say it. Just think about it. Meet me for drinks later."

"I'm busy tonight."

"In the morning then. For coffee or whatever you want. Name the place and time, and I'll be there."

She shook her head, torn between wanting to

appease him somehow and worrying that her intuition was right. "I don't think that's a good idea."

She was relieved to see the Roadhouse in the distance. Her feet couldn't get her there fast enough. They walked in silence a minute, her spiked adrenaline driving her forward.

Almost to the parking lot. Almost to the walkway.

"Come on, Lucy. Look at it from my perspective. My bride, the woman of my dreams, walked out on our wedding. She disappeared, and I worried myself sick, thinking the worst. Then she turns up, and she not only doesn't love me anymore, she doesn't even remember me."

Almost to the door. "That's not my fault."

"And now she's with someone else." He took her arm, forcing her to stop. His brows pulled together, his lips in a thin line.

He blew out his breath low and slow as Alma Walker shuffled past, giving Lucy a curious nod.

"I didn't say it was your fault," he said once Alma was inside. There was a strained edge to his voice, one that sparked a flash in her mind. A memory so vivid it instantly replayed.

It was the night before their wedding. He said something in front of his friends that made her feel stupid and clumsy. When she called him on it later, they argued. His voice was strained, his anger barely reined in. Eventually he apologized. They ended the night with a lingering kiss.

The morning of her wedding, she couldn't shake the uneasiness in her stomach. Even as she slipped into her beautiful gown, she knew she had to clear the air before they said their vows. Her friend from work, Anna, was serving as her maid of honor. Anna was a stickler for traditions. Bad enough Lucy was having a courthouse wedding. She'd never be in favor of Lucy seeing Brad before the ceremony.

They entered the courthouse through the side door.

"I'm going to touch up my lipstick," Lucy said. "Can you go on over to the waiting room and make sure our guests are comfortable? Make the introductions?"

"Of course." Anna's heels clacked down the hallway, and Lucy turned down a short hall to await Brad's arrival. He was due any moment according to his text.

Her heart beat up into her throat. She closed her eyes, breathing deeply, trying to calm her anxious spirit.

Immediately visions of Zac Callahan formed in her mind. His beautiful gray eyes, looking at her as if she were the only woman in the world. The soft scruff of his beard against her temple. His tender kiss pressed to her lips. His strong arms wrapped around her. Her heart pounded as an ache spread like a disease through her middle.

Stop it, Lucy!

"Did you hear me?" Brad squeezed her arm. "Lucy."

She turned her eyes to his. He kept talking, but his words faded, the memory of their wedding day clinging to her like a barnacle on a boat.

She hadn't loved Brad, not really. She'd settled for him. She'd still been in love with Zac.

She was dreadfully lonely after leaving Zac. Brad came into her life soon after her arrival in Portland. He helped fill the void. She liked his company, liked him. He was smart and, for little bits of time, he could make her forget how terribly she missed Zac. She didn't want to be alone forever, and Brad was a man she could love without needing him so desperately. He was safe. Just the sort of man she should spend the rest of her life with.

She tried to go back even further in time and remember her last moments with Zac. But the slate was blank.

Only when she tried to remember what happened next did the memories begin to flow again.

A car's engine hummed outside the courthouse door, and Lucy prayed it was Brad. They'd have a discussion, he'd settle her nerves, and everything would be fine. All these jitters . . . cold feet, that's all it was. She just needed a quiet moment with Brad before she pledged her life to him.

His voice boomed through the door well before he did. He had that kind of voice, especially when he was on the phone. After several seconds she realized he was going to finish his call outside. He was using his business voice. It was sharp and firm. But this time she heard a quiver of nerves beneath the confidence.

"I told you, Bill, I'm taking care of it."

Lucy leaned her head against the wall, heedless of the hairdo Anna had worked so hard on.

"Well, be more patient. I said you'll have it by the end of the day, and you will."

Lucy frowned, turning her ear toward the door, her stomach twisting with dread. After their wedding they were headed straight for Paris. Her bag was already in his car.

"I'll have it wired," he was saying. "If you'd leave me alone for two seconds, I'd get inside and get this taken care of."

A moment later when he burst through the door, Lucy pressed back into the doorway, the pieces falling into place.

"Lucy! Are you even listening to me?" His grip on her elbow had tightened painfully.

She jerked it away, the remnants of her memory

fading fast, her vision filling with his deceitful eyes.

Her body tensed as heat flooded through her. "You were using me."

"What?"

Her legs had gone weak, and her fingers were numb, but her thoughts were crystal clear. "I remember. I overheard your phone call at the courthouse. You owed somebody money. You were only marrying me to pay your debt."

Something shifted in his eyes before the shutters went over them. "That's absurd. You must've misunderstood. It was just a business call." He reached out, his voice gentling. "Lucy, you know how much I love—"

"Don't." She stepped away. "Don't you touch me. And don't talk to me ever again. I knew there was something fishy about you, about all of this. I felt it from the beginning. You never loved me at all."

"Lucy . . . don't be this way," his voice wheedled.

"If you contact me again, I'm getting a restraining order. Stay away from me."

His face hardened, the corners of his eyes tightened, and his lips curled up into an ugly snarl.

The door behind her crashed open, and Lucy jumped.

Zac took the porch steps in one leap. "I warned you, Martin."

"Wait." She held her hands out. "It's fine. He

was just leaving." She turned a dark look on Brad as Zac arrived at her side. "Weren't you."

A tense moment hung between them, swelling as the two men glared at each other.

Then Brad tore his eyes away, looking Lucy up and down. "Know what? He can have you. You're clumsy, you talk too much, and your redneck twang drives me up the wall."

Zac leapt forward, and Brad scuttled backward, palms up, all false bravado. "Touch me, buddy, and I'll sue you for all you've got."

"Show your ugly face around here again, and I'll tear you limb from limb. Try me."

With a final scowl Brad straightened his shoulders and sauntered away.

Zac stood in front of Lucy, his back rigid. Only when Brad was out of sight did he turn to her. "What happened? Did he hurt you?"

"No, I'm fine. But I remembered something, Zac. I remembered my wedding day." She told him the story, and he listened patiently. "He only wanted me for my money," she said after she'd gotten the whole story out. "I almost married someone who was just using me."

"Thank God you found out in time."

She gave a wry laugh. "Yeah, just in time to konk my head, get amnesia, and lose seven whole months."

"And come back into my life, don't forget that." He pulled her into his arms, pressing a kiss to the top of her head. "I'm grateful for all of it."

She breathed in deep and blew it out as she snuggled into his arms. "Me too."

Maybe the road back had been twisty and curvy, but they'd arrived just the same, and her life couldn't be more perfect.

Chapter 35

The next Saturday Lucy dressed in shorts and a V-neck T-shirt for their evening together. She blow-dried her hair upside down to give it extra oomph and put on a touch of makeup. She was applying lipstick when a tap sounded at her door.

She opened it to find Zac looking handsome in jeans and a black T-shirt. In the dim lighting of the hallway, his tightly trimmed beard was merely a dark shadow, giving him a roguelike appearance. He gave her that crooked grin, making her want to lay a big kiss on those gorgeous lips of his.

"Is this okay?" She waved toward her clothing. "Where are we going?"

"I'm not telling, but you look perfect." He took her hand and set a warm kiss in her palm. "Come on. Lola's waiting."

"Lola? We're taking another woman on our date?"

"You'll see."

She followed him out the back where a black motorcycle leaned in the alley. She gasped.

He gestured to the bike. "Lucy . . . meet Lola."

"You have a motorcycle? Oh, she's Riley's. I remember now."

"He asked us to run her from time to time, and I thought today was the perfect opportunity."

Something happy bubbled up inside even as butterflies flapped their wings in her stomach. "I've never been on a motorcycle."

"But you want to. I see the sparkle in those pretty blue eyes." He spared her a wicked grin as he stowed her purse by a duffel bag that was tied down to the back.

The temperature was perfect, around seventy degrees, and a light breeze blew. She frowned at the smoke-colored clouds obscuring the sun. "I hope it doesn't rain."

"It wouldn't dare." He slipped a helmet over her head. "This might be a little big for your tiny noggin."

"Hey . . ." She gave a mock glower, which disappeared when he dropped a kiss on her nose.

"You haven't heard from dipwad, have you?"

"Surely haven't. I don't think I will now that he knows I won't fall for all his nonsense."

"If you hear from him—"

"I'll tell you first thing."

"Good girl." He finished her strap, then put on his own helmet and straddled the bike.

Glimpsing the small sliver of seat behind him, her heart gave a little quiver. She climbed on, squirming until she was settled. She thought she heard a groan, but then the engine rumbled to life and she grasped the sides of his shirt.

"Hang on!" he called over the growl of the engine.

She grabbed on tighter when he accelerated. The bike leaned as he pulled out onto the street, and she gave a little squeak. Zac navigated through town, finding the road that wound along the shoreline. As he increased the speed, the wind tugged at her shirt and pebbled the skin on her legs. She wrapped her arms around him, pressing into the warmth of his muscled back. She lost count of the turns and closed her eyes, enjoying the ride.

When he slowed the bike a few minutes later, she loosened her grip and leaned back as the engine went quiet. They were at a quiet cove. About a half mile of pebbly sand stretched along the shore, and tree-covered hillsides sheltered the inlet. The scent of pine mingled with the salty tang of sea air.

She smiled up at Zac. "It's beautiful! Wait, have I been here before?"

His eyes glinted with amusement, his lips twitching. "No."

She nudged him. "Hey now, it was a legitimate question."

"You're so cute. Carry the blanket, Forgetful."

He grabbed the duffel bag, and she followed him down the sandy trail toward the beach. The sun peeked out for just a moment, dazzling her with the way it sparkled off the water.

Waves rolled onto the rocky shoreline beside the cove, splashing against the boulders with a loud roar. Maine had so many offshore islands that the water tended to ripple quietly ashore.

"There's real surf here." She thought of the map at the visitor center that she spent so many hours studying, and mentally followed it north. "This is Seal Cove." The boardwalk from town ended in a trail that led here.

"Very astute, Miss Visitor Center. Keep your eyes peeled. You might see a few of the little buggers frolicking in the surf."

She helped him spread the blanket on a flat area, and they anchored it with the duffle bag and their shoes.

He unzipped the insulated duffle. "Hope you're hungry."

"Starving. You packed a picnic in that duffel bag? What happened to my beautiful picnic basket?"

"It wouldn't fit on the back of the bike. Besides, it would've been a dead giveaway. We've got roasted chicken, Aunt Trudy's potato salad, pretzel rolls from the bakery—"

"I love those!"

His eyes danced with humor. "I know, goofy. I was there when you ate a whole basketful."

She gave a mock gasp. "I did not."

He gave her a look.

Okay, so she kind of did.

"And . . ." He pulled out one last container. "Brownies with chocolate chips and vanilla icing. Made by yours truly."

"Aww . . . my favorite." She took the container. "They're still warm. Let's eat them first."

He gave her an indulgent smile, adding a shrug. "Whatever the lady wants."

She plated a large square, and Zac took two of the corners. She bit into hers. It was warm and chewy, and the chocolate chips were still melty.

"Mmm, these are so good."

As they snacked, they talked about the money she'd inherited and some ideas for investing it locally.

"Have you given any more thought to that community center you wanted to open?"

"I have. I just need to find the right space and make some kind of business plan."

He washed down his bite with a sip of Coke. "What about the old firehouse? It's up on the market now that they've moved to their new building."

She could picture the old brick station with the red doors rolled up on warm, sunny days—an open invitation to come inside and mingle. "That would be perfect."

"It's too outdated for their use, but it already has an outdoor basketball court, and there's plenty of space inside."

"I love that idea. I'll check into it."

After talking about the firehouse and her dreams for the center, Zac told her about a local band he was trying out the next weekend, a country cover band that was popular in Bangor.

When they were finished with the brownies, they decided to keep the rest of the food cooling while they dipped their toes into the water. The ocean was cold, the waves tugging at her calves. The pebbly sand was rough against her feet.

Zac took her hand, and they walked along the water's edge. It was so peaceful here, just the sounds of the waves washing ashore and the cry of a seagull as it soared overhead.

Zac stopped suddenly, squinting down at the water. "Wait. Do you see that?" He pointed down near their feet.

Lucy squinted through the glassy surface of the water. A wave rolled in, stirring up sand. "What is it?"

"Down there, look. It's hard to see."

She leaned closer, peering through the murky water. "What? I don't—"

Zac reached in, his hand coming up with a scoop of cold water. The splash reached her neck and shoulders.

She sucked in a breath as she jerked upright.

Zac had darted a few feet away, wearing a cocky smirk. "I can't believe you fell for that."

"I can't believe you did that." She reached into the water and picked up a handful of wet sand. "You're going to pay for that, Zac Callahan!"

He turned to run, getting in a few long strides. But she was too close, and she caught up with him when he hit the soft sand.

She leaped onto his back, but her weight didn't even faze him. She pulled on the neck of his shirt and dropped the handful of sand down his back.

"No, you did not."

He twisted, reaching behind him, and maneuvered her weight. Next thing she knew the world was spinning, and she was upside down over his shoulder.

She squealed, clutching the back of his shirt. "Put me down!"

"Ooo-kay . . . if you insist." He started toward the water.

"Zac! Don't you dare. I'll tell your aunt Trudy!"

"She'll say you deserved it. She always sticks up for me. I'm her favorite."

His feet hit the water and kept going. She pounded his back. "Zac! Put me down!"

"I think I just felt a mosquito on my back." He was knee-deep now, which meant up to her thighs.

She swatted his butt. "I don't have anything to change into, you wretched man."

"Sounds like a personal problem to me." He loosened his grip on her legs, letting her slide down his front.

She clung to him like a monkey, wrapping her arms and legs around him, pressing her face into his neck. "I'm not letting go. If I go down, you're coming with me."

"Ayuh? You sure about that?" He wiggled his fingers into her ribs.

Laughter bubbled out as she flinched away, losing her grip on his neck. "Stop it! Get out of the water, Zac Callahan."

Their eyes aligned, his sparkling with amusement. "I've got wet sand sliding down my jeans, Georgia. Give me one good reason why I should let you off the hook." He poked her in the ribs again.

She wiggled, laughing. "Because you love me."

Her laughter stopped abruptly. *For gosh sakes, Lucy.* She winced, biting her lip. "I didn't say that. You did not just hear that. Let's go for a swim. Come on, throw me in. I'm ready. Go ahead."

She drew a deep breath, puffing her cheeks out, and held her nose, closing her eyes. Yes, it was ever so much better with her eyes closed.

Zac didn't move. Didn't so much as flinch.

"I'm waiting," she gasped, her heart thudding.

Why did she have such a big mouth? Disappearing under the surface sounded most appealing. Maybe she'd never come up again—

leastwise not till he left. Then she wouldn't have to see the look of pity she was sure was on his face.

But he hadn't moved, and it was dawning that she was going to be stuck in this awkward moment of her own making.

She opened an eye, peeking out. His face was inches away, and the look on his face . . . it was a job for both eyes. She opened the other one, releasing her breath, letting go of her nose.

His eyes pierced hers, twin smoldering pools. Her heart gave a lurch. Those eyes. Lord have mercy, it was like they reached clear down to her soul.

"Oh, sure," she said with a nervous laugh. "Now that I want in the water, you're not letting me go."

"It's no fun if you want it."

The rough texture of his voice made a pleasant scrape somewhere deep inside. His breath whispered against her lips, firing up neurons hither and yon.

"Well, now, that's not very nice."

His eyes lowered to her lips. "Sometimes I'm not nice."

"Just—just sometimes?"

"Only when it suits." He lowered his mouth to hers, brushing softly.

Once. Twice. His breath was warm and sweet, and she tasted a hint of chocolate. She tightened her arms around him, cupping his warm neck with her palm. He deepened the kiss, pulling her closer until his heart thudded against hers.

He swayed with the pull of the surf as it ebbed and flowed. That was her last rational thought before the rest of the world disappeared: the sultry breeze, the rippling water, the cries of seagulls. Gone. It was just Zac, and his beautiful mouth doing things that kindled a fire deep inside.

A moment later he eased back, pulling a whimper from her throat. Her heart thudded so hard she was sure he could feel it.

He leaned his forehead against hers, and she got lost in his eyes, the charcoal flecks mesmerizing her. She could hardly believe she was back in his arms. She'd missed him so much, she wasn't sure how she'd made it those seven months without him.

Two years ago he'd worked his way so quickly and so deeply into her heart. He'd unraveled her in so many ways. He still did, and she couldn't fathom life without him.

"I do, you know," he said on a soft breath.

"Hmmm . . . ?" She played with the hair at his nape.

"I love you, Lucy."

Her heart did a slow roll even as fear struck a match. "Again?" she teased.

"No." He gave her a long, slow look. "Still."

An ache opened up inside so big she could've

fallen into it. Her eyes stung. What had she done to deserve this man? She felt the same way, burned with it. She'd never stopped loving him. She knew that now. Burned with the need to tell him. But her words got caught in her throat, forming a hard lump.

Why couldn't she say them? It was only three little words.

Just say it, Lucy.

He dropped a kiss to her nose. "We should eat before the food goes bad."

She cleared her throat. "Yes, we should." Then she eased away, somehow both relieved and disappointed that the moment had passed.

Chapter 36

After eating their picnic lunch, Zac suggested a hike to Sawyer's Point to watch for seals. The point was about a half mile away and sat on a small cliff above the water. It was a popular place for photographers to capture Summer Harbor's lighthouse.

Lucy scanned the clouds on the horizon. They'd grown darker as they'd eaten. "The sky's not looking so great."

He gave the clouds a passing glance. "It'll go around us."

"That's pretty optimistic, Boss."

He pulled her up. "Just call me Pollyanna. Let's go."

The trail wound through the evergreen forest, heading north. The tall canopy above sheltered them from the outside world. Inside the bubble it was cooler and noisy with the playful tweeting of birds and nattering of squirrels. Zac set a leisurely pace, their footfalls quiet on the thick carpet of pine needles.

When they reached Sawyer's Point, they sat on the cliff top, her back against his chest. They rested up and watched the waves roll ashore. In the distance the white lighthouse squatted on the point jutting out from Summer Harbor. Folly Shoals was visible too, a dark hump in the sea.

There were no signs of seals, but snuggled against Zac's chest, Lucy couldn't bring herself to care. Especially when he brushed her hair aside and pressed a kiss to the side of her neck. His hot breath warmed her skin, and the scrape of his beard set off a shiver that traveled clear down to her toes.

"It's breezing up," he said a few seconds before lightning flashed in the distance. A low rumble followed.

"Uh-oh," she said.

"That's our cue."

He helped her to her feet and they started back down the trail, moving more quickly, hoping they could beat the storm. It wouldn't be much fun riding the cycle in the rain. Zac helped her down the steep parts of the trail, and minutes later the path opened to the beach.

The sky overhead had grown dark and angry, and the air was thick with the smell of rain. A bolt of lightning flashed and thunder cracked as the first drops fell. The wind whipped Lucy's hair, and she pushed it back from her face.

Zac gestured toward the road. "Go get your helmet on," he called over the storm's clamor. "I'll get our stuff."

"I'll help."

He didn't argue as she trotted behind him toward the blanket, now blown into a clump beside the empty duffel bag.

She went for the towels as Zac began packing the bag. As she gave one of the towels a quick shake, the wind ripped it from her grasp. She darted for it, catching it midair, then reached for the other one. The rain began in earnest as she snagged the blanket, not bothering to shake it out.

She dropped to the sand beside Zac, who was stuffing things into the bag as quickly as he could.

Suddenly an image of Zac stuffing the same duffel bag flashed into her mind, and Lucy froze as the scene played out in startling clarity.

He'd been wired and restless all week. Stressed out over his finances and torn between the Roadhouse and helping Beau and Riley get the farm up and going in time for the Christmas season. He'd hardly called or texted her, and the only date they'd had in the last month was the meal at the Lobster Hut the weekend before.

What if his feelings had changed? What if he'd realized he'd made a huge mistake? What if he didn't want to marry her anymore?

The thought struck terror into the very marrow of her bones. Something dark and dreadful bloomed inside, growing bigger as the days passed and Zac seemed to avoid her. But her love for him was so big and wide she pushed the dark feeling down each time it clawed to the surface.

But tonight . . . tonight everything seemed to be coming to a head. She dropped by after work to go over last-minute wedding details and found him in his bedroom, dropping clothes into a duffel bag.

She stopped on the threshold, something dark and ugly welling up inside at the sight. The feeling that took her back years to the house on Oak Street.

"What—what are you doing?"

He spared her a glance, his face inscrutable. He shook his head. A shadow flickered in his knotty jaw as it flexed.

Dread wormed up her spine. "Where are you going?"

He threw some socks into the bag and pushed the drawer shut with a bang. "I have to get away. I need a break."

The words, so familiar, swirled in her mind,

dredging up memories she'd shoved to the deepest reaches of her heart. A heavy fog rolled in, suffocating in its thickness. She was suddenly six years old, watching her father pack as her legs quaked beneath her.

A cold fist locked around her heart.

Zac's movements were quick and angry as he muttered about a no-show band, complaining customers, unreliable employees, needy brothers, but the sound of his voice was drowned out by the *whoosh* of blood in her ears.

Her breath felt stuffed into her lungs as her heart thrashed against her ribs. She worked hard at the basic task of breathing.

He's leaving. He's leaving you. You knew he would.

Of course she did. That's what people did. They left her. First Mama, then Daddy. How had she been so stupid as to give her heart away? The walls of her chest closed in.

Idiot!

Her heart pummeled her ribs. She should've known. She should've known!

You're not enough to hold anyone. When will you learn?

The backs of her eyes burned as she remembered clinging to her dad, begging him to take her with him. But he handed her off to Mrs. Wilmington as if she were a sack of garbage, and he never came back.

· · ·

"Lucy, hurry up!" The words snapped her back to the present.

The rain pounded her, running down her face in rivulets. Zac was putting the last things into the bag, and her eyes settled on him, seeing him in a new light.

She remembered the days following her concussion, remembered what he'd told her about the end of their relationship. She'd been so confused at his explanation. It hadn't made any sense—that she would just leave for no reason at all. Up and disappear. Not from Zac. She never would've done that.

Her eyes narrowed in on his face. "You lied." The storm snatched her words, swallowing them whole.

He zipped the bag, hitching it on his shoulder as he stood. His eyes drifted past her, then came back, concern lining his forehead. "What's wrong?"

"You lied," she said, louder this time.

Lightning flashed and thunder rumbled, shaking the ground beneath them.

"What?" He reached out. "Come on, let's get out of the rain."

She frowned at his outstretched hand, rain dripping into her eyes. She blinked the moisture away. *"You* left *me."*

His brows pulled together. "What are you talking about?"

Her heart pounded in her ears. The sand dug into her knees. A gust of wind tugged at her damp hair. "I remember now. That last day." She fixed her eyes on his. "You left me."

He tilted his head, his stormy eyes searching hers. "When I went to Bangor for the weekend?"

Her eyes burned, filling. "You left me."

Something flickered in his eyes. Something warm and tempting. He planted his knees in the sand across from her, reaching out.

She flinched away.

"No, Lucy."

"Yes, you did!"

"It was just a break."

"Exactly," she said over the howling wind. That was what people said when they left you forever.

He shook his head. "I was stressed out and upset, still dealing with losing my dad. We were getting married in a week. I went to Bangor to blow off some steam with my friends, that's all."

"That's not what you said."

"Yes, I did. I must've. Why would I leave? This is where I live. I have family here. I have a business here."

"So did my dad, and that didn't stop him."

The dark, ugly feeling inside expanded until she felt she'd burst with it. She needed to get away. Far away. She stumbled to her feet and turned toward the woods.

Chapter 37

Zac's mind spun with everything Lucy had just said. Why would she think he'd left her? He'd loved her so much. Still did. Maybe he hadn't come out and said where he was going or for how long, but this was his home. Their wedding day had been right around the corner. It made no sense.

"Lucy, wait." He dashed after her, wiping the rain from his face.

She kept going toward the trail back to town, struggling in the deep sand, the wind ripping at her clothes, the rain pummeling her.

"Lucy!" In three long strides he caught up with her. He grabbed her arm and turned her.

"Let go!" Her hair was plastered to her head, her blue eyes frantic, filled with pain. Her lashes were wet, with tears or rain, he wasn't sure.

He'd never seen her like this. "Wait . . . Think about it, Lucy. I came back a couple days later, didn't I?" He skipped the part where he'd found her gone. Where he'd panicked, calling her dozens of times before finally admitting she'd left of her own free will. Where he'd ended the night bawling like a baby.

"You misunderstood."

"You barely looked at me. You were angry."

He loosened his grip, stroking her arms. "Not at you. I was dealing with a lot of stuff. I shouldn't have run out on you like that, but, honey . . . you were the best thing in my life. There was no chance of me not coming back. No chance at all."

Something hopeful flickered in her face before her eyes shuttered.

She pulled, already backing away.

He tightened his grip. "Talk to me." Something she'd said earlier surfaced like a buoy. "Your dad . . . you told me he died, but you just said he left you. I don't understand."

She tugged for release again, giving him a flinty look. "I don't want to talk about it."

She gave a final pull, so hard he was afraid he'd bruise her if he didn't let go.

She stumbled backward as he released her, backpedaling until she caught herself. She turned and scrambled for the trail.

He stepped forward. "Lucy, come back!"

Dangit!

"I'll take you home." He rocked on his feet, the urge to go after her fighting with the instinct to give her space. He ditched the duffel bag and traipsed after her. "Lucy! Come on! Just let me take you home."

"Leave me alone, Zac!"

He barely heard her words over the howling wind. Lightning flashed and thunder rumbled, shaking the ground. The rain came harder, shards of water drilling into his skin.

She entered the trail, her quick strides taking her under the canopy of the forest. A moment later she was lost in the maze of pines.

Chapter 38

Lucy had no idea how much later it was when he entered town. The sun had sunk over the hills and darkness was closing in. Her clothes were stuck to her skin, her hair plastered to her head. Water had seeped into her sandals, turning her toes to prunes. But none of the physical discomfort rivaled the hollow ache that had opened up inside, dark and yawning.

Her feet moved quickly, her legs hurting, but she couldn't stop. Stopping would mean she'd have to think, and she didn't want to think.

Why did her memory have to come back now? Just when things were going so well? Just when she and Zac were finally happy?

Why, God? Why can't things work out, just once?

Her phone buzzed in her pocket, but she ignored it. Her eyes burned, and she blinked against the pain. Lightning flashed over Mulligan's Hill, and a sharp clap of thunder followed, making her jump. Her eyes dropped to the Roadhouse, a hulking shadow in the distance.

Where was she going? *What am I supposed to do now, God? Help me.*

Her pace slowed as she stared at the building through the rain. She couldn't go back there. She wasn't ready to face Zac yet. She was confused and angry. And the fear . . . it raked its cold fingers inside, clawing for the surface.

His words began playing in her head, but she chased them away. She couldn't think about it anymore.

She had half a mind to leave. Go back to Portland. Her feet itched with the desire to run. Her heart raced, thudding in her chest like a kick drum. Her throat closed up, blocked by a knot the size of a golf ball.

Help me, God.

Something pulled inside. Something she'd never felt before. A hard tug in her spirit, telling her to stay. She balked at the notion.

A rumble sounded. Thunder, she thought at first. But the sound grew closer. An engine.

Please, God, not Zac. Not yet. I just can't face him.

She kept moving toward town, head down against the driving rain. She was too vulnerable to face him just yet. Too weak. She'd fall into his arms regardless of her better judgment. Regardless of the fact that she'd fallen way too hard. He'd gotten all the way down to the soft spot of her heart, and already it was breaking in two.

Again.

As the rumble grew louder, she made herself turn. A red truck eased alongside the curb. Eden's worried face appeared through the rain-dotted window as she inched it down. "Lucy?"

The truck rolled to a stop beside her. Beau was driving, Eden's son in the middle.

"Get in," Eden said.

Lucy crossed her arms against the chill. "That—that's okay. There's no room, and I'll—I'll get everything all wet."

"Lucy Lovett, get in this truck right now." Eden threw open the door, lifted Micah into her lap, and dropped the booster seat in the back.

Lucy grabbed the door and slid inside, shutting it quickly. Water trickled down her legs and into the upholstery.

As Beau pulled away from the curb, Eden reached over and raised the window.

Lucy wasn't thinking straight. "Sorry. I'm getting your seat all wet."

"No worries." Beau reached behind the seat and handed her a jacket.

"Thanks." The word wobbled between her chattering teeth.

"What in the world?" Eden studied her with concern in her eyes. "Why are you out in this? And what's wrong? Did something happen?"

"W-we were over at S-Seal's Cove. We—we had an argument."

"You and Zac?" Eden asked.

Lucy nodded and clamped down on her chattering teeth.

Beau turned his sharp eyes on her, emotion tightening the corners of his mouth. "And he let you walk home? In this?"

"I—I ran off."

"I'm going to knock him upside the head." He accelerated through the green light.

Lucy suddenly realized he was headed for the Roadhouse. A chill passed over her, pebbling her skin.

She grabbed Eden's knee. "Wait. Wait, I c-can't go home. Please, I don't want to go there. Just—just drop me at the library or something."

Eden gave her a look. "We're not dropping you at the library. We'll just go to my place. You can get a shower and change into something dry."

"I don't want to r-ruin your plans."

"You're not ruining anything," Beau said. "I'll drop off you girls, then I'll take Micah for ice cream."

"Yes!" The boy pumped a fist.

"If you're sure." Lucy turned to look out the window, watching raindrops slide down the pane like tears.

The shower chased the chill from Lucy's skin, but deep inside a cold fist remained clamped around her heart. She slipped into a pair of yoga pants and a faded blue T-shirt. Her clothes tumbled in the dryer off the kitchen, the metal of her shorts button clanging intermittently. Eden had offered to let her use Micah's bed for the night, and Lucy was taking her up on it.

She tucked her feet under her on the sofa. Her left temple throbbed with the pain of an oncoming migraine, and Lucy massaged it. She'd checked her phone after her shower. Zac had called twice and sent several texts. She sent a quick response letting him know she was at Eden's. He immediately offered to come get her, but she told him she needed a little time.

She looked up when Eden entered the room with a steaming mug.

"Thought you could use some hot coffee."

"Thanks." She took the mug and sipped. The hot brew warmed her esophagus, but the strange chill inside remained, reaching down to her bones.

Eden moved a pile of Legos from the other end of the sofa and sat down. "Want to talk about it?"

Lucy shook her head. "I'm so confused."

"What happened?"

The memory of that day last fall pushed to the surface again, replaying in her mind, bringing familiar pain with it.

"I remembered. I remembered what happened all those months ago when I left."

Eden's brows lifted. "But that's good . . . isn't it?"

"I don't think so." Lucy filled her in on what had happened, how she'd come to Zac's apartment to find him packing. How he'd been so angry and distant. How she'd panicked and left.

"But at the beach he said he was only going away for the weekend—that he had to blow off some steam with friends. That I'd misunderstood."

"Why would you have thought he was leaving for good?"

"I don't know, I—now I realize it doesn't make any sense. But then it made perfect sense. He'd been distant and he was so angry, and he said he needed a break."

"And you thought he meant a break from you?"

The dark feeling surged inside, vast and heavy, weighing her down in its awfulness. Her chest tightened, making it hard to breathe. Her eyes burned, and she dug her nails into her palms.

"It—it just brought everything right back." Her throat closed over the rest of the words. What was wrong with her? It was so long ago. How many tears would she shed over her dad's abandonment before she finally got beyond it?

The couch squeaked as Eden shifted toward her. "Brought what back?"

Lucy released a humorless laugh as tears slid down her face. "It's a long story." A painful one. One she wasn't sure she wanted to relive again.

"I don't have anywhere to be."

She'd never told anyone. She'd locked the

memory up tight in a shadowed corner of her heart. Would letting it out ease the suffocating feeling? It was hard to believe it would get anything but worse.

"I know it's scary," Eden said. "But talking might help. Shoot, I needed therapy after everything my late husband put me through. If you push stuff down long enough, it'll eat away at you. I hope you know you can trust me."

Eden was the closest thing to a best friend Lucy'd ever had. That was downright pathetic, seeing as how she'd only known her two months.

She was starting to wonder if maybe that was her own fault.

"I never told Zac. I've never told anyone." She felt that tug in her spirit again. It gave her the courage to speak.

She started with her mom's death and the changes it had wrought in her childhood. She told about coming home from school to find her dad packing his things, about his peeling her off him and dumping her into the neighbor's arms.

"Oh my gosh. That's horrible. I'm so sorry you had to go through that."

Lucy wiped at the tears. "He was all I had. He was supposed to be there for me no matter what."

"No wonder you reacted like that when you found Zac packing."

"You don't think I'm crazy?"

"Not at all." She reached out for Lucy's hand.

"Jeez, you should've seen the way I reacted to Beau at first. I was so messed up. Our reactions don't always seem rational, but they make perfect sense in light of our experiences."

"There's a part of me that wants to pack up and leave again. A big part, if I'm honest. Even though Zac explained. That doesn't make any sense."

"When Zac left, it must've triggered all that anxiety you have about being abandoned. And you've just remembered it all, so it's as if it's happening all over again."

Lucy stared at Eden, her burden easing at the realization that her friend understood. "That's *it*. How come you get it?"

Eden gave her a wry grin. "Girl, I've been there. But trust me on this, running doesn't solve anything. The same old problem will keep cropping up until you deal with it."

The thought of dealing with all those old emotions made her want to curl up in a corner. "I don't know if I can."

"Trust me, you can. God'll give you the strength just like He did for me. And someday He'll use what you're going through now for a greater good. Just like He's using what I went through to help you now."

That seemed so far away. So out of reach.

"Just keep telling yourself the truth. Your emotions will catch up eventually."

"The truth," Lucy whispered as she swallowed

against the pain at the back of her throat. "I don't even know what that is anymore."

Eden squeezed her hand. "Be patient. Pray about it, and listen to God. He'll help you figure it out. And I'm here for you, sweetie. I'll help in any way I can."

Chapter 39

Zac arrived at church half an hour early the next morning. He'd spent a sleepless night tossing and turning, scanning Lucy's two short texts repeatedly, trying to read into them. Was she angry? Confused? Afraid? About to bail?

He turned off his ignition and settled back in his seat to wait, yesterday's conversation replaying over and over. Questions surfaced.

Why had she assumed he was leaving her last fall? Why hadn't she talked to him instead of running away? Why had she referred to her dad as leaving? Obviously there were things he didn't know.

He wanted to understand. He couldn't forget the pain he'd seen in her eyes yesterday. The anguish on her face. His leaving had hurt her. Destroyed her.

He'd hurt her. The thought of it made his heart twist. It was the last thing he'd ever wanted to do. Every instinct drove him to protect her, to make her smile, make her laugh. But he'd been so worried about his own problems the day he'd left that he hadn't even given her a single thought. He'd been in an ugly mood, and he could see now how she could've taken it personally. There'd been no gentle word of reassurance, no sweet goodbye kiss to reassure her that everything would be fine.

And when he'd returned from his weekend trip to find her gone, he sure hadn't given *her* emotions a second thought. He'd been too worried about his own feelings. Too busy holding up his shield of righteous indignation.

He pinched his lips together. *How's that for selfish, God?* Clearly he needed a refresher on the Love Chapter.

A car pulled into the lot, and he whipped around, hope pumping in his heart.

But it was only the organist, Mrs. Pritchard. He gave her a wave as she passed in her silver Buick.

The parking lot slowly filled. Beau and Aunt Trudy arrived with fifteen minutes to spare. His aunt made her way into the chapel while Beau headed toward Zac's truck.

Zac put down the window, eager for any news he might've received through Eden.

But his brother only greeted him with a dark look. "Really, Zac? You let her walk home in a storm?"

"She said she wanted to be left alone. What

was I supposed to do? Force her onto the bike?"

"You could've stayed with her."

His stomach sank to his toes. All right, so it wasn't his most brilliant moment. "Have you heard anything this morning?"

Beau gave him a long, withering look. Probably just to make him suffer a few extra seconds. "No," he said finally. "But they should be here any minute."

"Do you know what happened? Did she say anything?"

He lifted his shoulder. "Just a recap of your argument. There was other stuff Eden didn't feel she should tell me."

Zac dropped his head back on the seat, closing his eyes for a long second. "This is killing me. I was hoping we'd get a chance to talk before church."

Beau checked his watch. "You might start with an apology."

"No kidding, Sherlock."

Beau held up his palms. "Hey, don't shoot the messenger."

Zac had more questions than he'd ever fit in before church. There was so much he didn't understand. But he did know one thing. He couldn't lose Lucy again. He knew only too well what kind of pain and suffering that entailed. And call him stupid, but he didn't think Lucy wanted to lose what they had either.

"Any other words of wisdom?" he asked, half sarcastic, half desperate.

Beau read straight through the sarcasm. He gave Zac a long look, his eyes softening around the corners. "Try to be patient. I get the feeling she's dealing with some heavy stuff."

He reminded himself of that when Eden pulled into the lot a few minutes later. The passenger seat was empty.

Lucy had almost been relieved when she'd awakened at six o'clock with a full-blown migraine. Thank God she wouldn't have to face Zac yet. She found some ibuprofen in Eden's medicine cabinet and took a prescription-strength dose. It probably wouldn't touch the pain, but her migraine meds were at the Roadhouse.

She woke briefly when Eden slipped into the room to gather Micah's clothes and said she wasn't going to make it to church. Then she promptly fell asleep and didn't wake up until almost two o'clock. She couldn't believe she'd slept so late. Then again, she'd been up until almost three in the morning, crying and praying and crying some more.

The sleep had worked wonders on her migraine though. And the praying had helped her assimilate her thoughts. She'd come to a realization in the early hours of the morning. She didn't know what the future held. But she knew what she had to do next.

The sound of the TV filtered through the walls, and the smell of coffee lingered in the air, pulling her from bed. She brushed her teeth and face. Her eyes were swollen and her hair was a frizzy mess, but she couldn't find it in herself to care. She followed the smell of the brew down the stairs.

Eden was sitting on the couch, Micah napping in her lap. A stair squeaked under Lucy's feet.

Eden looked up. "Hey . . . you feeling any better?"

"Much." She cleared the huskiness from her voice. "Is it too much to hope there's still coffee?"

"There's half a pot warming. Help yourself."

"Bless you."

"I'm surprised you're not at Beau's," Lucy said when she returned to the living room. Sunday dinner was a tradition for the Callahans. She'd only just started joining them. Her heart plunked to her heels at the thought of Zac. How could she long for him and be afraid of facing him at the same time?

"I didn't want you to wake up alone."

"You didn't have to do that. How was . . . church?"

"Church was fine, but I suspect you're really asking about Zac?"

She was desperate for news of him. She'd been so distraught yesterday that the look on his face hadn't registered until she was quiet in bed last night. The feverish intensity of his eyes. The protective posture of his body. His emotion-choked voice. And finally that last pained stare. The memory of it slayed her.

She took another sip of the hot brew, willing the caffeine to kick in. Her hand trembled in midair. "Is he—is he okay?"

Eden ran her fingers idly through Micah's hair. "Depends what you mean by okay. He's worried about you. He's desperate to talk to you. He stopped by about half an hour ago. Brought your purse." Eden tilted her head. "He looks so pitiful, Lucy. Those big gray eyes all bloodshot, his face all haggard. You should put him out of his misery."

Lucy felt a sharp pinch in her chest. "He told me he loved me yesterday, before everything happened."

The corner of Eden's mouth lifted. "That can't be much of a surprise. I assume the feeling's mutual."

The admission formed in her throat. But before it moved to her tongue it got sucked into the cold, hollow place inside. It shouldn't be so hard to admit her feelings.

What is wrong with me, God?

It wasn't normal to hold back such a big piece of herself, was it? Whatever was going on, it was tied somehow to her father, and she was going to get to the bottom of it, no matter how much it hurt. Zac was worth it.

"Do you have any idea what you're going to do? I mean, you're welcome to stay here as long as you need, but I hope you'll try and work things out with Zac."

She wanted that more than anything. But God had laid something on her heart last night, something so solid and real it felt like a block sitting on the center of her chest. And there was only one thing that would relieve her of the weight.

She met Eden's gaze. "I need to go back home, to Savannah. I'm hoping to get a flight later today." Having money did come in handy. A month ago she couldn't have afforded a last-minute ticket.

Eden's eyes had tightened in a wary look. "Lucy . . . you can't do that to him again. From what I heard—"

"No, not permanently. I'll be back soon, I promise. And I'm going to stop by his place and let him know what's going on and let Miss Trudy know I'll need a few days off. I spent a lot of time in prayer last night, and it gave me clarity. There's something I have to do, and I have to do it alone."

Lucy's hand shook as she knocked on Zac's apartment door later that afternoon. Her knees were as flimsy as cooked spaghetti. Her heart hammered against her ribs, and her empty stomach twisted. She was so hungry for a look at his face. So desperate to be in his arms again.

Despite her need to get a grip on what was happening inside her, she didn't think she'd be able to refuse if he tried to kiss her.

She knocked again, but she was beginning to think it was a lost cause. She hadn't noticed his truck in the parking lot, but then, she hadn't really looked for it either. She'd been too lost in thought.

When one more knock proved ineffective, she took the stairs down to her room and packed what she'd need for a couple days. When she was finished, she went out to the restaurant again and peeked into the kitchen.

Cal, his cook, turned from the grill. "Hey, Lucy."

"Hey, Cal. You know where Zac is?"

Cal shoved a plate under the warmers and grabbed two orders from the wheel. "I think he's at Beau's house."

Her heart sank. As much as she'd been dreading his questions—questions she didn't have answers for—she'd really wanted to see his handsome face before she left.

"Oh. All right, thanks."

She checked her watch as she wandered through the dining room. Her plane left in two hours, and she still had to drive to Bangor. There was no time to stop at the farm. She exhaled deeply, frustration bubbling up.

She didn't want to talk about this over the phone. She wasn't ready to talk about her dad, and she knew Zac would somehow pull it all out of her whether she was ready or not. He might even talk her into staying. And she had to go home. Needed to sort this out once and for all.

A text was too impersonal, but a letter . . . a letter was perfect. She went to her room and pulled a sheet of paper from the notebook on her bedside table.

He was trying to be patient. He really was. He'd stopped by Eden's after church with Lucy's purse, but she'd been sleeping. At least that was what Eden had said. She wouldn't have lied. Would she?

He lost all track of the Red Sox game on Beau's TV. Couldn't even remember who they were playing. Next to him his brother let out a dissatisfied grunt. Aunt Trudy's knitting needles clacked across the room. The savory smell of beef stew hung in the air, turning his knotted stomach.

His phone had been annoyingly quiet all afternoon. Despite its silence he kept checking for texts. He was pulling his phone out for the umpteenth time when he felt a *thwack* to the back of his head.

He turned a dark look on Beau. "Hey . . ."

"Call her already."

"You told me to be patient," he said.

"There's patient, and there's stupid."

"For your information I stopped by before I

came here. She's sleeping. I don't want to wake her." God knew if her night had been like his, she needed it.

He fretted through the rest of the game, finally giving up during the seventh inning stretch. He swung by Eden's on his way home, but there was no answer at the door.

When he pulled up to the Roadhouse, his eyes fell on the empty space where her car was usually parked. A dark, heavy feeling bloomed inside.

No. Not again. *Please, God. I can't take it if she's left again.*

Defeat closed in around his neck like a noose as he strode toward Lucy's room. In his mind's eye he could already see the perfectly made bed, the empty closet, the clean dresser. He'd seen it all before. He had trouble swallowing against the hard knot at the back of his throat.

When there was no answer to his knock, he opened her door. She always kept the room picked up, the bed made. He checked the bathroom first, dread tightening the noose. The countertop was empty, her curling iron gone, along with her hair spray and cosmetics.

With anxious feet he moved toward the closet, his heart beating up into his throat. His hand closed over the knob, turning.

At the sight of her clothes his breath rushed out. He gripped the doorframe with trembling fingers, his eyes scanning the closet. There were quite a few empty hangers. His eyes dropped to the floor where her favorite heels were lined up in a neat row. The tension drained from his shoulders. She'd never leave those behind.

Maybe Eden had brought her over to get a few things. Maybe she needed a few days away. He remembered his own escape last year—the one that had caused all this. Maybe she was just stressed and needing a little space. With everything she'd been through with her memory loss, he could hardly blame her. That didn't make it any easier though.

He treaded upstairs to his apartment, sadness falling over him like a heavy fog. He had to talk to her. He needed to hear her voice and know she was okay.

He pulled his phone from his pocket. She wouldn't answer though. He was sure of it. Just like last time and the time before that. All those familiar feelings washed over him. His hands felt tied behind his back, and the helpless feeling knotted his muscles all over again.

Come on, God. Cut me some slack here.

He unlocked his door and flung it open so hard it bounced against the wall. Something fluttered off the ground, landing at his feet. A sheet of notebook paper, folded in half. He bent down and grabbed it, opening it.

Lucy's neat script filled the page. Equal parts of dread and hope filled him as he began reading.

Dear Zac,

I stopped by to see you before I left town, but you weren't home. I've been all messed up since yesterday, and I know you have been too. You must be as confused as I am. The memory that came back has really thrown me for a loop. I don't know what to think. But I do know you were telling me the truth when you said you weren't leaving me last year.

I've been praying about this, and I need to go home to Savannah. I have unfinished business to deal with, and I need to do it alone. I have some work to do on me. It will be hard, and I can't tell you how much I'm dreading all the feelings it will dredge up. But I think it will be worth it if it helps me move forward.

I know it's asking a lot, but . . . please be patient with me, Zac. I'm sorry to leave you with only a note and with so many questions, but trust me when I say I don't have any answers for you yet.

I haven't booked my flight back to Maine, but I don't anticipate being gone longer than a couple days. I would appreciate your prayers.

XXOO,
Lucy

Chapter 40

Magnolia Memorial Gardens was located outside of Savannah to the southwest. Mature trees towered over the grassy landscape, shading the gently rolling hills. Colorful flowers proliferated even in the August heat. Despite the well-manicured setting, the narrow, grass-edged lane winding through the cemetery lent it a country feel.

Lucy hadn't been here since they'd buried her mother, and those memories did nothing to calm the storm welling up inside. She'd never been to her dad's graveside. He'd died while she was away at college, and she hadn't gotten word until several days after his funeral.

Her aunt's arrangements, she remembered now, had been handled from Portland. Audrey had requested no funeral or memorial and only the simplest of arrangements.

It was only a vague sense of direction that led her to the back of the cemetery where the grassy lawn met the woods. Towering pine trees formed a canopy overhead, blocking out the evening sun. She'd arrived last night and had dithered away a whole day, dreading this moment.

She parked the rental alongside the drive and stepped outside. Even though the sun was setting, the heat felt blisteringly hot after the coolness of the car's air-conditioning, and the air was so heavy with humidity it was hard to breathe. The scent of magnolias swept by on a hot breeze.

Lucy wandered around the garden, searching for her family's plots. Her clothes were damp and sticking to her skin by the time she found her aunt's no-fuss marker.

Going by some distant recollection, her eyes wandered back a row to the base of a white pine. She followed the direction of her gaze and stopped at the foot of her mother's grave. Heart pounding, she read the inscription on the flat marker:

GLORIA JEAN LOVETT
BELOVED WIFE AND MOTHER
NOV. 2, 1965—SEPT. 19, 1996
GRACE WAS IN ALL HER STEPS
HEAVEN IN HER EYES
IN EVERY GESTURE DIGNITY AND LOVE

A knot formed in Lucy's throat as the marker blurred. She closed her eyes, her mother's image blooming in her mind's eye. The wind whispering through her brown hair, the smile sparkling in her blue eyes, the smell of sunshine and flowers on her soft skin. She breathed in a steadying breath, words clogging her throat, the loss still fresh after all this time. The one person who'd loved her right.

Thank you, Mama.

She bit her lip, helpless against the tears that flowed down her cheeks. Her eyes drifted to her dad's marker, an avalanche of emotions flooding in. Her feet were rooted to the spot. The walls of her chest closed in, smothering her with their weight. She labored to draw in a shallow breath. Her heart pounded too quickly, and fear sucked the moisture from her mouth.

That cold, dark pit opened up inside, filled with so many emotions she could barely contain them. She was helpless to find words. Lucy Lovett, whose words tumbled too easily from her mouth.

She focused on her mother's marker, not able to think about her dad just yet. She didn't try to stop the flow of tears, just let them come, all of them for her mother.

One thing at a time. One memory at a time.

She wept until she became aware of darkness falling around her, then headed back to the car. Exhaustion weighted her shoulders like a leaden cape. Despite the powerful grip of grief, she was disappointed in herself.

Why did I even come here?

She hadn't even been able to look at her dad's marker, much less process her feelings. She was a coward. She wasn't strong enough to face her past. She pointed her rental toward town as she drew a steadying breath.

She thought of Zac, waiting back in Summer

Harbor. Fear swarmed like a hundred angry bees at the thought of going back. Her love for him crippled her. How could she need him so much and be so afraid at the same time? The conflicting emotions swirled in her head until she was dizzy with them.

What if I lose him again?

She well remembered the early days in Portland now. The memories had come flooding back the night of the storm. She'd wept for weeks after she'd left Zac, and after that had moved numbly through her days, her heart broken into a million pieces. She had never put it back together. Had simply settled for someone less. Someone manageable. Someone she could stand to lose.

Zac was different altogether. She already knew how it felt to be without him. A fist closed around her heart, squeezing tight. She didn't know if she could bear to lose him again.

Zac helped unload the bread, then went to the front and turned down the chairs. Keeping busy was the name of the game. He'd been unsettled since Lucy had left. He'd reread her note a dozen times trying to reassure himself, but nothing soothed the anxiety threading through him.

He hadn't heard from her, and neither had Eden. What if she decided not to come back? It was that thought that had kept him on his feet for the past twenty-four hours, minus six hours of tossing and turning.

Come on, God. Give me something here. A call, a text. Something.

She'd asked for space, and he was trying to give it to her. But a pain had taken up residence in his gut, and his legs were weak and shaky.

This felt too much like last time, despite the note.

He checked the time, then rushed to pull the last few chairs down so he wouldn't be late in Skyping Riley. He'd scheduled the call last week when everything was flowers and sunshine. He always tried to be upbeat, hoping to keep his brother's spirits up, but he was going to have to dig deep today.

He went to his office, pushing next week's schedule aside. He needed to do payroll and make a trip to the bank. He was grateful for things to do.

He opened Skype, and the call came in right on the dot of eleven. A second later Riley's face appeared on the screen. He seemed older, somehow, than he had last time they'd Skyped. He supposed war could do that to a person.

Riley's eyes crinkled at the corners as he gave a two-finger salute, reminding Zac so much of their dad that he felt a pinch in his gut. "Hey, bro. Good to see your ugly mug."

"How's the military treating you, bud?"

"Aw, not bad. I'm keeping busy. Just finished a game of Madden with the guys. There's a tournament going on."

"Are you winning?"

"You kidding? There are guys here who are practically professional. It passes the time though."

"That's true. Before I forget, Aunt Trudy wanted to know if you need anything in particular. She's getting ready to send a care package."

"God love her. I could use some Chapstick. And I've really been craving your atomic wings. If you could throw in a bottle of that sauce, that'd be great. And candy to give out to the local kids."

"Consider it done."

"Thanks, man. How's everyone back home? Roadhouse busy?"

"Ayuh, it's keeping me on my toes. Beau's gearing up for fall activities at the tree farm. Hayrides, bonfires, and stuff. He's got quite a few groups scheduled already."

A wistful look came over Riley's face. "Fall in Summer Harbor . . . man, I can almost smell it. Decaying leaves, wood fires, the scent of rain. It's so freaking hot here—over a hundred most days."

"A dry heat though."

Riley made a face as he swatted the screen. "That was me, whacking you in the back of the head."

Zac dredged up a smile. "Didn't feel a thing."

"So, what's Aunt Trudy up to? I got a letter from

her a couple weeks ago, but she doesn't say much about herself."

"She's slowed down since Lucy started at the visitor center. Guess she's getting a lot of knitting done. I did find out something interesting . . . She and Sheriff Colton used to be an item."

Riley reared back. "What? When?"

"Back in high school. She told me recently. Sounds like they were pretty serious. Then Colton left for college and things fell apart."

"How did we not know this?"

"Grandpa didn't approve, so they kept it on the down low."

"They sneaked around?"

"More or less. I don't know exactly what happened between them, but she has bad feelings toward him."

"That explains why she's so prickly. Must've been something pretty big to hold a grudge this long."

"Oh, I don't know. She can hold a grudge with the best of them. I'm recalling a certain blueberry pie incident."

Riley made a face. "I was twelve. And I didn't know it was for the bake-off. Jeez, she wore me out over that for years."

"Well, imagine how Colton feels."

Riley gave a wry laugh. "Guy must be a glutton for punishment. She must've been over the moon for him if she's that torn up over it still.

Maybe it's not just the Callahan *men* who only love once, like she's always saying."

"She loved Uncle Tom."

"Yeah, but there's love and there's *love,* know what I'm saying?"

Boy, did he. The kind of love he had for Lucy knocked his legs right out from underneath him. "I hear you."

Riley settled back in his chair, running his fingers through his buzzed hair. "So what about you? Gonna tell me why you look like you haven't slept in a week?"

Zac gave a tight smile. "Don't know what you're talking about. Everything's fine."

"And I'm sitting on the beach with an umbrella drink. Cut the crap. It's Lucy, isn't it? She leave again?"

Zac's jaw locked down tight. "She just went back to Savannah for a few days. She left a note."

Riley rolled his eyes. "Aw, you gotta be kidding me."

"It's not like last time. She's coming back. She just has stuff she has to work out."

"Man, she's got issues, bro."

"No kidding, Captain Obvious. That's why she went home."

"And left you in the dust just like last time."

"That was a misunderstanding." He gave his head a shake. It was a long and convoluted story, and frankly, he didn't feel like defending Lucy at the moment. "I'm not getting into this with you. You got your own problems."

"If you're referring to Paige, I've made a decision. I'm telling her how I feel when I come home."

The tension oozed from Zac's shoulders. He settled back in his seat, adjusting the screen. "Really?"

"There's a lot of time to think over here. Things are more, I don't know, black and white. You gotta seize the day before it seizes you."

Zac didn't even want to know what caused that kind of thinking. "So why not tell her now?"

"She'd appease me just to keep my spirits up—after she faints dead away from shock. I want an honest response, and I'm not going to get that if I'm halfway across the world in a war zone."

"Probably right. She worries about you."

"How's she doing anyway? You see her much?"

"She was at the farm Sunday for dinner. She's doing well. She always asks about you."

The corner of Riley's mouth ticked up. "I'm glad she's spending time with the family. Keep an eye out for her, will you?"

"Sure, bro." He thought of the picnic lunch she'd had with Dylan Moore a few weeks ago. Lucy told him they'd gone out on a couple dates since then. He sure hoped nothing came of it, for Riley's sake.

Riley looked over his shoulder where a few of his buddies were messing around. He turned back to the screen. "Hey, sorry to make it so short, but I gotta run. I'll be praying about Lucy. Hope it all works out, man."

"It will. Take care of yourself. Love you."

"Love you too."

They signed off, and Zac leaned back against his seat, feeling just as unsettled as he had before the call.

Chapter 41

Sunlight poured through the slit in the hotel curtain, making Lucy wince. A headache pounded behind her left eye as she checked the time: 9:37 a.m.

She couldn't believe she'd slept so late. She'd dropped into the bed without supper and slept through the night.

She showered before hitting the local Waffle House for a quick breakfast. It was another hot, humid day, the kind that made breathing feel like deliberate suffocation. Or maybe it was just her internal struggle making her feel that way.

A Starbucks coffee in hand, she hit the streets in her rental, wandering around her aunt's neighborhood. Stately old brick homes. Oaks with Spanish moss draping from their massive branches. Friendly people, always ready with a smile and a wave.

She drove by her aunt's estate, but the gates in front of the long, straight lane were locked up tight. There were no real memories there anyway.

She had a whole free day in her hometown and no place to go. No old friends to look up. Not a single person she'd kept in contact with that she could invite out for lunch. She'd even lost touch with her friends from college. Girls who'd once shared every detail of her daily life.

She'd met many fine people in her travels, and had grown close enough to several of them to call them friends. But where were they now? A few e-mails and texts had come and gone. Had she even bothered answering?

After her concussion, she'd thought the names of her current friends were lost with her memory. But the truth was, she hadn't had any real friends. Even Anna, her maid of honor in Portland, was barely more than an acquaintance.

What was wrong with her?

Her car seemed to turn of its own volition into her old neighborhood, seeking something familiar. The houses seemed smaller than they were when she was a child. The lawns less kept, the trees so high overhead they provided a continuous carpet of shade. She turned onto Oak Street, spotted her childhood home, and pulled to a stop along the curb.

It was a modest two-story with a lovely veranda. The swing swayed lazily in the morning breeze.

The black shutters needed a coat of paint, and the gutters drooped helplessly from the roofline. The area that had once proliferated with flowers was a barren space filled with brown grass and weeds. She was glad her mama couldn't see what had become of her glorious garden.

Lucy stared at the house, that familiar sadness welling up inside. What had she expected? That she would come here and remember all the happy times? There had been many. Why did the painful ones always outshine the good ones?

Her eyes drifted next door to Mrs. Wilmington's house. She looked in the backyard, almost expecting to see the woman hanging her sheets on the line. But years had passed. She must've been in her midsixties back then. Her former neighbor had likely passed. Lucy pulled from the curb, that unsettled feeling building in her middle.

What now, God? I don't even know why I'm here. There's no one to see, no one to talk to. Why did You bring me back here?

She might as well return to the hotel. Maybe she could check on this evening's flights. She could always fly standby. She turned onto the road leading to the hotel. The midday traffic was worse than she remembered. Road construction blocked the street ahead, so she followed the detour signs, heading in a direction that took her out of her way.

She sighed. Just her luck. This whole trip was a

bust. Not to mention a waste of money. She was no closer to figuring out her problems than she'd been when she'd left Summer Harbor nine months ago.

She followed the flow of traffic several miles along the detour route. A few minutes later the route took her into a familiar area. She gave a laugh of disbelief as she recognized the entrance to the Magnolia Memorial Gardens.

Are You kidding me?

On a whim, she slowed the car and turned in, following the narrow lane to the back of the cemetery. She parked along the roadside and shut off the engine. The hot air swallowed her up as she stepped from the vehicle.

Déjà vu, she thought, as the familiar dark feeling welled up inside. She must be a glutton for punishment.

The ground was hard and dry beneath her feet as she trudged to the one marker she hadn't been able to face the day before. She was going to do it. She was going to go straight back there and stare his headstone in the face.

Her heart pounded in her chest, finding a new rhythm. The ugly spot swelled inside, taking up room her lungs needed. She marched on anyway, heat prickling the back of her neck. Her eyes narrowed on the marker, and her footsteps quickened.

She stopped at the foot of the grave, her breaths

coming rapidly, blood whooshing in her ears.

She glared at the marker. "It's me, Daddy. I've finally come back to see where you're buried. Maybe I should've come back earlier, but you didn't really deserve that, did you? You missed out on most of my life, you know. So much has happened. After you dumped me with Aunt Audrey, she shipped me off to boarding school. She had no idea what to do with a little girl—as you must've known."

The words bubbled out as fast as she could think them, the anger fading as she went.

"I did well in school though. I got your smarts, as Aunt Audrey liked to say. I even got into Harvard. That's where I was when I found out you died. I didn't go to your funeral though. I didn't even know about it until it was over, which is really kind of appropriate.

"I've done a lot of traveling since then. Aunt Audrey said I got that from Mama. She called it 'wanderlust.' Her lips always curled as she said it, and not in a good way. I got the feeling she didn't approve of Mama, but I always told her she was the best mother in the whole world. She was, you know."

Her eyes stung with tears, and a knot welled up in her throat.

"She would've been so disappointed in you, Daddy. She would've beat you over the head with a broom for leaving me like you did. And you know what else? You would've deserved it. You don't just leave a child like that. You were the only one I had. The only one I could count on, and you abandoned me. You weren't the only one hurting, the only one missing her. How could you think only of yourself? I needed you."

Tears washed down her face, one after the other. A boulder sat in her chest, heavy and unmoving. "I needed you so badly. I'm messed up now. I don't connect with people, not in any kind of lasting way. I have no idea what's become of my boarding school friends or my college friends.

"The real problem is . . . I'm afraid, Daddy. I'm so afraid of letting anyone too close, because if I do, if I let myself care too much, they'll leave me, just like you did."

The thought stabbed her in the gut, a sharp pain that got her attention in a way nothing else had. In a moment when her guard was completely down, the truth had come pouring out. She sucked in a deep breath, then another.

"I've let all my friendships slip away. I've left every boyfriend I ever had—and that includes two fiancés, Daddy. Two of them! And the one who managed to really slip under all my defenses . . . I had one foot out the door our whole relation-ship. And I left at the first glimpse of trouble.

"So here I am, Daddy." She shrugged, looking skyward. "I have no one. I chase away everyone who cares about me. I leave them before they can leave me. I'm so afraid of being treated the way you treated me that I've—I've become *you*."

The words resonated inside, sending an earthquake through her system. Aftershocks followed, sweat snaking between her shoulder blades.

Her legs buckled, and her weight sagged to the ground, her knees planting in the thick grass. Her eyes widened on the marker as a tingling sensation spread through her chest. Her breath escaped in one short puff, her lungs clocking out.

"I've become you." A hot breeze swept her words away.

How many people had she abandoned? She counted them off: the boarding school friends she'd left in the dust, the college friends she'd lost contact with, the boyfriends she'd brushed off, the fiancés she'd jilted.

Zac.

She'd done to him what her father had done to her. The weight of it crashed down on her, pushing on her shoulders, crushing her. Her eyes filled with tears again as she remembered the pain of abandonment. She would never forget the feeling. The endless, hollow ache that had swallowed her whole. She squeezed her eyes shut, rubbing at the ache centered in her chest.

Why, God? Why did I do the most hurtful thing to the one I love the most?

She opened her eyes, unseeing, puzzling it all out. But no matter how long she thought about it or how many answers she had for her past behavior, the fear remained. It was a heavy black weight that sat on her chest like a lead brick.

"What am I supposed to do with the fear?"

Her eyes swept across the terrain, unseeing. Until they passed a flash of color beside her mom's marker. They came back to the spot, lingering on the blue clusters of star-shaped flowers. She must be seeing things.

She squinted at the vibrant buds as she moved toward them, then knelt in the grass. She brushed her fingers through the velvety blooms, memories surfacing.

It'll bring courage to your heart, Lucy.

Her mom placing a tiny bloom behind her ear when she had to apologize to a neighbor for breaking a window. A vibrant bud in her cereal bowl on the morning of a big test. A vase of blooms when she had her tonsils out.

She breathed a laugh, looking heavenward, her eyes burning as she scanned the radiant blue sky. It was as if God had placed them here just for her.

There seemed no other explanation. She hadn't seen them yesterday. Plus the plant was an annual, and while it reseeded well, there were no other starflowers in sight.

The weight lifted from the center of her chest. She drew a deep breath, the action stretching out lungs that had grown tight. She blew it out, the darkness seeping slowly away.

She was no longer a child, believing a tiny bud might magically take away her fears. But there was a God who loved her enough to give her courage in the face of that fear.

I will never leave you nor forsake you.

The quiet whisper in her heart stole her breath. She knew that. Of course she did. But did she believe it all the way down to the core of her being? Or had she held God at arm's length all these years, afraid He'd leave her just as her daddy had? She thought of all the surface prayers, the skimming of Scripture, the wandering of her mind in church. She hadn't kept up her relationship with God any more than she had with all those friends.

Well, no more.

Her eyes fell to the marker beside her, the minimal inscription on her father's grave a sad indicator of a life misspent.

"You know what, Daddy?" She rose to her feet, her legs regaining their strength. A light, fluttery feeling bloomed in her chest as she brushed the dirt from her hands.

"God's not like you. There are plenty of nice folk who aren't like you. And I don't want to be like you either." Her voice was sure and strong. "The people who love me deserve better. I've got a good man. He loves me. He'll never leave me."

The words sank down deep, filling in the empty places. Filling them to overflowing.

He'll never leave me.

He was always there for his family. He'd been there for her when she was sick, even when he'd been reeling over his dad's death. Had come for her in Portland when she'd needed him so badly. When he'd had no good reason to help her. When he'd owed her nothing but bitterness over the way she'd left.

She could overcome her fears. She could act courageously in the face of those fears. There was no way she would knowingly do to Zac what her father had done to her. She loved him far too much for that.

After one last look at the vibrant starflower, she turned to her father's grave. "I forgive you, Daddy," she whispered, giving the headstone a sad smile.

Then she turned and worked her way toward the car, over the pine-strewn lawn, feeling the weight of a thousand boulders lifting from her shoulders.

Chapter 42

Once Lucy made her decision to return to Summer Harbor, she was suddenly eager to see Zac. She understood herself much better now. It was as if someone had shone a light into the dark recesses of her heart, illuminated her deepest fear. Her past behavior made sense now, and she needed to share what she'd learned with Zac. Needed to look him in the eyes and tell him how she felt, how she truly felt. She shook with the need to tell him.

But obstacles crowded her path. She had to wait a day for the next flight. Then her first plane was delayed. She paced the terminal, her legs trembling as though she'd had twelve shots of espresso. It finally took off an hour late, and when she arrived in LaGuardia, she hit the ground running, desperate to catch her next flight. She finally boarded the plane, breathless and jittery. Her knees bounced all the way to Bangor, making the woman in the next seat glare at her.

It wasn't until she pointed her car toward Summer Harbor that a terrifying thought emerged.

What if she was too late? What if Zac had decided she wasn't worth the effort?

Suddenly the excess energy channeled into nerves. A hard knot tightened in the pit of her stomach, constricting as she wound along the two-lane highway. By the time she entered the town, darkness had fallen, shrouding the hope that had blossomed inside.

When Lucy pulled into the Roadhouse parking lot, the Open light by the front door was off. There were three vehicles in the lot, including Zac's truck: the cleanup crew.

She pulled into her parking slot and shut off the ignition, the beam of her headlights extinguishing against the weathered shingles. Her hands trembled as she removed the keys, and her lungs worked to keep pace with her heart.

It had been four days since she'd left that note. Four days since she'd heard from him. He hadn't texted or called.

You asked him for space, silly.

But that meant he'd had space too. Space to reconsider the cost of loving her. It had been high for him in the past. She knew that now.

How many second chances did one person deserve?

Fear spread its cold, dark tentacles through her entire body. They encircled her heart, squeezing. Tightened around her lungs, impeding their expansion.

What if he said no? What if he didn't love her anymore? What if he . . .

Left her.

Her breath came in little gasps. Her heart kicked against her ribs. Her mouth dried. She closed her eyes against the familiar assault of fear.

Help me, God. It's only fear.

She knew the enemy by name, and she called it out.

The image of the starflower flashed in her mind, hardy stems poking through hard earth. The vibrant blue flower was so real in her mind she could almost touch its tiny petals, almost smell its delicate fragrance and taste its sweet flavor.

Give me courage to take the next step, God. I'm helpless without You.

She eyed the darkened entrance of the restaurant. Zac was beyond that door, and she wasn't letting fear stand between them. Not again.

Pull it together, Lucy Lovett.

Her tight grip loosened on the steering wheel. She reached for the handle and opened the door, stepping out into the night. The familiar tang of the ocean filled her lungs as a cool breeze swept over her skin.

Her shoes crunched on the gravel as she made her way toward the entrance. Time slowed, making the short stretch feel like a mile. By the time she mounted the steps, her heart was pounding like a drum.

Interior lights illuminated the obscured glass. She reached for the handle. The door swung open quietly, and she stepped across the threshold, her eyes drifting across the room. Someone was putting up chairs, someone else pushing a broom.

Her eyes swept past them to the bar where Zac stood over the register, hands in the drawer. The sight of him stole her breath. A lock of black hair had given up its position, probably hours ago, flopping over his creased forehead. His brows were a dark slash over his deep-set eyes, his lips drawn into a tight line.

He was standing where he had been when she'd first seen him. But there was no upbeat tune playing on the jukebox tonight. No baseball game blaring from the TVs or sounds of happy chatter. Only the scrape of a chair. The quiet brush of the broom.

The jangle of the cash drawer as Zac pushed it closed.

He looked up from the register, his eyes catching on her. He froze, a fistful of cash clutched in his big hand. The lines in his forehead smoothed, and his lips parted as his gaze raked over her.

Her feet stopped, grew roots, as her heart palpitated. She searched his familiar face. The bristle of his jaw. The soft curve of his upper lip. The straight line of his nose. Her gaze landed on his piercing gray eyes, and for the first time in days, her soul settled into place.

She loved this man. She loved him so much. The love—it was stronger than the fear. This need to love him the way he deserved to be loved. To put his needs before her own.

Perfect love casts out fear.

She'd heard the scripture more times than she could count, but she hadn't understood until now. When her concern was for Zac, her selfish fears evaporated. As love for him consumed her, the fear lifted, setting her free.

"I love you," she blurted.

The room came to a standstill. Gone were the swish of the broom, the clattering of the chairs. Three sets of eyes stared back.

Her face heated as she searched Zac's face for some clue as to his response, but his eyes were unfathomable. She bit the inside of her lip.

"Can I get you guys to clear out?" His eyes never left hers. The scrape of his voice was the most beautiful sound she'd ever heard.

The employees scuttled from the room.

Zac skirted the counter slowly, moving toward her with that masculine grace, his eyes intense, holding her captive. Something shifted in his face as he neared. Something hungry and determined.

Her breath caught and held, her lungs incapable of expansion. So much to say. So much filling her, she wanted to burst with it. "I have so much to—"

His mouth closed over hers, deliberate and demanding, his arms drawing her against him.

She clung to him in relief, surrendering to his kiss. It wasn't too late. He still wanted her. Still loved her. The proof was in the possessive swoop of his lips, the sure grip of his embrace.

The kiss slowly morphed, gentling until she felt as if she might melt into a puddle. He cupped the back of her head, and she slid her fingers into the softness of his hair. The spicy scent of him washed over her, bathing her in need.

He'd been so patient with her. Far more so than she deserved. Her fingers tightened at his nape as love for him overwhelmed her.

"I love you," she gasped into the space between them, needing him to believe her.

He paused in his tender ministrations, his lips hovering over hers. His eyes opened, searching hers.

"I never stopped loving you," she said. "Not in all the time I was gone."

Something in his eyes shifted, warming. His lips curled upward. "Neither did I, Georgia."

His lips met hers in a lingering kiss, soft and coaxing. She lost herself in his touch, her heart racing with desire. When her mouth parted, he took full advantage. His arms tightened around her and he lifted her off her feet, bringing her to his level.

She wanted to stay right here, right in his arms for the rest of her life. There was still so much to say. But he wanted her, loved her, without explanation, and that alone made her feel as if she would burst with love for him.

A moment later he drew away, setting his forehead against hers. "I missed you."

"I'm sorry I was gone so long. I had so much to sort through and—"

"Are you okay?"

She breathed a laugh. "More okay than I've been in all my life."

"Then that's all that matters."

"I have so much to tell you." She glanced down at the distant floor and gave him a tiny grin.

"Maybe you should put me down so we can talk."

"Oh no." He scooped up her legs, cradling her easily. "I'm not letting you go anytime soon. At least a month or two."

"Your staff might find that rather odd."

"I don't care what anyone thinks."

She roped her arms around his neck as he carried her into his office and settled on the couch with her in his lap.

"I guess you're serious about this not letting go stuff."

His eyes flashed. "Darn right. You can talk from here."

She could live with that. She snuggled into the curve of his arm, letting his warmth seep into her. "I guess, first of all, I should set something straight. Back when I told you my dad died, that wasn't the whole story. He didn't die until later, not until I was in college."

He tilted his head, his brow creasing. "But you said your aunt raised you . . ."

"That's right. She did." Lucy drew a deep breath and told him everything that had happened— everything—from her idyllic early childhood to the trauma of her mother's passing to the day she came home to find her father packing.

She met his eyes, needing him to understand the depth of her pain. "He was leaving me. He said he just needed a break, but I knew . . . I knew. I was kicking and screaming as he carried me to the neighbor's house, and I was so afraid."

He winced. "Ah, honey. I'm so sorry."

She swallowed against the knot in her throat. Blinked against the burning behind her eyes. "That day last fall . . . when I came here and found you packing . . ."

Realization dawned on his face. "You thought I was leaving you—just like your dad."

Her eyes filled, and she blinked against the tears.

"Aw, baby . . ." He cupped her cheek, looking at her with such conviction. "I wouldn't do that. I will never leave you."

The words made her soul sigh. "I know that. I know that now. Leaving you was the biggest mistake of my life. I've left so many people in the dust because of my fears. But losing you was the worst. It scared me so badly. I swore I'd never love again. In Portland I settled for Brad. He never had my heart, so I knew he couldn't break it."

He pressed a gentle kiss to her lips, the barest of brushes, their breaths mingling between them. "It's all in the past now."

He swept her tears away as she told him the rest of the story. Everything from her despair that first night in Savannah to her epiphany at Daddy's grave the day before. Everything just tumbled out, unedited and raw.

He listened, only an occasional murmur or sympathetic smile to urge her on.

When she was finished, she felt as light as a helium-filled balloon. "I've been thinking I might start seeing a counselor, just for a while. Just to get all my thoughts and feelings squared away. I don't want anything to spoil what we have."

"Whatever you want, honey. I'm proud of you. Is there anything I can do?"

She placed a palm on his bristly cheek, relishing the familiar feel of it. "Just let me love you."

He gave a hint of a smile. "I think I can manage that." His eyes pierced hers, growing in intensity, the color deepening to smoky gray. "For the rest of my life, if you'd like . . ."

Her gaze sharpened on him. Her heart beat up into her throat. Hope bloomed, colorful and breathless and beautiful.

"Marry me, Lucy." His low voice rumbled in her chest. "I want to spend the rest of my life loving you."

He was so much more than she deserved. "Oh, Zac."

"I'm not letting you get away again."

"I'm not going anywhere," she said on a soft breath.

He kissed her. Long and slow and sweet. A low hum worked its way through her, making her dizzy. Her love for him was deeper than the fathomless sea, bigger than the clear blue sky, brighter than the noonday sun.

When he drew away a moment later, it was only to tuck her close, resting his cheek on her head.

Drained, she curled into his chest, clutching his shirt. She drew in the smell of him and exhaled quickly so she could do it all over again. His heart beat strong and steady against her ear. That was her Zac. Strong and steady.

"I will never leave you." His words echoed through her mind, a promise her heart would remember always.

Epilogue

Two months later, Zac hadn't let up on his promise to keep Lucy close. He watched her skirt a table, then stop at a booth to take an order. When she'd offered to fill in for one of his sick servers, he hadn't complained. He loved having her nearby as he worked. Watching her hitch the tray on the curve of her waist, seeing her flash that dimple when she laughed, hearing that soft, slow drawl that drove him crazy.

Realizing that he was wiping down a clean bar, he tossed the rag behind the counter. It was just nearing suppertime but the restaurant was slow, only a handful of booths filled. He was surprised since Boston College was playing UMass tonight.

He intercepted Lucy as she headed toward the kitchen and pulled her behind the partition, dragging her into his arms. "I can't wait two more months, Georgia."

"We've been all through this. Things'll be slower around here in December, and we can get away for a whole week. You said so yourself."

He let out a low growl. "I changed my mind."

"Your impatience is most charming," she said in that drawl of hers. She turned that smile up at him, drawing his eyes to her sweet lips.

He liked to keep things professional when they were working, but those lips . . .

He tried not to. He really did.

His lips brushed hers in a slow, soft kiss that made him wish they were someplace else. Like on his sofa or in his office. Mindful—just barely—of his surroundings, he drew away.

She set a hand on his chest, giving him a look that gave him second thoughts about pulling away.

Before he could act on the impulse, she pulled her phone from her pocket. Her engagement ring —the one he'd saved from before—flashed on her finger. Nothing had ever looked so right.

She pinched her lower lip as she frowned at the screen. "Uh-oh. Sounds like Eden needs me." She turned those baby blues up at him. "Think you can do without me for a while? It's pretty slow so far."

He knew it was crazy to be disappointed, but he loved having her here. "What's going on?"

"Maid of honor stuff, apparently."

He made a face. "Her wedding's not till next summer."

She lifted her shoulders, giving him a look. "We've practically been attached at the hip for two months."

"I like you here." At her long look he gave a heavy sigh. "Fine. Go on."

Her lips turned up as she patted his cheek. "Stop pouting. I won't be long."

And then she was gone, leaving him to his work. The next hour dragged. It didn't help that he checked his watch every fifteen minutes. He refilled the paper towels in the men's bathroom and was checking the soap dispenser when one of his staff came for him.

"Phone call, Zac."

He made his way to the bar and picked up the extension. "Zac here."

"Hey, Zac, it's Pastor Daniels. How are you?"

"Pastor . . . I'm just fine." After asking about his pastor's day, he worked around to the purpose of the call. "What can I do for you?"

"Well, we have a group meeting here at the church tonight, and I was wondering if we could get some wings."

"Of course." He took the order, then asked, "Delivery or pickup?"

"Well, that's why I asked for you . . . I was hoping you might deliver them yourself. See, we have a baptism scheduled tomorrow, and it seems there's a leak in the baptistery."

"Sure, I'll check it out." Not like he had anything better going on.

After hanging up, Zac busied himself with next week's schedule, and when the wings were ready, he grabbed the two sacks and headed toward the church. He parked his truck and stepped out into the night.

The October evening was cool and perfect, the sky just turning a radiant shade of pink. Maybe when Lucy got back, he'd start a fire in his fireplace. They could cuddle up and watch a movie or just talk awhile.

His steps quickened at the thought. She'd been pretty busy lately between work and her community center project. She'd bought the firehouse and was already making plans for its renovations. They'd spent many hours dreaming together about the purpose it would serve. He loved the way she lit up when she talked about it.

He dashed across the half-full lot and up the steps, pulling at the heavy, oversized door. He crossed the threshold and drew to an abrupt halt at the sight before him.

"Lucy."

She stood in front of the closed sanctuary doors, facing him.

His gaze fell over the simple white dress that hugged her compact curves, over the small bouquet of tiny blue flowers. His eyes cut back to hers.

Apprehension flared in her eyes. "Hey there . . . I hope this is all right."

Was she kidding? The upcoming two months had been stretching ahead like an endless highway. A smile spread across his face as his heart pounded with joy.

"All right?" His eyes searched hers, noticing the silver sparks flashing in the blue depths. "Honey, you just made this the best night of my life."

Her lips curled up as her eyes turned glassy. She blinked back the tears. "Oh, thank God. I was so worried. I know you wanted to move it up, but it seemed like it took you forever to get here, and then I started second-guessing myself."

"I would've been here sooner if I'd known you were waiting for me." He took her in, his woman, his true love, his bride. His heart felt so full. "You're so beautiful, Lucy. Inside and out. I'm the luckiest man on the planet."

She flapped a hand in front of her face, then dabbed at the corners of her eyes. "Stop that. You're going to ruin my makeup, and Eden worked awful hard on it."

He remembered the text from Eden that had set all this off. "Maid of honor stuff, huh?"

There was a glint of amusement in her eyes. "Well . . . it's true now."

She gestured toward the high square windows in the sanctuary doors, and he peeked inside. Pastor Daniels stood at the front with Beau on one side, Eden on the other. Mrs. Pritchard waited at the piano, her back ramrod straight. His eyes drifted over the people seated in the sanctuary. Aunt Trudy, Sheriff Colton, and so many other friends and neighbors. All of them waiting for the moment he'd been dreaming of for so long.

"I can't believe you did all this."

"There's a suit for you in the men's room. And we're Skyping Riley in so he doesn't miss anything."

He looked at her in wonder. She was amazing. And she was all his. "How in the world did you pull this off? We've hardly been apart the last two months."

She grinned. "Lots of texting. And good friends. Really good friends."

He reached up, cupping her soft cheek in the palm of his hand. "Thank you for doing this. I can't wait to hold you all night long—to make you mine."

His gaze fell to her lips. He should wait till after the wedding. But he'd never been good at waiting where Lucy was concerned. He bent low and gave her a long, slow kiss. She didn't seem to mind his jumping the gun. Her lips were soft and pliant and tasted sweet as honey. His heart sighed when she roped her arms around his neck, and he fervently wished the bags in his hands would disappear.

The sanctuary door burst open, and Zac reluctantly drew away.

A flush crept up the pastor's face. "Whoops. I guess it's a go then?"

Zac gave him a pointed look. "I'm not sure if we have time, what with the baptistery leak and all."

Lucy elbowed Zac.

Pastor Daniels had the grace to look sheepish. "Well, there is a slow drain." He cleared his throat. "I think I'll just give you two a moment," he said as he disappeared behind the door.

Zac leaned into Lucy, eager to pick up where they'd left off.

But she set a firm hand on his chest. "Oh no, mister. We have a plane to catch tonight, and right now you have a date with a suit. You can have all the kisses you want . . . *later.*"

It was only the "later" part that gave him the motivation to step away from her. He held up the bags. "What am I supposed to do with these?"

"Put them in the reception hall. I'm already famished, and we have guests to feed."

When he started backing down the hall, she lifted a playful brow. "Don't you even want to know where we're going?"

"As long as I'm alone with you for days on end, it'll be just fine."

"St. Lucia should fill the bill then—just you and me and miles of white sand."

Paradise. "Sounds like heaven."

She gave him a slow, sweet grin as he backed away, her dimples coming out to tease him. "I'll see you at the end of the aisle, Zac Callahan."

"I'll be there."

Then he hustled down the hall. Suddenly he couldn't wait to see her walking toward him. Couldn't wait to slip that band on her finger. Couldn't wait to make her his forever bride.

Discussion Questions

1. Who was your favorite character and why?

2. What was your favorite scene in *The Goodbye Bride*? What did you like about it?

3. Zac was hesitant to trust Lucy again after she left him. Discuss the role of trust in a relationship. Has someone ever broken your trust? Did he or she manage to earn it back? Can trust be restored to its previous level once it has been broken?

4. Lucy and Zac experienced many hardships on their journey toward love. Have you ever gone through difficult circumstances only to later see God's hand in them? Discuss.

5. If you could have permanent amnesia about a specific event or period of time in your life, would you sign up? Why or why not?

6. In Lucy's need to avoid being abandoned, she became like her father, leaving people before they could leave her. Have you ever experienced a similar phenomenon?

7. Fear prevented Lucy from having meaning-ful relationships. What are some other ways fear can spoil relationships?

8. The starflowers at her mom's graveside were like a sign from heaven in Lucy's time of need. Have you ever experienced something similar?

9. The Bible says, "There is no fear in love; but perfect love casts out fear" (1 John 4:18). What does this mean to you?

10. Riley is in love with his best friend but is far away serving in the military. What do you think might happen upon his return?

Acknowledgments

Writing a book is a team effort, and I'm so grateful for the fabulous team at HarperCollins Christian Fiction led by publisher Daisy Hutton: Katie Bond, Amanda Bostic, Karli Jackson, Elizabeth Hudson, Jodi Hughes, Becky Monds, Becky Philpott, Kristen Golden, and Kristen Ingebretson.

Thanks especially to my editor, Becky Philpott, for her insight and inspiration. Thanks also to editor LB Norton, who has saved me from countless errors and always makes me look so much better than I am.

Author Colleen Coble is my first reader. Thank you, friend! Writing wouldn't be nearly as much fun without you!

I'm grateful to my agent, Karen Solem, who's able to somehow make sense of the legal garble of contracts and, even more amazing, help me understand it.

Thank you to Mainer Susan Faloon, who kindly agreed to read this manuscript to make sure I'd gotten the setting details right. Any errors that made it into print are mine alone.

Kevin, my husband of twenty-six years, has been a wonderful support. Thank you, honey! To my sons, Justin, Chad, and Trevor: You make life an adventure! It's so fun watching you step boldly into adulthood. Love you all!

Lastly, thank you, friend, for letting me share this story with you. I wouldn't be doing this without you!

I enjoy connecting
with friends on my Facebook page,
www.facebook.com/authordenisehunter.
Please pop over and say hello.
Visit my website at the link
www.DeniseHunterBooks.com
or just drop me a note at
Denise@DeniseHunterBooks.com.
I'd love to hear from you!

About the Author

Denise Hunter is the internationally published bestselling author of more than twenty books, including *Dancing with Fireflies* and *The Convenient Groom*. She has won the Holt Medallion Award, the Reader's Choice Award, and the Foreword Book of the Year Award and is a RITA finalist. When Denise isn't orchestrating love lives on the written page, she enjoys traveling with her family, drinking green tea, and playing drums. Denise makes her home in Indiana where she and her husband are raising three boys.

Learn more about Denise online!
DeniseHunterBooks.com
Facebook: authordenisehunter
Twitter: @DeniseAHunter

Center Point Large Print
600 Brooks Road / PO Box 1
Thorndike, ME 04986-0001 USA

(207) 568-3717

US & Canada:
1 800 929-9108
www.centerpointlargeprint.com